Books by Thomas Williams

TSUGA'S CHILDREN

TSUGA'S CHILDREN

By
Thomas Williams

Random House
New York

Library of Congress Cataloging in Publication Data

Williams, Thomas, 1926–
Tsuga's children.

SUMMARY: Two children enter a secret valley within a
mountain and encounter a people with whom they share a
strange kinship.
[1. Fantasy]   I. Title.
PZ4.W7275Ts   [PS3573.I456]   813'.5'4   [Fic]   76–53466
ISBN 0–394–49731–7

Manufactured in the United States of America
2 4 6 8 9 7 5 3
First Edition

For Ann and Peter

Contents

TSUGA'S
CHILDREN

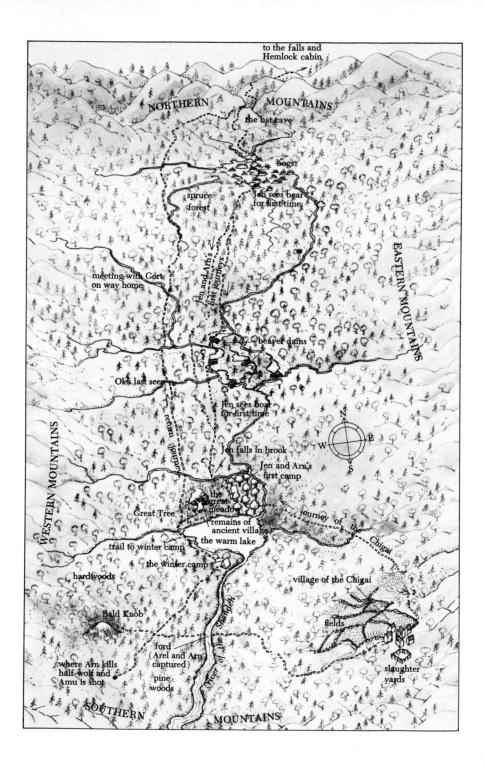

1

The Cabin
in the
Wilderness

Once there was a family named Hemlock who lived, in
another time, near the base of Cascom Mountain, a high
bold mountain of hardwood trees, dark evergreens and
granite crags. There were no other houses for a hundred
miles of forests and meadows and swamps, lakes and rivers blue and unnamed where the swift animals lived in
their ways, running and flying, and the slow animals
blinked away their long years.

Tim Hemlock was a hunter, a maker of things, and a
farmer; he and Eugenia had cleared the kitchen garden
and their two small fields and held them open against the
shadowing woods that always wanted to creep in, fill the
openings with trunks and roof them with leaves. Tim was
a silent, thoughtful man, kind enough to his family and to
his animals, though at times he seemed to hear voices that
made him sad and stern. He watched and listened a great
deal, as a man must in the wilderness, but there was more
to his watching and his silence than he ever told his family. He worked and cared for them, that they knew, but
he would never tell them what he waited for, what he
might hope to see in the shapes of the storm clouds over

Cascom Mountain, or to hear in the voices of the wind.

In the Hemlocks' log cabin, Jen, who was seven, was helping her mother with the big wooden butter churn, spelling her mother while the clabber was new and the crank easy to turn. Arn, who was nearly ten, was out in the cold storage cave dug into the hill behind the cabin, helping his father cut the venison jerky they would dry in long strips in the short-lived October sun. For it was fall, the time before the cold storms would come with the white hiss of snow over the mountain. They were preparing for the long dark season when the days would be short and the wind like knives, when their cow, Oka, and their ox, Brin, and the two goats and the pig would barely heat the small barn with their bodies. The barn was barer now, for their bull, who had been the brother of Brin, had wandered away from the pasture in the spring and never returned. And Oka's calf had died at birth. In the cabin the fireplace would burn by day and ember by night, eating the precious cords of hardwood Arn and his father had stacked under the long eaves after Brin had hauled them from the woods on the iron-shod sledge.

In the kitchen Eugenia was singing, her long brown hair in braids Jen had woven, her blue eyes as clear as the October sky. She sang the butter song. Sometimes Jen sang along with her, but sometimes she just listened to her mother's sweet voice as she sang:

> "Out of night comes daylight,
> Out of thin comes thick.
> Oka knows how butter grows,
> So turn the paddles quick."

In the storage cave, on the thick maple table by the door, Arn's knife sliced the dark red venison into long, thin ribbons. His father was quicker and his ribbons of meat thinner and longer, but his father told him he was doing well.

"You must be quick and careful with the gift the deer have given us," he said. "Remember, we do nothing for the deer as we do for Oka and Brin, the pig and the goats. The deer feed themselves and nearly starve every winter, and we don't help them at all, so their flesh is a gift to us."

"Like the salmon in the river," Arn said.

"Yes," his father answered.

Now, the Hemlocks were all expecting the Traveler, who came once a year in his long canoe. Every once in a while Arn and Jen would stop what they were doing and look down into the valley to the river, wondering with excitement if they could see the Traveler's canoe in the distance as he poled his way up the rapids to the last landing of all. Every October he brought them lead ingots for rifle balls, a twenty-pound keg of black powder, flint, needles, salt, oil, steel, iron dogs and strapping. If Tim Hemlock had had a good year of hunting and a good winter at the forge beside the barn (where Arn pumped the bellows for his father), and if Jen and Eugenia had a good winter making deerskin moccasins decorated with porcupine quills they cut into beads, bleached and dyed and strung on thread, there would be skins and fur, Tim Hemlock knives of steel and deer horn, and beautiful moccasins to trade. Then the Traveler would return to his canoe and bring them licorice, powdered chocolate, tea, and other things they enjoyed but didn't really need.

So it happened that Jen, having taken her turn at the butter churn, went to the door thinking she might be the first to see the Traveler's canoe on the blue river. As she opened the door she jumped back with a cry, for standing there, absolutely still, was a person, a small person all in brown, her brown deerskin dress touching the ground. It was an old, old woman, her hair thin and white, her old face as brown as her deerskin clothes. She didn't speak or change her expression, she just stood there with her bright old eyes staring at Jen. Her face was covered with deep wrinkles that crisscrossed like the cracks in the mud of a dried pond. Between the wrinkles her skin was as smooth and shiny as dark wax. In her hands she held a basket woven of water reeds.

Jen's mother had heard her cry and came quickly to the door. She was startled too, because the Hemlocks hadn't had a visitor other than the Traveler for many years.

"Who are you?" Eugenia asked, but the old woman didn't move or say a word. Only her brilliant old eyes moved from Jen to Eugenia, then into the open door of the cabin as if she were looking for someone else.

"Go tell your father," Eugenia said to Jen, who made a wide circle around the old woman and ran to the storage cave where Arn and her father were working.

"There's an old brown woman!" Jen said. She felt like crying, she was so upset. "At the door! She scared me!"

Quickly they all went to the cabin, and the children, who soon looked to their father, saw a strange expression on his face when he spoke to the old woman.

"Who are you?" he asked, yet his face was puzzled, as though he shouldn't have had to ask the question at all. He seemed to be trying to remember.

When the old woman saw him she moved for the first time, nodding her head, then holding out her basket to him. He took the basket, still puzzled, and nodded his head three times. The old woman, her face as unchanging as wood, nodded three times in answer. And from that time forward, Tim Hemlock never again tried to say words to the old woman.

He handed the reed basket to Eugenia, then pointed to the cabin, made his hands into the shape of a roof, pointed to his heart, then to the old woman, and moved his hand in a slow sweep toward the door, bidding her to enter. She did, walking so smoothly it seemed she had no feet but glided over the ground. She went straight to the bench beside the fireplace and sat down, her worn and ragged deerskin skirt still covering her feet. Her hands were knobby; the brown fingers seemed to bend at the wrong places, the joints swollen and painful-looking. But with smooth motions she seemed to be speaking with them just the same. She cupped her two hands, pointed to the basket Eugenia held, then made one hand act as the cover of the basket, and opened this hand as she nodded. They all knew that Eugenia was to open the basket.

The children came up close to look. Inside the basket were various small objects, each wrapped carefully in a basswood leaf. First there were mushrooms, on top because they were fragile. There were corals, pink, white and light blue, morels that looked like brown sponges, puffballs of pure white that when sliced and fried would taste like meat, beefsteak mushrooms that looked like their name, and oysters because that is how they looked. And then there were some beautiful orange and yellow mushrooms the Hemlocks had never seen before and wouldn't have dared to try if they had.

Beneath the mushrooms were perfect little birch-bark boxes fitting side by side. Eugenia took them out one by one and put them on the big oak table. On the top of each box was a picture of a plant cut into the birch bark, and inside each box was a different-colored powder, fine as flour. Arn, who liked to collect wild food, thought he recognized some of the plants in the pictures. There was goosefoot, arrowhead, roseroot, kinnikinic, glasswort, purslane and dock. But some of the plants he couldn't recognize. One box, full of a fine brown powder, had on its cover a picture of a gracefully drooping human hand.

"She says they're a gift for us," Tim Hemlock said.

"But what are all those powders?" Eugenia asked.

"I don't know, but they're a gift, so we'll put them on the shelf," Tim Hemlock said, and they did. They put the little boxes on the shelf over the fireplace, where they would stay dry. The old woman never moved or said a word, but her eyes were bright.

In the following days they ate the mushrooms they knew were good to eat, but left the orange and yellow ones in their leaves on the shelf.

Days passed, and the old woman sat on the bench by the

fireplace. She sat quietly, hardly moving, all day long. During the early morning hours before dawn and just after, she was gone, but then she returned to glide quietly to her place on the wooden bench. She ate very little and was no trouble, but after a week or more Eugenia began to get a little upset. She and Jen were out by the watering trough where Tim Hemlock and Arn were working, and she asked Tim Hemlock how long the old woman was going to stay.

"It isn't that she's a bother, but she looks at me all the time and it makes me nervous," Eugenia said.

"And she smells funny," Jen said. "She smells like sometimes when you're taking a walk in the woods and there's a warm sort of animal wave of air, and you don't know where it came from."

"If I could only *talk* to her," Eugenia said. "Who is she? What is she doing here?"

Eugenia asked because sometimes Tim Hemlock and the old woman did talk, with their hands, and no one else could follow their meanings beyond something simple like "Would you like some more soup?" which was easy enough to understand.

"I'm not sure who she is," Tim Hemlock said slowly, the puzzled look on his face. "But I know we must let her stay."

Later, when he and Arn and Jen were in the barn feeding the animals, Arn said, "How do you know how to talk to her, Dad?"

"I don't know," his father said. "My grandfather—your great-grandfather—Shem Hemlock, could talk that way. Once, when I was a boy, when I was about your age, Arn, and one of the Old People came by my father's house, my father told me that. But he couldn't do it. I don't know how I know how to do it."

"Is the old lady one of the Old People?" Jen asked. She was scratching the broad muzzle of Oka, the cow.

"She must be the last one, if she is," Tim Hemlock said.

"Were the Old People always old, like her?" Arn asked.
"No, it's that they were here before us."
"And they're all gone?"

"Men have thought so for many years," Tim Hemlock said, and the children, seeing their father's thoughtful, silent mood come over him, said nothing more.

They had been told before about their grandfather, and of his farm many miles, hills and valleys away, how it had been destroyed by a great forest fire when their father was a young man. Their grandfather had moved back toward where the people all lived together, but their father had left the blackened farm and gone deeper into the wilderness. "I went deeper," Tim Hemlock told them once. "Something called me to go deeper toward the mountain."

But the mountain was always a forbidden place. No man went to Cascom Mountain. There were old legends about the gods the Old People had abandoned when they died away, and how the gods, being immortal, still lived lonely and bitter within the mountain.

One evening, a cold, late November evening when the winter had snapped down hard and all the small cabin windows were furry with frost, Tim Hemlock said, "The Traveler isn't coming this year. It's too late. The ice is forming on the river."

They had all been thinking this, but it was too important to talk about. Now they all sat in silence, for without powder and ball, and oil, salt and steel and flint, the winter would be long and hard at best, and at the worst they might starve. Jen saw the fear in her mother's blue eyes and went to her, to stand between her mother's knees and look up into her eyes that had turned dark, like the blue of a stormcloud you think is sky until you see it is really part of a dark cloud. Jen put her head against her mother to feel the warmth.

Arn was silent too, because he knew how little powder and ball his father had left. Each year the Traveler could bring just so much of everything, because of the long hard journey up the river, so in the fall they were always short of supplies. He looked up at the long flintlock rifle that hung on its deerfoot racks on the log wall, at its full stock of bird's-eye maple, and at its brass fittings engraved with animals and plants. From its tang hung his father's beaded leather possibles bag, the small priming horn and the large powder horn, now only half full of black powder.

The old woman sat more quietly than all the rest, but now her bright eyes were upon Tim Hemlock, and she began to speak to him with her hands. He replied, and soon their hands moved swiftly, seeming to dance in the air, Tim Hemlock's great horny working hands and the old woman's small bent brown ones gleaming in the firelight.

After watching this for a while Eugenia cried out, "What are you saying? What are you saying?" She was close to tears.

Tim Hemlock and the old woman stopped moving their hands, and he turned to Eugenia. "She says the Month of the Iron Ice will be the worst," he said. "I can't quite understand all she wants to tell me."

"It's not right!" Eugenia cried. "Why can't she talk?"

"She doesn't know our language." He saw how unhappy Eugenia was, so he went to her and put his arm around her. There was nothing he could say to reassure her, other than a lie, so he said nothing at all.

The children looked at the old woman, who sat as still as wood, the orange flickerings of the fire reflecting from her dark face.

It was Jen who first thought she saw something stranger and deeper in the eye hollows of the old woman than any of them had ever noticed before. She said nothing about it because even though the old woman wasn't supposed to know their language, she couldn't talk about her right in front of her as if she weren't there.

But late that night, after everyone was asleep, Jen woke up with a strange question in her mind, as though something had called her awake. The children slept on the loft at one end of the cabin, where it was warmest. Jen got up and put her quilt around her shoulders, for the fire had burned down low, and even on the loft it was bitter cold. She went around the log partition that separated her bed from Arn's. It was dark; from the fireplace came only an occasional spark of flame that would dimly light up the rafters before it died down again.

"Arn," she whispered. She had to feel for him, and found the very top of his head, which was the only part of him that wasn't bundled up in his quilts and blankets. "Arn!" she whispered again. "Wake up!" She patted him on the top of his head.

"Umph grumph," he mumbled.

"Wake up!" she whispered.

"Wha?"

"Shh!"

"Wha mattuh?"

"Wake up!"

Then he did wake up all the way. "What's the matter?" he whispered. "It must be the middle of the night."

"It is. But there's something very peculiar we've got to find out about."

"In the middle of the night?"

"Yes, because she's asleep."

"Who's asleep?"

"The old lady. She goes sound asleep. I've watched her. She sits there just like always, but she goes sound asleep. And there's something we've got to find out. I don't know why. But it's her eyes. There's something funny about them."

"I know that," Arn whispered back.

"But this is really strange. I'm scared to go down and look by myself, so you've got to come with me."

"I don't like the idea."

"I don't either, exactly, but it's something we've got to do."

"You want to look at her *eyes?* How can you do that if

she's asleep? And suppose she wakes up?"

"We've got to take that chance. We've got to, Arn. I don't know why, but we've got to."

Arn could tell that she meant it. His little sister was only seven, but when she made up her mind, it was made up. And he was curious, too, even though he was scared. So they fumbled around on the loft in the dark, finding clothes and putting them on, and Jen followed Arn down the ladder.

In the dying flickers of the fire they could see, across the room on her bench, the upright figure of the old woman sitting as straight as if she were awake. But they also heard the long, even breaths of sleep. Slowly, as quietly as they could, they crossed the room. The smooth breaths continued. They were both trembling with fear, yet they had to go toward the shadowy old woman who sat so stiffly upright in her sleep. What were they doing? They both thought this, but something seemed to make them move quietly, in stockinged feet, toward the very presence they feared.

"We've got to have a candle," Jen whispered into Arn's ear. "We've got to be able to see her face." Though it seemed even more dangerous, Arn took the candle from the table and lit it noiselessly from a small flame in the fireplace.

Nearer, the old woman's smell grew stronger. To Arn it was like the first puff of air from the paunch of a deer as his father's long knife cut it open to free the tripes from the body, or the way the very leaves could hold and keep the news of a black bear's passage through them, so the hairs on the back of your neck stiffened almost before you could remember what the smell meant, and then when you knew, and looked around quickly for your father, it seemed that your stiffening hairs and not your nose were what had told you. To Jen it was the smell of small animals just after being born, a vixen licking her still-damp kits deep in a moist cave. She had smelled it in the early spring when it came in a warm wave of air.

Closer and closer they came, the old woman's body never moving at all, just the regular, even breaths. They had thought they were getting used to the old woman's presence in the cabin, but now, at night, when everything was asleep, on this strange quest they knew must be guilty because they were so quiet about it, she seemed to loom above them.

Arn held the candle up before the ancient sleeping face. If the eyes had opened at that moment, Arn was sure he would have died of fright. But the eyes didn't open. The wrinkled face shone, brown as polished wood, shining squares and diamond shapes and triangles cut by the deep cracks. The old woman's mouth was closed, her lips folded and collapsed at the outer edges. Gray hairs curled and straggled from a black mole on her sunken chin.

And then as if in a dream Jen found her own shy arm reaching out toward that face. She came closer, closer, till she felt the warm, rich air of the old woman's breath on her hand. She reached toward the brown, wrinkled eyelid and lifted it up from the sunken eye.

What they both saw then was so strange that in their wonder they almost forgot to be afraid, for in the eye was no pupil or iris but a clear lighted glasslike globe in which they could see with the clarity of a bright winter day green spruce trees and a great crystal waterfall, and behind the wildly flashing water a dark mountain. Over its gray rock, black clouds rolled and climbed against a dark sky.

When they had seen the waterfall, the mountain and the clouds just long enough so they would never forget them, ever in their lives, Jen let the old skin of the eyelid settle once again. With a long glance at each other, but not a word, they crept back from the old woman, put the candle out, and climbed back to the loft, where they slept, each one, a sleep full of dreams of the ominous beauty of a mountain, surging clouds and falling water.

2

Tsuga's Black Gate

Early the next morning Jen and Arn woke up to hear Eugenia putting wood on the fire beneath the hissing kettle. It was cold, bitter cold even on the loft. They kept their bedclothes around them right up to their noses, not wanting to make the jump out of their warm beds into their frosty clothes.

But then all at once they remembered what they'd seen in the middle of the night, and they were both amazed and a little frightened by what they'd done.

"Jen," Arn whispered across the partition between their sleeping places. "Jen, do you remember what I remember?"

"Yes," Jen whispered back. "It must have really happened."

"I think we'd better not tell," Arn said. "What do you think?"

"I'm not sure why, but I think so too."

"Come on, children," Eugenia called up to them. "I can hear you're awake. It's hot porridge, cornbread and honey for breakfast!"

That sounded good, so they gathered up their nerve

and were soon down the ladder in front of the warm fire, both of them, toasting themselves on one side and then the other. The old woman hadn't yet returned from whatever mysterious place she went before dawn, but both Jen and Arn cast an occasional guilty look at her place on the wooden bench by the fire.

Tim Hemlock soon came in from the barn, knocking the snow from his outer moccasins by the door where it could be swept out with the round rush broom. He had milked Oka and the nanny goat, cleaned up and fed Oka, Brin, the pig and the goats. He put the two buckets of milk on the cooling shelf in the pantry where it was coolest in the cabin (but not freezing), and before he could take off his deerskin parka the door opened again and the old woman, all in brown deerskin, glided in as smoothly as if she had no legs. Just as always, her wrinkled, brown old face without any expression except that look of the very old that seems to say, "How heavy the sky is to hold up," she went straight to her place on the bench and sat down.

It was as if she had no idea the children had seen into the depths of her eye.

The days grew colder and shorter as the winter came down upon them from over the dark bulk of Cascom Mountain. Cold squeaked in the rafters, in the window frames, in the frost-white hinges of the door. For a hundred miles the evergreen trees turned from green to almost gray in the terrible cold. Those trees that lose their leaves in winter creaked their bare branches against the cold sky. The snow came and came again, until the paths to the barn and outbuildings and to the storage cave in the hill were almost tunnels in the white. Tim Hemlock, when he went hunting for the meat they began to need more desperately than in any winter they had ever known, moved across the high snow on his longest, widest snowshoes. In the late afternoon, just before dark, he would come back exhausted, his eyebrows white with frost until they melted in the warmth, hang up his unfired flintlock rifle on its pegs, remove his ice-stiff leggings and parka to hang them by the door. The children knew how tired he was from the cold, the deep snow and the long journeys he had made. His face grew thin and gaunt, and one place on his cheek where he had once been frostbitten turned bright red as he sat slumped before the fire. It made the children afraid to see their father so tired, though he pretended to be cheerful when they sat down together for supper, even though the portions were growing smaller day by day.

One day when the sky was nearly black even in the middle of the afternoon, when a blizzard was hovering over Cascom Mountain ready to come howling down, he came in exhausted, limping from where he'd fallen and hit his knee on his snowshoe. Eugenia got him a bowl of hot potato soup, and he blew his tired breath across it, holding its warmth in his cold hands. He seemed too tired even to speak, but finally he said to Eugenia, "We're going to have to slaughter the pig."

This was a big disappointment to the Hemlocks. They had paid the Traveler many moccasins and several knives for the little piglet he had brought them the year before, hoping that it would begin to fatten on the fall mast and corn. But this pig ate and ate and never grew very big or fat at all. He was a rangy, long-snouted pig, more like a wild pig than a domesticated one.

"There may not be enough feed for Oka and Brin, and we can't live without them. We just can't feed the pig any longer," Tim Hemlock said. "I don't think this blizzard will hit till tomorrow night, so we've got to do it in the morning first thing."

"There won't be much fat or meat on that pig," Eugenia said.

The old woman looked from one to the other as they spoke, just her eyes moving in the dark old sockets.

So the next morning, just after first light, there was blood in the snow, bright red as it dissolved down into the crystals of ice. The pig died quickly, never knowing, stunned by a sledge hammer, then bled as he hung from his hocks on a tripod of saplings. Arn helped with the skinning and the cutting of the lean meat. Eugenia and Jen saved the entrails and all the blood they could. Nearly everything was saved, even the four split, pointed hooves, for what could not be cured or boiled down would be eaten, fresh, and what could not be eaten fresh was put into a wolf- and bear-proof cache at the roofpeak to be frozen by the winter itself. But when they had finished, that afternoon as the first stings of the blizzard began to be felt, they had gotten very little meat from the pig, and even less of the precious fat that gives energy against the cold.

Arn and Jen thought about the pig. They hadn't ever got to know him very well, the way they did Oka and Brin —especially Oka, who was Jen's favorite. And now the pig was no more, just chops and lean roasts, uncured bacon slabs, spareribs, parts for head cheese and sausage casings, a skin to be made into leather, and marrow bones. Jen wondered if the other animals knew what had happened, if they would miss his company in the chilly dark barn. Especially she wondered about the goats, whose bright eyes with their strange oblong irises seemed to know more than they said. The pig's pen was empty; they must all know that.

The winter never let up at all; it seemed to the Hemlocks that it had already lasted for years. The jerky, the smoked and pickled venison, the smoked salmon from the river and the frozen pork were soon gone. All the nourishment had been tried from all the marrow bones. They had flour, some cornmeal and some dried vegetables, a few potatoes that had sprouted and were wrinkled and punky. Oka's and the nanny goat's milk were terribly important to them. Tim Hemlock had to spend most of his days out searching for game because he didn't want to think of slaughtering Oka or Brin or the goats. They all knew he would, though, if he had to.

"I don't know where the deer have gone," he said to

Eugenia one night when the children were asleep. "They haven't yarded up this year in any of their regular places. They're just gone. Nothing seems to be out this winter— not a moose or a fox, not a rabbit, not a red squirrel, not a white-footed mouse, not a partridge. All the animals seem to have gone from the forest."

As he spoke, the old woman's eyes were upon his tired face. Tim Hemlock hadn't tried to speak to her with his hands for a long time, and now he just shrugged hopelessly, as if he could think of nothing to say. Eugenia could see how tired he was.

The firewood corded beneath the eaves was getting low, too, so they burned the wood sparingly now, and the cabin was not cheery and warm as it was most winters. There was never a fire in the forge next to the barn. It seemed the forest they had known so well had forsaken them. It was their home and it had always been stern but bountiful to them, but now it was barren, nothing but cold snow and mute frozen trees.

In December the paths between the barn and the storage cave did become tunnels, cold blue light filtering down through the snow ceilings. While this protected the paths from the harsh wind, they were breathlessly cold inside, like the middle of a block of ice.

It wasn't the happiest Christmas that year, though they tried to make the best of it. Tim Hemlock cut the top from a balsam fir, just the top that stuck up out of the snow, and brought it into the cabin, but they couldn't decorate it with candles because they had no tallow. Jen and Arn got the parts of the manger scene from the loft and set it up at the left of the tree, the baby and his parents carved from wood, as were the goats and cows. The little dolls looked cozy and warm in the hay-filled manger. To the right of the tree they set up the small circle of carved wild animals with the deer and the smaller tree in the center, the tree a branch cut from the balsam fir. But they had no saddle of venison, their traditional Christmas dinner. All they had was potato and corn soup with dried chives in it, and some bannock.

After dinner, when they sang "Silent Night, Holy Night," Eugenia could not keep the tears from her eyes. Tim Hemlock, as he always did on Christmas Eve, went into the back sleeping room and put on the cape of deer-skin and the deer mask with the antlers, then entered the main room walking slowly and sedately like a deer. He silently looked around the room, then took a place at the table. Eugenia took the maple-sugar doll she had made that morning, holding it carefully on the wide blade of a knife, and presented it to the deer, who tasted it, then removed his costume and divided the candy doll among them all. The old lady watched all this with her bright old eyes, and accepted her piece of the candy with a nod.

They were gathered around the fire and it was time for a story, so Tim Hemlock told them a story he had heard from his grandfather, about Tsuga, a great hunter of the Old People, whose other name was "Wanders-too-far." Jen and Arn knew the story by heart, but they always liked to hear it because while telling it their father changed. His eyes grew brighter, and an excitement came into his voice and gestures that made him seem more like them.

"It is said," Tim Hemlock began, "that the Old People never saw their gods, only heard their voices in water, wind and thunder." He went on with the old story, telling them how Tsuga, hunting far into the wilderness, came upon a strange mountain and climbed up into its valleys, where he came to a gate of black stone. The deer trail he was following stopped at the stone. Some versions of the story, Tim Hemlock's grandfather had told him, said that the stone was hung on great hinges, others that it was a teetering stone that could turn on its fulcrum. Tsuga reached forward to touch the stone and heard the voice of thunder, so he drew back, afraid, because the thunder was all around him though the sky was blue.

In spite of his fear, Tsuga was still curious, for he had always gone over the next ridge to see what was on the other side, crossed the widest rivers, followed his quarry until he found it. He stood trembling before the stone gate, then reached forward to touch it. To his wonderment it turned slowly, opening into blackness from which a deep voice came. "Where are your children?" the voice asked in the sad tones of the wind. "Where are your children?"

"They are safe at home," Tsuga managed to say, though his voice trembled.

"There is no safe place," the windy voice answered.

"Why can't I see you?" Tsuga asked, his curiosity overcoming his fear.

"Your eyes see only that which you must kill. Where are your children?"

It was more wind than voice now, and it faded into the sound of an autumn wind in the trees as the black rock slowly turned shut again.

Tsuga returned to his home place, a journey of many days. He read the sun for direction by day and the stars by night, not stopping except to eat cold jerky and bannock when he grew weak from hunger. Bear, deer, wolves and all the animals of the wilderness showed themselves to him without fear, as if they knew that he would not stop to hunt them. He neither strung his bow nor unsheathed his knife on the long journey, and when he reached his home he found that all his foodstores had burned and his family was near death from hunger. Although he was so weak himself he could hardly string his bow, he knew that he must find food for them. Just as he turned from the entrance to his hut a dry wind came through the trees with a long sigh, and a graceful white-tailed deer, a doe, stepped from the forest, its eyes sadly upon him, to wait for his arrow.

"All the rest of his life," Tim Hemlock said, "Tsuga sought to find the Black Gate again, for it was the one passage he hadn't traveled through, but he could never find it. When his children's children were grown and he was an old man with white hair and wrinkled skin, he went alone on a long hunt from which he never returned. The people said he must have found the Black Gate at last."

Wind cried at the cabin's small windows, and a puff came down the chimney so that the fire hesitated for a moment in its climbing. Tim Hemlock was silent, his eyes staring thoughtfully beyond the warm room. Arn wondered where his father's thoughts had gone, and just for that moment felt lonely.

After they were in bed, where all of them except the old lady went early in order to save firewood and keep warm, Eugenia said to Tim Hemlock, "But why is that old woman here? She just sits there and never says a word and eats what little food we've got. Why did she have to come this winter?"

"She eats very little," Tim Hemlock said. "And we couldn't turn her out into the cold to die."

"Of course not. I didn't mean that! But if she'd only gone away in the fall! Why did it have to be this terrible winter she came here?"

"I don't know. When I try to ask her who she is and where she came from, she won't answer. She doesn't seem to understand the questions. But they're simple questions in that language. Maybe she's just an old wanderer who's survived all the rest of her family. If she lives through the winter, she'll go on to somewhere else. She believes that she's paid for her keep with those boxes and mushrooms, you know."

Eugenia sighed. "Yes, I know, but what good are all those powders?"

"Found things," Tim Hemlock said. "Wild greens, mushrooms, tubers and herbs. There's so much we don't know."

"But what do you talk about with your hands? Couldn't you ask her?"

"She tells me riddles. She won't answer my questions.

I'll have to find them out some other way."

"What questions?"

"I hardly know the questions, and you wouldn't know the answers," Tim Hemlock said. He seemed so weary and sad, Eugenia tried not to show how his answer had hurt her.

But the children, on the loft, heard their mother and father talking, not the words but the unhappiness and danger in their voices. Their mother and father were unhappy and it was not just because the Traveler hadn't come and the winter would be long and hard. They had both wondered why they hadn't told about what they'd seen in the old lady's eye. The reason, they both knew, was that they didn't want to upset their mother and father in any way.

"Arn," Jen whispered, "are you awake?"

"Yes," Arn whispered back.

"It wasn't a very happy Christmas, was it?"

"No."

"I wonder what Tsuga's children were like," Jen said.

Arn thought awhile. "Maybe they were like us. But I guess not. They were Old People. And maybe the story's just made up anyway."

"Maybe the old lady is one of the Old People," Jen said.

"Did you ever see her tracks in the snow?" Arn said. "They're funny-looking. They're moccasin tracks, but they point in, sort of, and don't look right."

Jen said nothing for a while, and then she said, "We're the only children we've ever known. Maybe other children aren't like us."

"When you were just a baby a stranger came by here. I was five and I can remember. He said he had a little boy just like me."

"I can't remember," Jen said.

"He was all brown, all dressed in brown deerskin and he had brown hair and he was brown all over, that's all I can remember except what he said about me."

"Did he say anything about me?"

"Not that I remember. You were just a baby anyway."

"I don't know what a baby looks like, except maybe the little Jesus, and he's just a wooden doll."

They were silent for a while.

"I wonder if Tsuga had a little girl my age," Jen said.

The
Iron Ice

It was on the first day of February, the coldest month of all, that disaster struck the Hemlocks, and struck twice on the same bitter day. Oka's milk began to dry up. She gave less than a quart that morning, and soon after milking time a weakening sickness had come over Tim Hemlock, with a high fever. He was suddenly so weak he could barely stagger back through the tunnel from the barn and slump down sweating and shivering before the small fire.

"Something strange is happening to the air," he said. "There's a change coming."

"What kind of change?" Arn asked.

"I don't know. Everything seems heavier," his father said.

Eugenia, Jen and Arn couldn't feel anything strange, so they worried about him even more, thinking that it was his illness. They wrapped him up in the great bearskin robe, heated water to put his feet in when he shivered, put cool damp cloths to his forehead when he grew hot. No one paid any attention to the old woman, who sat still as a carved wooden statue, always watching.

Later, toward noon, they began to notice something strange too. First it was a tiny noise that seemed to surround them, the kind of indistinct noise you think might be in your head, so you shake your head and it seems to go away, but while you're not thinking about it, it sneaks back into your ears and there it is again. As it grew, each of them began to wonder if the others heard it, a small, watery sort of noise, a trickling noise such as they hadn't heard since the cold closed in upon them in late fall. Louder and louder it grew, until all at once they asked each other, "What is it? What's that noise?" It seemed to come from all around them.

Arn went to the door and opened it. He was met by a wave of heat. Warm, balmy air pushed in upon him from the open doorway, air as warm as a hot summer day. The roof of the snow tunnel had fallen in, and bright blue sky and sunlight flashing on the snow—light he hadn't seen for weeks—hurt his eyes and made him blink. The trickles of melt water were almost a roar as they cascaded from the cabin eaves and the roofs of the forge house and the barn.

"It's like summer!" he said. The warm air came flowing into the cabin, coating the table and chairs with a fine mist when it touched their colder surfaces.

"It's the false spring!" Eugenia said. But they had never seen the false spring so warm. Soon they were sweating in their heavy winter clothes.

"It won't last long," Tim Hemlock said. In his father's low, weak voice Arn thought he heard some dread, and he shivered for a moment in spite of the warmth.

But the sudden summery air was glorious to the children, who had been cold and even colder because they were a little hungry all the time. Jen hadn't been to the barn to see Oka for several days, so she put on her waterproof boots—the ones with the spruce pitch on the seams—and waded out between the walls of snow in the mud and slush of the path to the barn. She opened the door upon the barn's cold air, glad she was bringing in the warmth to the animals.

"Oka?" she said, her eyes just beginning after a minute

to get used to the hay-smelling dimness. She felt her way along a wooden railing until she could see again. "Oka?"

She was at Oka and Brin's stall. She heard the heavy movements of the large animals. The floor creaked, the warm smells surrounded her, stronger as the summery air poured into the barn. There was Oka's broad wet nose, her wide cow face and bent-over ears, her brown eyes that seemed so kind. Oka gave a deep sigh and a low humming sound in her throat to let Jen know that she was welcome in the dim dusty winter home of the animals. Brin, who was always calmer and quieter than Oka, gave a smooth moo that was half breath, half voice, but he remained back in the square stall, lying down in the hay with his thick forelegs bent in front of his great broad brisket.

Sometimes Jen thought she could talk to Oka, but sometimes she wondered if they ever really understood each other. Maybe she made up Oka's words in her own mind and Oka hadn't really said them at all. As for Brin, he never really felt like saying much. She never heard the thoughts of the goats. They seemed so quick and neat and clever, but she never could understand them.

But Oka did say things to her, answered her questions in ways that seemed too strange for her to have thought up all by herself. They were cow thoughts, ruminant deep slow answers, as heavy in themselves as Oka's great body and bones. "Oka knows how butter grows," the butter song went, and those seemed to be Oka's words too.

"My father's sick, Oka," Jen said. "And you didn't give much milk this morning. Are you sick too? I hope you aren't."

As Oka moved her head slowly, sighing, her jaw sliding slowly from side to side, Jen seemed to hear deep, echoing words. They were about a calf, a brown and white calf with long awkward legs and a handsome bony head, and how her milk was rich with cream then as she turned the warm air and sweet clover grass into richness and sustenance, the giver of life. But now she was sad, sad down through the hollow four-chambered depths of her cowness, heavy, heavy with sadness for a place she had once been long ago, a wide meadow and a bony calf, sweet water and the green heat of the grass.

Jen was filled with sadness to hear of the deep yearning of her friend. She had always been so grateful for the milk and butter and cheese that Oka gave them. Oka was the giver of life, and now her sadness made Jen sorrow for the beautiful rich meadow and the bony long-legged calf, as if she, too, had been happy and calm there once long ago.

Even before Jen could get back from the barn to the cabin another change in the weather came moving inexorably down from Cascom Mountain. The warm air passed through the small openings of the farm, slid wetly across the cabin and the outbuildings to be followed by a deep cold, not a wind but a change as palpable as a moving wall. On her way back to the cabin Jen's boot soles wanted to stick frozen to the slush that was turning to clear ice. She almost had to leave one of them on the doorstep. It wanted to stay there, as if it were a tree with roots deep into the sudden ice.

In the cabin they all felt it too. The wet snow on the roof creaked like a great fist as it turned into ice. Tim Hemlock, shivering by the fire in the bear robe, said, "Now everything will freeze solid. Everything will be as hard as iron."

"Iron," Arn said. He seemed to remember something about iron, ice as hard as iron.

"We'll have to chop the wood loose from the piles with axes," Tim Hemlock said wearily. "And the doors. All the doors will freeze hard shut."

Iron ice, Arn thought. When had he heard that?

As the days passed the cold never let up. It sent its probing chill to find chinks or cracks in the cabin. And each day Tim Hemlock got worse, as if the cold had found a way in and was freezing his throat and chest. He could barely drink the thin hot soup Eugenia made for him, and finally he lay on a straw pallet before the fire, trembling and gasping for breath. Arn, as best he could, wearing all the clothes he could put on and still move, had chiseled open the cabin and barn doors, and with Eugenia's and Jen's help, took care of the animals and chopped logs loose from the frozen piles to drag them in over the blue ice. They had to wear iron crampons strapped to their boots, the spikes barely digging into the ice that was harder than any they had ever seen before.

Each day Oka gave less milk. The nanny goat gave her usual small amount, but of course her udder was so much smaller than Oka's. The goats didn't seem to mind the ice and cold, as if they said, "We can climb anywhere, live on anything." Jen, who spent hours in the barn with Oka, thought she heard things like that from the goats, but their thoughts were cold and superior, not directed toward her at all.

One day when they had nothing for supper but a piece of bread, dried berries and thin milk, Tim Hemlock could no longer hear them or respond. He lay with his eyes closed, breathing short breaths as quick as a mouse's breath. He grew dryer and colder to the touch. Eugenia tried to keep him warm, to keep herself hopeful, but inside she was in despair. Her whole world seemed to be ending. She could not bear to live if Tim Hemlock weren't there. And what would happen to her poor dear children? The merciless cold would steal into the cabin, into their bodies and claim them forever for the far world of the dead.

Arn and Jen knew how bad their father's illness was, even though Eugenia tried to keep it from them. They found it impossible to believe that Tim Hemlock, who was always so strong, who had always protected them and provided for them, could be so weak and sick. It seemed impossible. But then all of a sudden they would know, as if they had awakened from a dream, that the strong silent

man could not speak to them or hear their voices or see
their tears.

That night at supper Arn couldn't eat his food. His small
crust of bread would not soften in his mouth. It was as
hard as iron. Iron, he thought. And then he remembered.
It was the old woman. They were all so worried and frightened about his father, they hadn't thought of the old
woman at all. She might have been a piece of wood sitting
there on the bench all day long. She had said once in her
hand language to Tim Hemlock, "The month of the iron
ice will be the worst." And now, certainly, they were in
the month of the iron ice. February. With these thoughts
he was awakened again to the strangeness of the old
woman, what she had brought with her as a gift when she
first came to the cabin. Yes, there they were, all the little
birch-bark boxes of powders upon the shelf, each with a
picture cut into its top. He remembered some of the pictures of plants: goosefoot, arrowhead, roseroot, kinnikinic,
glasswort, purslane and dock. Others he didn't recognize.
Suddenly he felt that it was time to open the boxes. For
one thing, all of those plants he recognized were good to
eat, and they were hungry. He got a stool and climbed up
on it so he could reach the shelf.

"What are you doing?" Eugenia asked.

"We've got to eat," Arn said. "Here, Jen, take these as
I pass them down."

"But we don't know what's in them!" Eugenia said.

"I do. Some of them, anyway." Somehow he knew he
was right, that it was almost too late but not quite. Then
he happened to see a movement out of the corner of his
eye, a brown thing moving. He looked, and was shocked
to see that the old woman stared brightly into his eyes.

She was speaking to him! Her arm was raised, her hand
limp at the end of her wrist, limply falling. Her hand
reminded him of something, of the picture of a hand. Yes!
He remembered that on the cover of one of the boxes was
a hand delicately poised like that. He found the box with

the hand on it and took it to the old woman.

She nodded, her polished, cracked old face unmoving but her eyes bright. She raised her arms and her hands began to move quickly, up and down, back and forth, her crippled old fingers moving too. He couldn't understand anything of what she was trying to say, and he felt hopeless again. But a strange thing happened, little by little. He would never know how it happened, but he began to understand everything; her gestures that a minute before were nothing but the meaningless twitches of an old woman's arms and hands suddenly began to mean water, box, powder, cup. Other movements suddenly meant open, pour, heat, stir, and finally all the different kinds of words—words for things and words for doing—came together almost as easily as the words he had spoken all his life.

When the old woman stopped speaking she nodded three times and he nodded three times back, then began his preparations. Jen and Eugenia watched in wonderment as he put just so much of the brown powder from the box with the hand on it into a large cup. He added hot water from the water pot that hung over the fire, added a pinch of kinnikinic and a pinch of glasswort and stirred the mixture with a wooden spoon. He got down from the shelf the two kinds of mushrooms they hadn't dared to eat before—the yellow ones and the red ones. They were dried out, now, and he put them together in the mortar and with the pestle ground them into a fine powder.

"But what are you going to do with those things, Arn?" Eugenia asked. "They may be dangerous!"

"I'm making medicine for Dad," Arn said, pouring the ground mushrooms into the steaming cup.

"No!" Eugenia said. "It might be poison! We don't know what those things are!"

"Are you *sure*, Arn?" Jen said.

"No, I'm not exactly *sure*," Arn said, "but I feel this is the right thing to do."

Eugenia, who knew that her husband was getting worse and worse, that he might die, finally saw that though it was a desperate thing to try what was unknown to them, they had to do it.

When the cup had been prepared according to the old woman's directions, Arn propped his father's head up in his arm and held the strange steaming broth to his lips. The steam was orange-yellow, almost as thick as liquid; Arn could see it entering his father's nose when he took his short breaths. Soon the breaths became longer, as more of the steam entered his father's body, longer and more easy. He could feel his father's neck begin to loosen and relax against his arm. Some color came back, little by little, into his father's face.

Finally Tim Hemlock's eyes half opened. Arn held the cup to his lips and he drank the brownish broth. When he had drunk it all his eyes closed again and he slept deeply —far too deeply for their voices to follow him. But it was at least a sleep of longer breaths.

They turned to thank the old woman as best they could. All winter she had been there in her place on the wooden bench. Every day the brown, silent presence was there.

But now she was gone.

They couldn't believe it. They looked again, blinking their eyes. But she was gone, all except for a pair of neat, short deerskin moccasins that sat side by side where her feet had been.

"But she couldn't go out in this cold without her moccasins," Jen cried. She went to the door, but all she saw was the blue ice, the air so cold it made her nostrils close when she tried to breathe. The ice was lower in the path to the barn, but everywhere it was rolling, slippery, blue-white ice, with not a sign of the old woman.

It was then Jen noticed that the barn door was ajar. Maybe she had gone to the barn! Quickly Jen put on her fur parka, boots and mittens and went through the deep cold to the barn to see.

When she came back she was sobbing. "Oka's gone too!" she cried. "Poor Oka! She'll freeze to death! She won't have anything to eat!"

Arn and Eugenia went with her to see, and it was true. Brin and the goats were there in the dim light of the barn, but Oka was gone. They couldn't tell which direction she had taken because no hoofprints would show on the ice. Was it the old lady who had opened the pen and the barn door? Had she taken Oka with her?

"Arn, when you fed the animals did you leave the barn open?" Eugenia asked.

"No, of course not," Arn said.

It was Jen who was the most upset. She loved Oka and was grateful to her for the milk and butter and cheese she gave them. To Arn, a cow was meant to give milk and that was that, and though he knew they couldn't afford to lose Oka, he couldn't understand why Jen was crying so hard.

"Oka will be hungry!" Jen cried. "Where can she go on the ice with nowhere to sleep and nothing to eat?"

They tried to comfort Jen, but she wouldn't be comforted. They dressed in their warmest clothes and with the aid of their crampons made a wide circle across the glare ice of the fields and the forest, but could find no sign of Oka, no tracks, no spoor of any kind. When they came back to the cabin where Tim Hemlock slept on the pallet before the fire, Eugenia made a soup of what they had for food, adding some of the powders that Arn had identified from the pictures carved into the birch-bark boxes.

Jen was quiet, and ate little of the soup. That night when she climbed up the ladder to the loft and crawled into her warm quilts, all she could see was Oka, somewhere deep in the strange wilderness, hungry and alone. Oka, who had been so generous to them, all alone in a cruel land so different from the warm green fields she yearned for, with no one to help her. Even now the deadly cold might have her down on her side, awkward on the hard, slippery ice. Jen couldn't think of anything else. She couldn't sleep in her warm bed when Oka was in the cold, so when everyone else was asleep she got up, as quietly as she could, dressed herself in her fur parka with the fringed hood, her fur-backed mittens, boots with the fur inside and the sharp ice crampons strapped to the soles—and stepped out into the moonlight where it was so clear she was in the frozen chill of the moon itself.

She didn't know where to go to look for Oka, but she had to go. First she would go to the barn and see what she might learn there. Maybe Brin, out of his warm, phlegmatic vastness, might have something to tell her. Or the clever goats, who seemed to know so much. They must have seen it all through the black slots in their yellow eyes.

She stood in the breathing barn, slits of moonlight and the briny smell of hay and manure around her, saying, "Brin? Brin?"

He moved a gigantic part of him—brisket or flank, she couldn't see that well at first—and rumbled deep inside one of his stomach chambers: *I am only a beast and do not understand much. Oka was warm and could help to hear the noises. She could smell wolf and bear when they were hungry, but she is gone and I am only an ox, strong but with few opinions.*

"But where did she go, Brin? Where did she go?"

She will follow the moon because how else could she see?

"But the moon goes over Cascom Mountain!"

Why do you ask anything of an ox? If I were a bull I would talk to you with my eyes and horns.

Behind her the goats tilted their heads at each other and stamped their feet, but their thoughts were beyond her understanding.

Jen didn't know if she'd heard anything at all but the movements of penned animals and the creaking of frozen timbers, but she had to go toward where the moon would set, toward where it was forbidden to go. Cascom Mountain was dark, sacred to the Old People, and only the Old People, if there were any of them left, could go there. It was said that the gods of the Old People could never die, and without their people they had grown mean and vicious.

But Oka knew nothing of this. If only she could catch up with Oka before she got to the forbidden place, she could lead Oka home to the warm barn. With her crampons she could cross the ice better than Oka on her slippery hooves.

Hooves, the goats said from behind her. She turned, not sure she had heard a sound. *We are all hooved here, split-hooved, even the one murdered and the ones gone away.* The goats shivered their manes and stamped their hooves on the board floor.

"But where did Oka go?" Jen asked, expecting no answer. Suddenly the nanny goat bleated—a loud, meaningless *caw* in the dim barn, and the male goat knelt and as quickly rose again to his four feet. They both seemed amused. Jen could not understand, was not sure she had heard anything at all, but she knew the unfriendliness, the cold distance between the animals' thoughts and her own.

4

The Mountain
and
the Waterfall

Jen took Oka's rope bridle from its peg and tied it over her shoulder. As she left the barn, carefully closing and latching the door upon its warmth, the frozen windless air came into her nose, into her chest. She knew she shouldn't go alone into the forest, across the crackless ice that was as smooth as the ice on a pond yet frozen into hills and waves.

Her crampons squeaked, complaining of the hardness, as she entered the frozen, silent trees.

As she left the barn, the cabin and the sheds, it was like going away, away, like diving into deep water away from the familiar light and air she could breathe freely. Her home passed far behind her, growing smaller, and only the trees, silver on one side and black on the other, kept moving toward her to pass behind. The sound of her steel crampons on the ice was the only sound in the forest, and even those small squeaks seemed to grow dimmer and more lonesome in the cold. The only colors were silver and blue-black, the spaces moving only as she moved through them. She stopped to call, "Oka? Oka?" but her voice was so small and helpless and alone, it frightened her.

The trees, standing frozen, made no answer. They were mostly spruce, forming a black mesh overhead, where their silence, without any wind at all, was unnatural. It was there that they had always whispered, even just a little, to each other. But the wind itself was dead. She would look down a long aisle of trunks to see moonlight at the end, the aisle so long and even, she thought it must be a road or path, yet when she came to the end there would be no end, just random spaces of ice and silent trees, which would again re-form to make other aisles going in any direction.

She followed the moon as it went across the sky toward Cascom Mountain, the black bulk of the mountain appearing only now and then through the boughs, but she felt it as a terrible weight pressing upon the world. She was going where her father and mother and brother had never gone. The dead air, which she had to breathe, took her inner warmth and sent it out, lost forever, in thin clouds of breath. Her feet were growing colder. She was tired from being hungry for so long. Oka's rope bridle, which had weighed so little before, grew heavy and hard, dragging her thin shoulder down.

"Oka! Oka! Where are you?" she cried, but her voice was lost. Nothing had ears to hear the small cry except herself, and all the name did was to make her think of Oka's brown eyes and kindly warmth—if the cold hadn't taken it all away. Oka could be as dead and stiff as the butchered pig, whose pink flanks had become so still and cold it didn't matter when the knives cut them into pieces of other things—pieces with other names that were not part of a living thing, like hams and bacon and chops. The pig was as quiet, then, as these hummocks of ice, but where had his life gone? Oka could die as easily, or any living thing. The frozen world wouldn't care.

"Oka? Oka?" she cried, and listened. There was no answer, none at all. It was as if her small voice stopped at her chilled lips, but she continued to place one foot forward, carefully so as not to fall, and then the other, going deeper and deeper, alone into the strange woods.

All the rest of the night she followed the moon's path. Sometimes, climbing a long slope through scanty trees, the moon's glare on the ice almost doubled its light. Then the trees would gather close again and crowd darkly around her so that their brittle lower boughs, like dry skeleton fingers, touched her as she passed.

Gradually the moon dimmed as it neared the icy rock of Cascom Mountain. Daylight began to rise in the east, behind her, and with that strange other light, at first dimmer but more vast than the moon, she began to hear a long and continuing sigh, as if the gods of the Old People were lamenting the disappearance of their race. The sound was at first a hushed sigh, but as she came nearer and nearer to the mountain, climbing its lower hills, the sigh grew into a more angry sound, then to a hiss like a high wind, then to a heavy roar, the deep sound of power.

She was afraid; she had never heard anything like this before. It seemed to come from a great mouth, the mountain itself roaring out of pain through a cleft or canyon. Finally, climbing slowly in her tiredness and fear, she came up over an icy knob where the trees parted and she found herself looking down and across a deep chasm toward the thunder itself—a great descent of rolling, folding white water that poured slowly over rock high above and fell, too slowly for its continuing roar, down the cracked ledges into the chasm below. Above the falls tall spruce writhed in a wind, against a black sky, the wind caused by the falls itself, all that thudding, hissing weight of the water descending into the chasm, where its roar was heard behind clouds of mist and spray that boiled up and coated the ledges with glittering ice.

It was the falling white river, the mountain, the twisting trees against the ominous sky she had seen, all silent then, in the old lady's sleeping eye.

It made her dizzy to see the immense falling of the

water and she held tightly onto a small spruce, trying not to think of herself falling, down, down into that depth. After a while she noticed that it was slightly warmer here. Maybe the friction of the water itself had warmed this place. Then she saw what looked like a path, a narrow ledge that led along the cliff toward the center of the falls. Cautiously, her ears filled with the roar of the water, she climbed down to the narrow path. She thought she saw tracks there. Yes, there in the melting ice was a deer track, its delicate wedges, and beside it the prints of larger hooves that might have been Oka's, they were so much broader than any deer tracks could be.

"Oka!" she called, but nothing could be heard over the rush and boom of water. She must go on, though the path, if it really was a path, was so narrow on the side of the cliff she felt hands, as if they were inside her, wanting to pull her over the sharp edge to fall into the chasm far below. The trail was as narrow as a shelf, and she could hardly believe where it seemed to lead. It could barely be seen as it followed the cliff's side, appearing and disappearing until it finally disappeared altogether into the swirling mist at the edge of the falls. Oka, if the tracks were really Oka's, and a deer had come this way and not come back. She had to go on.

Never before had she been so far from home, not even with her father, and he would never have come this close to Cascom Mountain. She was afraid, yet inside her fear was another thing, hard as stone, that said she would never give up no matter how terrible this path. Her father was sick, they were slowly starving, Oka was lost. She had to go on even if the whole world had changed to evil and would kill her. "I'll go on anyway," she said, not hearing her own voice over the deep roar of the water. She could feel her small voice but not hear it. "I'll go on *anyway*."

Maybe Oka was now a battered wet cow-corpse tumbling over rocks in the rapids below. In places the ledge was only a foot or so wide, sheer rock above, sheer cliff

below. Yet here and there she could find the broad print
of a hoof. "I'll go on *anyway,*" she said again, the small
silent voice all she could set against her fear.

Jen crept along the narrow rock shelf, the falling water
booming louder as she approached the falls, the bulk of
the water so great that for one awful moment it was more
substantial than the rest of the world; while the water
seemed to stop falling, she and the cliff hurtled skyward.
She grasped the mossy rock with both hands and shut her
eyes tightly, waiting and hoping for that terrible motion
to stop. When, after a while, she thought that the cliff had
grown steady, she opened her eyes and once again it was
the gray-green water that fell. And right in front of her,
in the moss, was the large print of one of Oka's hooves.
Oka had passed this way, yet the shelf of rock here was so
narrow, Jen couldn't see how Oka could have kept her
balance. Her wide cow sides must have had to scrape
against the cliff.

She shivered with cold and fear. Though it was warmer
here than back in the frozen forest, the dampness of the
mist came through her clothes. Oka's rope bridle, heavy
with the wet mist, pulled down on her shoulder.

The falls were green in their depths, heavy as falling
glass, but she kept on until the shelf of rock led behind the
long columns hissing on their way to the roar below, and
came to a narrow black hole in the wet rock directly
behind the falls. Ahead of her, mist churned across the
dark opening. She hesitated, trying to overcome her fear.
There was no other way Oka could have gone but into
that hole, unless she had fallen to the rocks and water
below.

That blackness in there was almost too much; to go into
a hole, a cave of blackness, was against everything she had
ever been taught. But now she examined that fear, as if
she were Jen who was seven and also another Jen, older
perhaps, who knew or had long theories about the animals
and their voices, a Jen who had looked into the old lady's

eye and seen this very place before and was too deep for the simple fears of childhood. No, she was not too deep for those fears; maybe they were the deepest of all—but something pulled her toward this opening into the unknown. She unstrapped her crampons, tied them to Oka's bridle, and began to feel her way in. The floor of the passageway was smooth, as if it had been polished by water or feet, and led slightly downward. She felt with her hand along the smooth wet side, her other hand feeling the damp air in front of her. As she felt her way along, the roar of the falls lessened, the retreating boom and roar sounding again like a long moan, now at her back and growing sad and low.

"Oka?" she called, but her voice came back to her strange, constricted by the rock into a high, piping noise that sounded as if it hadn't gone anywhere.

So she didn't call again, but saved her strength, feeling her way along. The passage turned sometimes, sometimes climbed and then descended. Her open, staring eyes ached to see any kind of light, as if her sight tried to breathe through them and they were being suffocated by the blackness. It seemed she had gone miles and miles in that blackness darker than night, darker than any void she had ever stared into before in her life.

She felt her way forward for so long a time, she began to believe that she would never get out of the black tunnel, that it would never end but just go on, deeper and darker with the dank cave smell into the under-parts of the mountain. But then, little by little, before she could identify what it was, the smell changed. It seemed at first wrong, and then very sad and nostalgic, for she was smelling, faintly in the stagnant air, the rich odors of leaves and earth, the warm, alive smell of autumn. But she knew that outside it was February, the frozen month; she had entered the stone passageway from a world of ice.

In that world she had left behind were her family and her home; with every small step she took she was leaving

them. If the warm smells and the increasing warmth of
the air were now more kindly to her, it was all too strange
and distant from the land she had left behind. She wanted
to turn back, feeling that at any moment it might be too
late ever to find her family again.

Then, far ahead, she saw the faintest gleam of light. She
had begun to wonder if her eyes worked at all, they had
been straining so hard in the utter blackness and finding
nothing, but now came that faint gleam of light, some
kind of daylight, certainly, so she went on a little faster.
She began to hear strange noises, small squeaks and soft
flutters that grew in intensity as she felt her way toward
the light. It was almost as though she felt the high squeaks
rather than heard them. Something else was happening,
too; the cool wall of stone she had been feeling as she went
along turned away from her, away from the distant light
where she wanted to go, and as the million piping squeaks
grew louder, she knew by the echoes of her footsteps, and
by the soft velvety flutters that were an invisible cloud all
around her, that she had entered a great room.

She could see nothing, just hear the high clamor and
feel a puffing sort of wind that came from above. She went
on, trembling, one foot feeling ahead, then the other. The
light grew larger and began to have shape. It must be a
hole in the stone, a tunnel; it must be a way into daylight.
Something soft was under her feet now, like an inch of soft
mud, and a smell rose that reminded her of the chickens
they had last year, before the red fox got into the coop one
night and stole them all.

Then, as if the distant hole of light were a great eye, it
winked out, glimmered, opened again and winked out, till
it was black as the rest of the space she teetered in, with
nothing to hold on to. She grew dizzy and nearly fell into
whatever the soft stuff was beneath her feet, and when
she got her balance back, in that vast absolute dark, she
had no idea where the light had been. It was like a game
she and Arn used to play, where one would shut his eyes

and twirl and then not have any idea where anything in the room was. But now she thought of Arn and her mother and father, all of them together in the warm cabin, with the fire blazing orange and silent, and here she was, lost in the mountain she had been told never to go near, surrounded by blackness and a high clamor of noise. If she tripped, or fell or gave up, she would fall into something soft and gooey that smelled like the earth beneath the chicken roost. She could not stand there, teetering on the edge of the unknown. She would be lost forever.

The light came slowly on again, not where she thought it had been before, but then her mind said no, that was where it was before. The whole black world turned gradually around, remorselessly, making her feel sick. The squeaking and the fluttering were less intense, now, and she realized that those sounds had been draining away in the darkness all the while the hole of light was black, as if they had drained out through the hole itself. This was still going on as she walked as fast as she dared toward the light. The sounds swept by her, flutters and squeaks and puffs of air. She could see them now, black specks against the light, thousands of them flowing out through the hole, dimming it, letting it wink open when their flowing numbers thinned, then closing off the light again. She came closer, to where the wind grew into a high rush and the piping became one constant myriad vibration in the center of her head. The specks were clearer now. Leathery wings beating, and black bodies; she was in a bat cave, but there was the way out, and she was getting closer.

As she began to be able to see the rocks around her she climbed faster toward the light. The bats still flowed all around her, none touching her with anything but the wind from its wings. The light grew and at first hurt her eyes. She saw blue sky and the tops of green trees, and she was stumbling, crying with relief to see daylight. Finally she got through the entranceway and ran to the side of the cloud of streaming bats. She was in a new warmth full of autumn smells, looking down across a mountain valley to a blue, island-studded lake, tall trees, a mountain meadow, all surrounded by mountain walls reaching up into glinting white.

The bat cloud rose above the cave entrance, swirling into a confused whirlwind in the brightness. Above the dark cloud and beside it, two great hawks turned and then fell into the cloud, which received them and let them plummet straight on through, each of the thousands in the hawks' way swerving aside from the arched talons at the last moment. But then there was a bump in the air. She could almost feel it. In all that flowing and falling there was a jar, a stoppage somewhere up in the swirling cloud, then another and another, before the two hawks broke out below the cloud to brake with their broad wings and cupped fan-shaped tails. Each had a broken bat in its grasp.

Another bat fluttered down and landed near her feet, one of its soft wings splayed out, blood on the dark furry body. It tried to fly, but one wing was broken, the fragile wrist of the bat's wing. She felt sorry for it, and bent down so she could see its clattering little fangs, and its nose, which was bare and pink and flat as a pig's snout. Large pointed ears stood out from its head, full of little white hairs. It was ugly, but she knew it was ugly only to her and not to itself. She wanted to help it. The bats in the cave were like a nightmare to her, and had frightened her badly, but really she had frightened them and caused them to fly out into the daylight where the birds of prey had an advantage they wouldn't have had at twilight or at dawn. In a way, she had caused this little animal to be hurt. But when she bent nearer to him he felt her presence, or saw from his pinhead eyes, or heard her in the echoes of his squeaking, and opened his mouth, coughing with hatred and fear, to display his white fangs. He couldn't fly any more and was doomed to die, but he didn't yet know it. Jen knew it, and knew that she couldn't help.

The bat cloud turned once more above the cave and then, as if sucked like smoke into a flue, came down toward the cave entrance. She scrambled away and hid in some ground juniper as the cave received its thousands and thousands again into safe darkness. The air was clear, warm in the low sun that was about to go behind the white rim of the mountains. The hawks were little specks now as they climbed toward the cliffs behind her. The wounded bat was gone. No, there he was beside a stone, not moving now, lying there in that extra kind of silence that meant he had suffered other wounds, and he was dead.

As the sun went down behind the distant rim, the air turned colder and the light turned around, growing golden as it was reflected from the snow fields high above her on what must be the eastern rim of the valley. But it was not winter down here. The sweet juniper smell mixed with all the live odors of fall. If Oka had come this far she might still be alive, maybe in that green meadow below, beyond the dark forest. With the thought that Oka might be near, she felt for a moment some of Oka's calm warmth, but then it all changed and seemed so impossible and strange that her fright and loneliness grew worse. She didn't know if her weakness came from fear or from hunger. Between her and her home was the bat cave. She didn't want to think of entering that shrill blackness again, and even if she did go back inside, she might never find her way across the vaulted cave to the narrow passage that led back toward her home.

"Oka?" she called, but her voice winged away and was lost in the far distances of the strange valley. She still carried Oka's rope bridle and the iron crampons, which were heavy, so she untied the crampons and left them on a rock near the cave entrance, keeping the bridle. She wanted to get away from here, to try to find the mountain meadow below, before dusk when the bats would stream like a black wind out into the darkening valley. Yet she was afraid that even in the meadow, if she could ever find her way to it, she would be alone; it would not be her father's field with the smoke from the cabin chimney rising nearby.

She could find no hoofprints on the broken rock around the cave, or see any in the dim light fading down into the cave itself, where she didn't dare to go look. She would have to try to guess which way Oka went, and hope to find her trail on the softer ground in the woods.

Her fur parka was too hot to walk in now, though she didn't leave it behind because she knew she would need it in the night, when the cold would slide down the snowy mountainsides into the valley. She wished she had taken her rucksack, and some rawhide to tie her parka into a bundle. Arn would have thought of that. He liked his gear so much. If only he were here she wouldn't be so much afraid. She was too young and didn't know enough to have come this far from her home, but it was too late now. She carried her parka under her arm, Oka's bridle over her shoulder, as she descended through the broken rocks. Trees and shrubs appeared as she descended. Darkness descended with her; like the cool air, it seemed to be seeping down to settle into the valley. She was weak from hunger; when she made a misstep her knees felt like warm water.

In the dying light she came to a bog she had to cross. As she started across it something moved very near her, something large as a tree. She felt the soggy earth depress toward it, as if the bog were a hammock, and then the thing rose higher and higher above her—it was a bear, with massive narrow shoulders and wide head. It looked down at her in the twilight, motionless now, judging. As with Oka sometimes, she seemed to hear deep rumbling thoughts that formed themselves into language. At first she wanted to cry out and try to run, but the slow deep thoughts came into her mind with the power of stillness and contemplation, holding her silent.

What is this small animal?

It is small enough to ignore.

Unless it is good to eat.

Jen felt the hard eyes looking down upon her, and at the same time she saw herself caught there, crouching down in the brush of the bog. She didn't look like herself, but like a dark bunch of fur and cloth and skin, with odors rising from her in the form of a dim bluish glow that wavered and changed like the Northern Lights. The bear's deep thoughts changed, grew more hesitant.

This small animal reminds me of an old danger.

I am not hungry.

I am not angry.

I shall move away.

The bear silently turned, his black bulk folded down, and the boggy earth moved again as he pushed steadily and quietly away through the brush.

She trembled, and took the deep breaths she hadn't dared to take. Every time she blinked the dark seemed to double itself and the low spruce trees along the side of the bog melted together into furry secret depths. A night bird screamed off in the forest as if it had been suddenly startled.

She didn't know which way to go. She waded through the bog to where the ground rose into the black spruce. She could see nothing here. It would be dangerous and even impossible to go on, now. So she did the only thing she could. She felt among the roots and dead needles until she found a place between two roots, a hollow where she curled up and tried to hide, crying a little but not daring to make a noise, her parka over her head.

5

The Hidden Land

Back in the Hemlocks' log cabin, back over the several long miles of iron-hard ice, through the frozen trees where no bird flew and no wind whispered, the cold light came.

Though Eugenia had got up several times in the night to put wood on the fire so that Tim Hemlock, sleeping on a pallet before it, might stay warm, the dawn brought a chill over the embers and gray ashes. The dawn's wan light came through the icicles that hung heavy from the eaves, webbed together like thick screens outside the small windows. Eugenia got up, shivering but with some new hope because of Tim Hemlock's easier sleep, and built up the fire, not as high as she would have liked, because the wood supply was very low, but enough so that soon the yellow warmth was felt around the hearth.

Arn called from the loft, "Jen? Is Jen down there?"

Soon they knew that Jen was gone. Not just outside, or to the barn, but gone. Arn came back from outside, rubbing his mittens on his cold nose, to tell Eugenia that he could see the marks of her crampons, like little ice-pick stabs in the ice, heading on a line toward Cascom Mountain.

"She's gone after Oka," Eugenia said. "Oh, Jen!" She turned to her husband, who slept on, his thin, wasted face dark and calm in his sleep. "Tim! Tim!" she cried, but he couldn't hear her.

Arn saw his mother's fear and before he even had time to think he said, "I'll go find Jen!"

"No," Eugenia said. "You must stay here and take care of your father. Feed him the broth you know how to make, and keep the fire going."

"But I could find her," Arn said. "I could find her all right. It's slippery out there and you could fall down! It doesn't hurt me to fall down. Sometimes I even do it on purpose!"

"I must find Jen," Eugenia said.

Arn saw that there would be no arguing with her, but he made her drink some hot broth before she left. She took some bannock with her in one of the deep pockets of her deerskin parka to give to Jen if she found her, and Arn helped her strap her crampons tightly to her boots. When she was dressed and ready she kissed Arn and Tim Hemlock and set out into the cold.

Eugenia knew only too well the old tales about Cascom Mountain and of those powerful gods deprived of their people. Yet Jen's trail of crampon scratches in the ice led straight toward that dark towering mountain to the northwest.

All day she walked and clambered over the ice, through the silent trees, until she heard the long sighing that turned to a dreadful roar, and came upon the last icy knob where Jen had stood to see and be buffeted by the roar of the falling water. When Eugenia saw the narrow path along the sheer cliff and knew from the tracks that Jen had taken it and not returned this way, she was afraid she could not make herself go on. She was afraid of heights. She could never trust herself not to almost want to fall. But she saw in her mind Jen's determined, sweet face and went on. Many times, on the slippery path, she thought she would give up and fall, or die of fear. The falling water seemed to want to pull her down, to argue with her in its demanding roar, telling her that all was lost, that she must let herself go and end her fear forever in the rocks and water far below.

The path thinned in places where she had to stop, her hands against the black rock of the cliff, and pray for her nerve and strength to come back. After what seemed hours, days, forever, she came behind the swirling mist of the falls, where the long tumbling columns of water fell beside her, so that all the world except for the narrow rock ledge she held to was falling. And then the path stopped, went no farther. It ended. In front of her was only streaming black rock. Below her the pulling water fell into the thundering mist hundreds of feet below. There wasn't a crack, a foothold or a fingerhold anywhere. She knew from the tracks that Jen had not come back from here along the path. She had to believe—there was no other thing to believe—that Jen and Oka had fallen and were gone.

In her sorrow she wanted to fall herself, to give up to her hopeless sorrow and let go. But she knew that back at their home were Arn and her husband, who were still alive and needed her. She clung to the rock, balancing herself against a cold voice from the water and rock that said, *Why suffer? Come, descend with the water and make it all end. Come, come down with us where it is all cold and gone.* She felt that power, that pressure as though arms dragged at her to pull her down. But she could not let go, and the bravest thing she had ever done was to hold on, to think of the family that was left and to turn and pick her way back along the ledge, though she found herself crying out of terrible weakness and despair. Away from the falls, into the freezing air, the mist that had entered her clothes turned them solid, and she had to crack the ice in them in order to walk at all.

It was long past dark when she returned, another almost full moon letting her see the trail and at the same time draining the warmth from the world like an evil magnet of ice in the sky. Arn was waiting; Tim Hemlock slept on.

"Jen's gone!" she cried. "She fell into the waterfall. I know she's gone!"

She was feverish and weak. Arn helped her out of her frozen parka and leggings and made her sit by the fire. He could not believe that his little sister was gone forever. He did not want to believe it and he wouldn't believe it; he would go and find her himself. He knew that his mother wouldn't let him go, so he didn't ask. He could see that she was exhausted and would soon be asleep, so he waited, thinking of Jen lost on the forbidden mountain and how he would have to go there too. He thought of not going, of staying here next to the warm fire, just him and his mother and father now, safe in the cabin. But he knew he would go, because his father couldn't. It was his duty. His mother was brave but she didn't know the wilderness the way he did. His father had taught him how to follow a trail as faint as a breath, to see an animal that wasn't there and to see it whole from a single scratch of a claw or a dropping. It was up to him now to use the knowledge his father had taught him.

And so, while the moon was still high and his parents both slept, he prepared himself. He took one of the little birch-bark boxes and put into it some of the brownish powder from the box marked with the drooping hand, some of the powdered purslane and dock, and some of the powdered mushrooms. He took the stale bannock from his mother's parka, a flint and some tinder from his father's possibles bag, forty feet of narrow hemp rope from the rack by the front door, the small but sharp sheath knife his father had forged for him a year ago, and a small iron pot in case he would have to cook. The birch-bark box, bannock, rope, flint, tinder and pot he put in his small rucksack. His knife he put on his belt, with a rawhide

thong to hold it in its sheath in case he fell. He looked up
at his father's flintlock rifle, but knew that it was too long
and heavy for him to carry, even though he had shot it
over a rest. If the Traveler had come this year his father
would have made him a smaller rifle, of smaller caliber;
together they had drawn the plans for it. But there was
no use missing what he'd never had. At the door he
strapped on his crampons, slung his pack over his fur
parka, and quietly left his warm, firelit home for the
moon-cold woods.

At dawn he came to the same icy knoll where Jen and
then his mother had faced the clamor of the falling water.
He knew at once that it was the same falls, the same black
rock and spruce-topped cliffs he and Jen had seen in the
old woman's eye. It all looked evil, but the old woman
could not be all evil. Hadn't she taught him, in the strange
language he now also knew, how to make the soothing
medicine for his father? Yet he knew that the greatest evil
is not easy to read, for it gives a little in order to take away
more. It is patient, and waits, speaking in convincing
ways. He knew this through all the old stories, where
death is real and comes to the good as well as to the bad.
He had hurt himself before, and had been in pain; he
knew what happened to all living things—trees, animals,
the pig they had butchered and eaten, the tall grass cut
down in summer and fall. But even so he found the tracks
along the narrow ledge, read them as his father had
taught him, and went on.

He never thought his body would betray him and make
him fall; if the ledge held, he would hold. He was tired and
hungry, but he was nearly a man, the only man in his
family who was not sick, and he would go on until he saw
for himself what had happened to his little sister—or until
what had happened to her happened to him.

He came to the narrow shelf of rock and found, behind
the hurtling columns of water, the same dark entrance
Jen had found. With the water hissing past him and the

roaring from below, he held on carefully and looked around. Yes, there on the rock were small scratches that must have been made by Jen's crampons. His mother, from her tracks and what she'd said, must have come just this far, and he wondered why she hadn't seen, or mentioned, the cave entrance. For a moment he thought he must be in the wrong place; but then he remembered his father having told him that tracks are as sure a sign as the thing that made them, even though they tend not to stick in the memory as well. He must believe the evidence of his eyes, and never forget. Jen, Oka and a deer had come here, as had his mother, and only his mother's tracks had returned. He knew that he was logical and practical, especially compared to Jen, who tended to hear odd voices and do things without thinking them out beforehand. Like the night she insisted on looking into the old lady's eye. She tended to do things like that, for reasons she could never explain.

What, he wondered, had made her go into this dank cave all alone, searching for a cow? What could have made her care so much for a cow? She had reasons, unreasonable reasons. He knew that he was going in because he had to find his sister and bring her back home. For a little while, even in his fear, he thought proudly of himself. But then a small voice said to him, Yes, but partly it is Jen's authority, her unknown reason, which lets you be brave enough to enter here. She went in first, alone; you go in second, with the possibility of finding company in that darkness.

He took off his crampons and tied them to his pack, tightened up all the straps so the pack rode high and easy on his shoulders. There at his belt was the knife with its bright, slightly curved blade his father had forged for him and he had filed and polished. He had selected part of a deer antler, taking care that it curved the right way for his hand and was the right thickness, and fitted it with rivets through the tang. Then he had carved a scabbard from two thin pieces of cured spruce, two pieces that he fit together and bound with buckskin, sewn while it was wet so that it shrank around the scabbard taut and hard.

He undid the thong and pulled the polished blade from its scabbard. It was sharp, honed and stropped sharp as a razor, and it gave him, through his pride in having helped make it, a feeling that he was ready, that this fine tool might help him in whatever he had to do. He turned as if to say goodby to the light. He did have flint and tinder in his pack, if it became necessary. But he knew that Jen hadn't any, and he would save the fire for dire need. Then he entered the cave.

The roar of the falling water receded as he felt his way deeper into the mountain, until it was only a faint sigh, farther and farther behind him. He could tell by the echoes of his cautious, sliding steps that the passage was narrow, so at least he wasn't worried about getting off the track. Several times he was startled by turns, descents, and once by his own cough and its strange, hard echo. His hand would go to the hilt of his knife. His eyes remained open, staring, searching for light. Sometimes he would shut them hard and see little star-flashes, but these, he knew, were only inside his head. He must make himself stop imagining monsters, dead things that still lived, pale organisms with tentacles that might wait to reach for his blind face. He made himself think of his purpose, which had nothing to do with monsters or old legends; he was to find Jen and, if possible, Oka, and bring them back home. He wasn't hopeful about Oka because it seemed such a crazy thing to have left the comparatively warm barn to go off into the ice. The cow must have lost her senses, or been let out, or led away, maybe by the old lady. In any of these circumstances other forces than mere cow stupidity were involved, and he didn't see how he could fight against them. But Jen could be talked to—if he could find her.

He kept going forward, and after a long time he smelled

the same rich, autumn smells Jen had. Finally he came to the cavern and immediately recognized the odor of bats, because he had once explored a small bat cave—a deep crack in a ledge, not far from his father's westernmost field. If there were bats here, there had to be an opening to the outside so that at dusk they could fly out in search of their food. He could see no light at all, and he couldn't feel the presence of bats, so it must be night. Beneath his feet was tangible evidence, a soft coating of bat dung. Now would be the time to use his flint and tinder—but then, much as he craved light, any kind of light, he knew that if there was an opening ahead, some light would show even at night, even from behind deep clouds, and if he looked at fire his eyes would not be sensitive enough to see it.

So he moved forward across the cavern floor, feeling ahead with each foot in case there was a crevice or a stumbling stone. Finally, after crossing the cavern in several directions, not knowing whether he might have been going in circles or zigzags, he did see just the faintest deep blue haze, and climbed toward it, over rocks and up a gradual incline of rubble, hoping desperately that the faint haze was not just some trick of his head. Then he saw a star. It blinked on, then off, but it was a star and it was as if he had been suffocating and could breathe again.

He hurried through the cave entrance and stood in calm air, yet after the closeness of the cave it seemed moving and alive. He could feel distance in it, and freedom. The clouds moved high over his head. An occasional star winked through. He couldn't follow Jen in the dark, so he moved some distance away from the cave and found some ground juniper, under whose prickly branches he could rest until morning. He thought of calling for her, but he didn't want to disturb the night, or to reveal his presence in this place he couldn't see. He was hungry. The thought of the bannock in his pack made his mouth water, but he'd brought that for Jen. Instead of thinking about food he would try to get some rest, even go to sleep.

When Eugenia awakened, back in the cabin, the fire was nearly out. Once again the gray light of dawn filtered wanly through the ice-covered windows. The cabin was cold—too cold, near to freezing. Immediately she felt its emptiness. Jen was gone, lost forever. Arn must be hungry; he wouldn't have eaten enough. She had failed to take care of her children. Her husband slept on his pallet, his breaths faint puffs of mist above his thin nostrils.

"Arn," she called softly toward the loft. "Arn, come and I'll make you some breakfast."

There was no answer.

Arn woke with the feeling that time had passed. He'd had a dream, a strange dream, but then, most dreams were strange. He dreamed he'd seen hundreds of people all at once, standing, talking, cooking over small fires, some of them going in and out of small log buildings and tents. He'd never seen more than five or six people together in his life, and those were his family and the Traveler and the old lady and a visitor he just barely remembered and Jen couldn't remember. That had been, he'd been told, when he was just three years old. All he could remember was that the visitor had been a big man dressed in brown, with a brown beard. But in the dream all the people were together, in what must have been a village, and none of them thought it strange.

Light rose in the eastern sky, slowly outlining the mountain ridges from behind, then bringing into its glow the snowy western cliffs on the other side of the deep valley. As the light grew his dream faded and he examined the valley in its bowl of mountains. Although the pale winter sun was the same, it was a different season here. The sun rose at a shallow angle that showed it would scarcely rise above the cliffs before it began to descend, but the valley was warm, as if this were the month of

September or October instead of February. The leaves of the small birches were yellow, just about to fall, and the high-bush cranberries down along the rock-slide were ripe, their small globes glowing red. Across the forest of spruce and balsam below was an unfrozen blue lake and a green meadow, and beyond another dark forest of evergreens a cloud of mist rose in slow swirls from what must have been a swamp or a pond. Here and there around the perimeter of the valley white water splashed and fell in streams from the snowline, across gray rock, to disappear into the trees below. The valley was alive, not hibernating like the frozen wilderness from which he had come.

He went back to the cave entrance to see if he could find any sign that Jen had come this way, and there upon a rock were her iron crampons, the small crampons his father had forged for her. Jen was nowhere in sight, but right there on the rock was the hard evidence that she had been here. He called for her, but got no answer, his voice thinning out across the distance. A mild wind moved the tops of the trees below, and the mist rose silently from across the valley. He untied his own crampons from his pack and put them beside Jen's, so that she'd know he was here if she came back to the cave. Remembering what his father had taught him, he looked for more signs before making up his mind where she might have gone. He found vague smudges of bat dung that might have been made by her boots; he found a spot of drying blood, which scared him until he found the dead bat folded in upon itself like a small gray glove and saw that the blood had come from its wounds. Two broad-tailed hawks circled far above, riding the air and watching.

Finally he decided that Jen would have gone down toward the far field by the lake. She would be following Oka, or hoping to find Oka, and that meadow would be a good place for a cow. Maybe he could pick up a trail farther down in the soft ground among the trees. He would find berries and water down there too, for he was hungry and thirsty and he would need energy to go on.

As the sun rose above the mountain wall the air grew warmer, so he took off his parka, rolled it as tightly as he could and roped it to his pack before climbing down the rock-slide. The cranberries were bitter, but he ate some anyway, and put some in his pocket.

When the trees rose around him like dark towers and the air dimmed into the cool green rooms of the forest, he thought again about the ancient gods that were supposed to inhabit Cascom Mountain. This valley itself must be part of the mountain, or in the mountain, if his sense of direction was right. He was certain his father had never been here. The valley was beautiful, with its strange warmth and fall colors. It was so easy to walk again, as he had last fall, on spruce needles instead of ice.

After a while he came to the same bog Jen had found. He saw where a large animal, probably a bear, had crushed the blueberry plants. Here, as in the woods, the ground was so fibrous and spongy no tracks could possibly show. In the opening of the bog he could see the shadows cast by the low sun, so he got his bearings again. The meadow and lake should be due south, where the sun would be by the middle of the day.

Before entering the gloomy corridors of the spruce he thought of home. He could turn around right now and find the bat cave, then, using fire, follow the passage back toward the waterfall and the world he had left. It was cold there, but only in that world would he find his mother and father and the cabin where he had been born. He would rather be shivering in front of a meager fire in that familiar room than here in this autumn warmth. He could turn around right now and go back. But then he saw in his mind Jen's iron crampons upon the rock. In his fear and loneliness he had begun to forget them, but they were there and they were Jen's and she was his little sister, who would also, in spite of her mad affection for a cow, be hungry and lonely.

He could turn around and go back. He could make his

body do it, but in a strange deep way the most important part of him, what he thought of himself, would still be here, left here forever in this alien valley. It seemed to him that when he came to this conclusion and could not escape it, something free and selfish and innocent left him forever, and he felt loss and sadness. Yet while he felt that loss and sadness he was a little less afraid. In a few months (if he lived that long, a new voice within him said) he would be ten years old, growing toward manhood. Ten was old, an age when tools began to stop being toys. The knife on his belt, though small, was not a toy, nor was his pack and the things it contained. *They'd better not be toys,* the new voice said. *Your father is not here.*

6

Toward
the Meadow

A small wisp of gray smoke came from the Hemlocks' cabin chimney. The cabin was set deeply in the ice, as if the ice around it were a clutching hand, cold rigid fingers curving over the roof and around the log walls.

Inside the cabin the air was dead cold except for a small space in front of the fire. Tim Hemlock lay sleeping on his pallet, covered with a bearskin robe, his thin dark face calm but not aware. Eugenia, bundled up in her parka, poked the fire carefully and fed it slowly from the last of the wood. She could do little else. She had gone once again onto the ice to follow Arn's trail, but came again to that blank wall behind the terrifying falls.

When she reached home she was so weak from hunger and despair she could barely chop loose and drag in the last of the wood and remake the small fire. All the food was gone except for the seed they would need to plant in the spring, carefully stored in hemp bags hung from the rafters. There was a bag of corn, bags of tomato, turnip, cucumber and squash seeds, beans and other vegetable seeds, and wheat and timothy. In a dark bin dug into the floor of the cabin were the precious seed potatoes. All this time she had tried not to think of using the seeds, but they must eat if they were to live, so finally she took some corn, found some seed potatoes with two eyes or more and cut them in half, and with the small amount of milk the nanny goat gave, made some chowder, which she fed to her husband with a spoon. He could not wake up enough to see her or talk to her, but took the thin chowder. When she lifted up his head and shoulders to feed him he seemed as light as a forkful of hay. Though he slept calmly and took his soup, he was growing thinner, his nose as shiny and sharp as a blade.

The spring on the hill had frozen over for the first time in her memory. When she had to go outside and chop into the blue ice with a mattock she could feel the warmth of her life itself drifting away into the frozen air. If the two of them were to live, they had to have warmth and food. But then she would think of her children, who must have fallen into the chasm of the waterfall and drowned, and she wondered why she cared whether she lived or died.

She knew that Tim Hemlock needed more nourishing food, so in the morning when she woke cold and stiff in the fireless cabin she dressed and went to the barn. She would take the male goat from the barn and slaughter him. This would take all her strength, but her husband needed the sustenance meat would give him.

There was silence as she entered the dim light of the barn. Brin breathed long breaths but made no other sound. When her eyes got used to the dim light she saw that the goats stood side by side, the male goat in his pen, the nanny goat in hers, not moving, staring at her through their strange yellow eyes. They didn't move their heads or stamp their narrow hooves as they usually did, but stared at her as though they knew why she had come. In her hand she held the rope noose. In her pocket, sheathed in its leather scabbard, was the short sharp sticking knife.

The goats stared at her. The nanny goat moved her jaws once, chewing, then stopped. *We know something,* the goats seemed to say through their unmoving attention. She could almost hear dry goat voices.

She turned away, shut the barn door and latched it, and went back to the cabin, where she put the noose and knife on the table and stood, dazed by her inability to do what she had to do. Tim Hemlock slept. She could not wake him. She would lie down next to him on the pallet, cover herself with the bearskin robe and wait for the final sleep. The small wilderness farm would die and be retaken by the forest. She must at least set the animals free, even though they would die too. All of these thoughts passed with unnatural calm through her mind as she stood looking down at her husband. But no, she could not leave him. She would burn the tables, benches, chests and chairs, make food from the seed corn, beans and potatoes as long as anything lasted. Maybe when the last of these were gone she would have the desperation to kill the goats. Even Brin. She knew how to load the flintlock rifle. The thought of entering the animal silence of the barn with that weapon dismayed her. They would know and she would know.

She poked the fire into life, sat down beside it on the still-warm hearth, reached for her husband's hand and held it in hers. Though still hard and calloused on palm and fingers, his hand had shrunk toward its bones.

If it were all going to be over—her life, her family—she could at least remember their times of happiness, and other hardships they had overcome, other bad winters. She and Tim Hemlock had been married when they were very young, back where the people lived. Her mother and father had died when she was a little girl and she had been brought up in the Hemlocks' house in the settlement. She could barely remember her mother and father. When she was sixteen and Tim Hemlock eighteen they had been married. She knew he would go deeper into the wilderness but she hadn't cared then. They were both strong and young. He could never explain why he had to live in this far country where there was no other smoke but the lonely smoke from their cabin chimney. It had always seemed to her that he was searching for something, not just wanting to get away from the other people. He was known as a strange, silent one. Like his grandfather, the people said, who had been a dark, quiet man who went his own ways and would disappear for weeks, even months at a time to hunt in the wilderness.

Many times she had watched her husband's face as he gazed toward the mountain, often in the early morning just at dawn when the sun shone on its long slopes and granite peak, making each tree and rock so vivid and near, the great mountain seemed closer and higher than it was, like a wall leaning toward them. His face would be perplexed, fierce with a kind of baffled curiosity. At night the children would sometimes get him to tell some of the legends of the Old People and their gods, and then he would tell them, smiling at the magic tales, that the ancient stories were just legends, and they shouldn't take them as the real truth. Yet he had never gone to the mountain.

He helped her teach the children how to read and count, to learn the things that people must know, but he was best at teaching them the skills of the forest.

For a moment she felt angry at him because he had brought his family so far away from the other people, who might have helped them now. But then she knew that it was his nature, that she had known it well when she was sixteen. Just for that one moment resentment flickered before it was drowned by care.

She remembered long evenings by the hearth when the children listened to the old stories, felt their warm bodies again as they hugged her goodnight, remembered how in the night she would know that they were sleeping on the loft, the heat from the hearth rising on winter nights. Now the loft was empty and she, too, was empty, even of tears. Where were her children? Tim Hemlock's son and daugh-

ter were gone away from them forever, taken by a cold
world that had no mercy toward the weak, the young, or
anyone.

As if in answer the wind pushed against the cabin and
the ice rang like struck iron.

Jen woke up just at the first silver paling of the sky, the
coldest time. Her feet had pushed out from under her
parka and were numb with cold, so she pulled her legs up
until she was all in a ball, but still she shivered. The cold
made her feel more alone in the strange valley. A white-
footed mouse sat on the root next to her face and looked
at her, then ran away terrified when she blinked her eyes.
She heard him scrabbling away across the frost-rimmed
spruce needles, so scared he couldn't remember for a
moment where his hole was. She knew what he thought,
feeling his terror and confusion at finding this large animal right in the middle of his usual morning path.

She seemed to remember the small voices or thoughts
of other animals who had come across her in the night,
their interested or frightened questions before they
moved away from her.

She got up long before the sun came over the mountain
rim, then went through the dark spruce toward where she
hoped the meadow would be. It was a green darkness
beneath the spruce, cool and moist. She walked for a long
time, quiet on the hummocks of needles, before the sun
rose. She never saw a hoofprint or a track of any kind, and
she worried that in going around and ducking through the
random tree trunks and dead lower branches she might
even be going in circles. She was still cold and shivery
from the long night and yearned to come out into an
opening where she could feel even the pale rays of the
winter sun. There were high boulders and thickets of
fallen branches and vines, all dim below the green roof of
spruce. When she had to cross a small brook one foot
slipped from a mossy boulder into the dark water and cold

knives of water went down over the top of her boot. She would have to find the sun in order to dry out her boot and stocking before she spent another night, or her foot might freeze as she slept. She knew how her heat would slip away through dampness.

She was running out of strength, so hungry she stopped to pry a small sphere of spruce gum from a tree and chew it. It would do little good but it made her feel a little better to chew on its sticky spruce-flavored bitterness, as if it were really food.

Ahead she thought she saw the broader light of an opening, and went toward it as fast as she could. It turned out to be an alder swamp, where dark stagnant water lay in random ditches between the twisted alders. She would have to go around it, out of her way. Many of the surrounding trees were poplar, yellow birch and ash that beavers had gnawed. Stumps, pointed and etched by beaver teeth, stuck up here and there. The alder swamp was probably the upper reaches of a beaver pond, which might be enormous. She would have to guess which was the shortest way around it. Her father or Arn could have told her, maybe, just by looking at the beaver trails that ran in shallow muddy depressions from the trees to disappear in the deeper water. She couldn't tell, so she decided to go to the right, unhappy that she couldn't go straight south, into the sun, where she believed the meadow to be —if it was, as she thought, about midday and the sun was in the south. She was mixed up, probably lost, twice lost because she was in this lost valley. Where was Oka, her friend? She wiped away her tears, saying to herself that they certainly wouldn't do any good at all. Her foot was squishy and wet, heavy as she walked.

Arn had come to the edge of a swamp where willows grew in thick bushes. "Willows make whistles," he said out loud. He had called for Jen many times that morning, but the spruce had absorbed his voice and he knew he couldn't be heard very far. But with a good whistle maybe

Jen might hear him. He took out his knife and cut off a
willow wand as big around as his thumb, cut off a piece
three inches long, then cut a notch for the hole. As his
father had shown him, he cut carefully around the wood,
bark-deep, and began to tap the bark with the back of his
blade to loosen it from the wood so it would slip off and
he could cut an air passage along the top of the wood.
Then it was a matter of adjustment until he got the shrill
sound he wanted. The whistle would last a few days until
the bark dried up and cracked, but in the meantime he
would have a whistle that could be heard twice as far as
any shout. When he was finished he tried it out, hoping
that if Jen heard it she would recognize it for what it was.
Their father had made one for her last summer and she'd
blown it until Arn's ears rang.

As he walked on toward the south, ducking branches
and stepping carefully over swampy places, he would stop
every once in a while and blow the whistle. He was hungry. He was pretty sure he could find some food one way
or another, but he felt he ought to find Jen first. She didn't
know as much about the woods as he did, and she hadn't
a knife or rope or anything useful with her, as far as he
knew. He had the stale piece of bannock he was saving for
her, his little iron pot and some of the old lady's powders.
If only he could find Jen he could give her something to
eat, at least.

Jen thought she was never going to get around the
beaver swamp. It went on and on, each part looking like
the last. The channels of dark water might have been
getting a little shallower but they were too wide to jump
and they were certainly over her boots. The bottoms of
the channels looked mucky too; she might sink in to her
waist if she tried to wade them, even get mired there. So
she kept trying to get around the swamp, stumbling more
and more because of weakness. Several times she fell
down just trying to step over branches she knew she could
have avoided if she were stronger. She had the desire to

give up, to lie down on the damp earth and cry, but she knew the swamp had to end somewhere and she had to get out into the sun and dry off before nightfall. It didn't help to know that the swamp was home to the beavers, who made it comfortable for themselves. They loved its clutter of edible branches and bark, its dank water channels. She could feel in the musty air their pride in their work, which meant life and comfort to them. But to her it was like a trap.

And always before her was the vision of Oka, large and kind, who might be in the meadow waiting to greet her with a soft moo of recognition. She could lie down next to Oka and be warm.

Finally the ground began to rise and the watery troughs grew farther between. The weeds and brush changed, and the trees were bigger. As she came around the beaver swamp, pines and juniper took over. Great thickets of naked blackberry stalks, their berries all gone, grew here and there among the juniper, so she had to choose between the springy juniper and the clasping barbs of the blackberries that hooked into her sleeves and pantlegs, an occasional barb going all the way through into her skin. It was almost impossible to climb over the juniper, which let her down and then pushed her up and made her lose her balance. She tried crawling below the branches of the pines, but those passageways always ended in juniper and clusters of blackberries that were like toothed arms wanting to gather her in.

She was trying to climb over a patch of juniper as high as her head when suddenly she fell right through its rough branches, the small juniper berries turning like tiny blue stars as she fell, and she was down on her hands and knees beneath the branches in a sort of tunnel. The ground was trampled by sharp hooves, and she smelled pig, the bittersweet, biting odor of pig, just like the pigpen in the barn at home, but here it was fiercer, more alive and wild.

She had a feeling she had never had before, only heard

about in stories, that she was trespassing. It was not her fault; she had fallen down into this passage by accident. But that didn't matter. She tried to climb back up through the juniper, but the branches that had let her fall were bent the wrong way and wouldn't let her get back out. By bending way over she could walk down the tunnel. *Boars,* she thought; this must be wild boars' property. Along the side of the tunnel the juniper trunks were slashed to the quick as if by scythes. As she moved along the tunnel she heard, or felt beneath her feet, a thudding like thunder heard behind a mountain, far off over the rim, but advancing. She tried to find a way out, up or to the side, but the branches and trunks were too thick, so she began to run, bent over, though she was not even sure which direction the thudding came from. She might be running toward it, or the sound might not be what she thought it was—wild boars' hooves shaking the earth.

The odor of pig was thick around her and as she ran she couldn't help thinking of the pig they had eaten, his long pink flanks and sparse yellow bristles, and the dense expression in his small eyes. Then had come the sledge hammer and he turned all to something else, not himself any more.

The thudding in the ground grew nearer. From weakness and tiredness she stopped; it would do no good to run on and on. And then, clear and sweet above the rumbling, came the cool song of a chickadee. She looked up to see the little bird perched above her head on the branch of a pine tree. The spreading lower branches of the tree had shaded out the juniper, which couldn't grow in the constant shadow of the pine. The chickadee looked at her and turned its head, its little black cap and bib nodding at her. "Chicka dee dee dee," it sang, and hopped to a higher branch. She could climb out of the tunnel on those same branches. The thudding grew louder, and with all the strength she had left and a little more given to her by her fear she pulled herself up onto the first branch and then climbed higher up the black trunk of the pine until she was as high above the boar trail as the loft at home was above the cabin floor.

The thudding grew, but now she was not in its path. The tree shivered but was strong; she'd always liked white pines because of their soft green wands of needles and their sturdy quietness. The chickadee hopped and danced from one branch to another as if it had no weight, not bothered at all by her or the approaching thunder.

Below her the first boar came by at a thumping, heavy trot. He was brownish black, with long coarse hair—nothing at all like the pig she'd known. He was four times as big as their own pig. His shoulders were huge, and from the long snout came four gleaming yellow tusks, two above and two below, as if he held in his mouth long curved blades that came out both sides. Other boars followed him, their shoulders high and their rear quarters sloping back down. Their smell rose from them, their hairy ears flopped as they trotted by. She seemed to hear in their huffing, grunting breaths a song or a chant made half out of words, though maybe the words were hers. *Root, root,* the thoughts said. *Food, food, mast, meat. We shall go where we may eat!*

The words, or the meanings of the words, came up from their panting travel as if the words, the smell and the thudding of the hooves were all one thing. She held tightly to the tree and did not move.

The last boar stopped short, his hooves sinking into the ground, and snuffled with his round flat pig nose to the right and left; then, slowly, as if he knew what he might find, he raised his big head toward her. His eyes glowed blood-red and his tusks gleamed with saliva—yellow-brown, bright ivory along their sharpened edges. She could not hear his thoughts at all as he stared at her, but the blood-red eyes seemed to reflect the blood she felt pulsing in her own veins. She felt small and unprotected; even the tree seemed to grow thinner as the eyes looked at her. She shut her eyes and held on as tightly as she could, and when she opened them again the boar was gone. He hadn't made a sound.

She wondered if he could have known that she had helped slaughter a pig, and eaten its flesh. Whatever he had thought had been too dark and secret for her to understand.

The sun was getting low, now. Its rays were dim and pale as they came through the branches over her head. The chickadee had gone and only a bluejay flew past, high above the tree, swooping and calling as it went on toward its destination. Another jay answered from far off. The air was colder. When she put weight on her wet foot she found it had grown just a little numb at the heel. She had to get moving. The boars had been traveling south too; she would have to follow them. She was worried about Oka. What would they do if they found her? Pigs ate everything they could find, but would they kill a cow?

Maybe the tunnel opened out after a way. The boars probably used it just to get through the juniper and blackberry thickets. If she was to move at all, she would have to go through the boar tunnel; there was no other way.

Just as she got out of the tree and dropped back into the tunnel she heard, from far away, a long high whistle. She couldn't think what bird or animal would make such a long whistling call. She would have thought about it more, but she had to get to the end of the tunnel as quickly as she could and find the green meadow she knew was there somewhere to the south.

If only she could reach the green meadow. The woods and brambles, the twisted branches, the swamps and blowdown were all against her. Boars could come along again and she didn't know what they might do. She was trespassing on their ground. Maybe the meadow didn't even exist, was just a mirage she'd seen from the bat cave. Or it could be nothing but muskeg, or sphagnum moss floating on a wide water hole.

Finally she came to a place where the boar tunnel did end in more open woods, where she no longer had to fear that something might be coming up behind her. Past the woods she came to a wide brook with waterfalls over rocks, and deep pools. She heard it first, coolly splashing and sighing ahead of her, and when she got to it, there just on the other side was the meadow, sloping upwards to the south, smooth with real grass. Clumps of trees were scattered across its smooth, undulating surface, green except in lower places where it had been touched into brown by frost. Several animals, maybe deer, grazed far out beside a great evergreen tree that stood alone. One of the animals was larger, shorter in its body. It had a white spot on its neck. At that distance she could just make out the white spot. It was Oka.

"Oka!" she cried, but of course the splashing brook was louder than her voice. She had to get across, to go to Oka, but the brook was too deep and wide. Rims of ice had formed on the boulders from the spray. But there, downstream, a tree had fallen across. She might be able to cross the brook on that tree. It was a big maple, rotten in its center and split all the way down to its upturned roots, but it would surely hold her if she could hold on to it. The trunk was icy in places from spray, but she went to it and carefully began to inch her way out over the brook, holding on with her arms and legs. She got almost all the way across before a rotten section of bark, punky wood and the sawdust of wood-boring insects gave way and rolled her off into the water.

Because of her clothes the shock wasn't immediate, but by the time she thrashed her way to the shallows and stood up, her clothes were numbing cold and so heavy they might have been made of stone. Icy knives enclosed her everywhere. She tried to walk but had to get down on her hands and knees and crawl to the bank, where she managed to stand up again. "Oka! Oka!" she cried as she searched the broad meadow. But the animals that had

been there had disappeared, along with the stockier one
she had thought to be Oka. Nothing moved across the
distance but several crows, far away, rowing across the air
on their slow black wings, so far away she couldn't hear
their cawing. They were in the sun, but it had left her and
the meadow. The top of the tall evergreen tree near
where she thought she'd seen Oka was touched with
golden light, but now it faded into a somber green full of
darkness. She must try to move her legs toward that tree.
If she stopped now, she would surely freeze. She would
fall into that terrible sleep she had been warned about, in
which cold pretends to be warmth and takes your life.

With the sun gone the air in its blank stillness pressed
against her; her sleeves were touched with white frost.
Her pantlegs rattled as she took the first steps, already
beginning to freeze solid. She walked in her freezing
clothing as if she were in armor, fighting her own clothes
at each step. The rope bridle, still looped around her
shoulder and under her arm, might have been made of
wood. Her feet were numb; the numbness was creeping
up her legs, creeping in from the tips of her fingers to her
palms and wrists. Though she staggered toward the tree
as fast as she could, it seemed as far away as ever. Once
she'd had a dream in which something she loved fled from
her and her legs and arms were in molasses, so slow, so
slow. But after that dream she'd awakened; this time it
was real.

From far away to the west came a long, whistling call,
and another, from some bird or shrill animal she was too
tired even to think of identifying. She was lying on the
ground, stalks of field hay sticking without pain into her
cheek. She couldn't remember falling, or hitting the
ground. Inside her chest she was still warm, in a small
round warm center there, but the warmth was growing
weaker, wanting only to rest, to sleep. Against the stubble
and the folded stalks of grass, her ear received a faint hum
as if from the earth itself, or from all the tiny living things

within it, all the plants and animals sleeping their winter sleep in the earth below the field. They were all merely sleeping, but the sleep she fell slowly toward was not the sleep from which one ever wakes. *Alarm! Alarm!* part of her said, a small voice within her crying out against the false warmth. The hum from the earth was like a lament, but it was indifferent toward her, as though it mourned the ending of life while knowing that other life would go on. But she heard the small cry of alarm and with her last strength got back to her knees and cried "Oka! Oka! Oka!" before she was taken back down toward the warmth of that false sleep.

7

Fire
and Food

Arn blew a long note on his willow whistle, then wiped it dry. The air had grown colder when the sun went behind the mountains, and his saliva tended to freeze inside the whistle so that it would give only a mousy squeak. He had seen no tracks or signs that could have been made by Jen or Oka. In patches of freezing mud he had seen deer tracks, doglike prints that must have been made by wolves, and splayed prints sunk deeply into the ground that looked like pig tracks. He had heard of wild boar but had never seen one. The wolves and the possible boar gave him a shiver and made him cautious. He kept noticing trees that he might climb in an emergency, and as he passed through the woods he seemed to be going from one climbable tree to another.

Now he stood at the brook and looked across it to the meadow, relieved to see that it was a real meadow, not just a bog. Several deer browsed upon it, far out near a large evergreen tree. When he blew his whistle again the deer looked up, freezing to stillness. Then, after a long look, they went back to browsing again. He scanned the whole meadow, all that he could see of it, but there was no sign of Jen or Oka.

It took him a while to find a way across the brook. By going upstream he finally found a place where all the rushing water had to flow within a deep crack in the ledge and he could jump across, being careful of the ice forming from the spray. He did slip as he landed, but he was ready and went down on all fours and held on.

Soon it would be dark. He whistled and called for Jen as he went into the meadow. If he could get to the rise near the big evergreen before dark settled in, he would have a better view, but he was tired and weak from hunger and it seemed so far.

He heard a strange call from the east. At first, before he could stop walking, he thought it was a night bird's faint scream. It repeated itself several times. He tried to think what bird would be calling in this freezing dusk. It might have been a goose, but all the geese must have gone south long ago. No, it had more urgency to it, more desperation. And then, as if the idea were very strange and he hadn't really believed that he would find Jen at all, he wondered almost with fright if it was Jen, and the call, that strange double sound, was the name *Oka*.

It had stopped, but before he went toward it he took a sighting on a tree that stood higher than the others there to the east at the woodline bordering the meadow. The call seemed to have come from just that direction, and even if it was dark by the time he got there he could still pick out that tree against the sky.

As he approached the eastern edge of the meadow, the woods loomed up like a black wall. Ahead of him on the ground was a grayish bundle that might have been an animal or a rock. He called, "Jen?" but the thing gave no answer and didn't move. Cautiously he moved closer, then closer still, until he could begin to see its shape. An arm there, silver with frost, a leg and a boot. It was Jen. He knelt beside her and felt her face, which was as cold as glass. When he rolled her over she was like a piece of wood, encased as she was in her frozen clothes. But she was breathing, very faintly. He saw at once she must have fallen in the brook and she would soon be dead unless he got a fire going and made some shelter against the night wind. She was too close to death now, so close he almost called out for his father. He wanted to call for him. His father would know what to do. *Dad, Dad;* he could hear the words forming in his throat.

But then he remembered that no one else was here and that he alone would have to try to save Jen. No one else could help him or tell him what to do.

First he got her under the arms and dragged her toward the woods, where he could find protection from the wind and from the frost, which was falling as the light faded. She was heavy from the frozen water in her clothes, but finally he got her beneath the trees, next to a tall pine tree and another, fallen one, where the two made a shelter of sorts from the wind. It was even darker in the woods, but by feeling around in the trees he found brittle dead lower branches which he broke off and carried back in armfuls to the place where Jen lay against the blown-down tree. From the edge of the field he gathered dry stalks of hay. By feeling the ground in front of Jen and kicking the woods soil and the rotting damp wood away, he made a place for a fire, then crumbled up the field hay into a pile. From his pack he got the flint and the tinder, a box of shaved, carefully dried, partly powdered wood that should begin to burn from just a spark. In the dark he arranged some of the tinder as best as he could, then held the jagged piece of flint over it and struck the flint hard with the back of his knife blade. Little sparks fell, jumped in arcs, spluttered and burned out before they could reach the tinder.

He kept trying. Maybe the cold air and the falling frost had dampened everything more than he knew. His hands, out of his mittens, grew numb and awkward, but he kept hitting the flint, getting small sparks that died too quickly. But then, finally, after a hundred tries, two sparks at once fell into the tinder and a tiny flame rose, no larger than the head of a pin. He held his breath, knowing that until it grew and gained color, any wind could put it out. It did grow, even giving a little light, now, so that he could see enough by it to carefully, carefully offer it a stalk of hay. Please take this, he prayed. Take this small offering, little flame, and don't go out. The flame grew until it was nearly an inch high, with a small wisp of smoke swirling above it. It must grow. It must. Carefully he fed it stalks of hay —not too much at once or it would smother. It had to be fed just enough, not too much, just enough to let it gain warmth and confidence. He could just feel its warmth now in his cold fingers; soon it grew large enough to think of taking twigs, then larger twigs, which he arranged like a tepee over it. And then branches, the fire's cheerful, hungry glow growing until it lit a warm circle in the woods among the standing, overhanging trees.

But it must be bigger if it was to thaw Jen's clothes and dry them out. It would have to roar and to singe the trees; its strength would have to make the branches above it move and toss in its rising heat.

He gathered branches, breaking off the dead ones that were small enough to break off, using his knife as an ax to hack the larger ones until he could break them off, until he had the fire roaring as high as his head. Parts of the fallen tree had broken off, and these he dragged around so their butt ends could lie in the fire. Then he made a high pile of whatever wood he could find, so he could feed the fire in the night.

Jen lay propped against the fallen trunk, still breathing, her eyes closed. The surface frost had melted from her parka and pants, and he could just begin to move her arms and legs within the frozen clothes. He pulled off her mittens, then the rope bridle, which creaked in its ice, then her hood, and finally managed to open her parka. She faced the fire and would be getting its warmth while he made a shelter.

He went farther into the dark woods until he found a grove of balsam firs, broke off the lower boughs and carried armfuls of the green and aromatic boughs back to the fallen tree. Weaving them together with dead branches propped against the standing pine and against the fallen trunk where Jen lay, he made an overhanging shelter, enclosed on the sides and in back, open to the fire in front. He was warm now from all this activity, so it was time to get Jen out of her wet clothes and into his parka. First he took the forty feet of narrow hemp rope from his pack and strung part of it between two trees on the other side of the fire to make a clothesline, then got Jen, who was now mumbling to herself, out of her clothes and wrapped in his parka. She seemed so small and fragile as he pulled the dank wet buckskin from her. Her hands and feet were still like ice, but the fire would warm them. He hung her clothes on the clothesline, where they began to steam, clouds of white mist rising from them into the trees above.

While her clothes were drying he found a flat rock and rolled it on its edge to the fire, went to the brook in the darkness, its rushing sound overcoming the crackle of the fire as he left the circle of warmth, and filled his small iron pot with water. Back at the fire he set the pot on the flat rock next to the flames. Then all he could do was gather more wood, tend the fire and hope that its heat would enter Jen's skin and blood and bring her back to life. Each time he came back from the darkness with a load of wood he stopped to feel her hands and feet.

And then one time he came back with an armload of dry pine branches for his woodpile and saw that she was coming awake. When her blue eyes opened, they seemed blind. Her face was always pale, but it glowed in the firelight as if light came from inside it, palely gleaming from her round child's face. Her eyes were round, too, staring at him but not knowing who he was for just a moment, then opening wider and turning gleamy with tears when she saw who he was.

"Arn! Arn!" she said.

Arn was suddenly so tired he had to sit down on the balsam boughs he had spread on the floor of the shelter. Jen finally stopped her crying. She was trying to move her fingers, rubbing her hands together in the fire's heat.

"Arn, I'm so cold," she said. "But you found me."

"I heard you calling."

"You came after me!"

"Well, sure," he said. He got the piece of stale bannock out of his pack and handed it to her. "You won't warm up enough if you don't eat something."

She took the bannock and bit a piece from it. "But you're weak too," she said. "I can tell. You've got to eat too, Arn. I'll bet you haven't had anything to eat. I can tell."

"We'll have to find something to eat soon," he said. He watched her avidly eating the bannock. His mouth watered and his stomach moved, constricting, wantingfood so badly it seemed to cry out from down inside him. He shut his eyes so as not to see Jen eat, but as soon as he did she pressed the last piece of bannock against his lips. His will said no, but he couldn't help himself and took the bannock in his mouth. It felt like life itself, but it was so small, like the part Jen had eaten, that it would do little good.

The water in the pot was steaming, so he put some of the powder from his birch-bark box into it and they drank the hot tea, careful to hold the pot by its bail and to drink from the side that had been away from the fire. Immediately they both felt more awake but even hungrier than before. Arn knew he had to find food. They hadn't had much to eat at all for weeks and they were both thin. The bones in Jen's wrists looked as if they would come through the skin at any moment. When he turned his head to look at the fire and to see how Jen's clothes were drying, his weakness made him dizzy and he had to put his head down between his knees so he wouldn't faint.

They told each other what had happened to them since the night Jen left the cabin. "I had to find Oka, Arn. I just had to," she said, almost crying again.

"All right," he said. "What's done is done."

"And I think I saw her just before I fell in the brook. She was out there by a big tree with some deer. I'm sure I saw the white spot on her neck."

"Didn't you hear my whistle?"

"I think I did once, but I didn't know what it was."

"We've got to find some food," he said.

"I thought for a while I was getting used to being hungry," Jen said. "But I'm not. My teeth hurt I'm so hungry." She held the iron pot in her hands, warming them.

"We're starving," he said. In spite of the fire he shivered with sudden cold.

Then he heard a sound not made by the fire. It was a scratchy sound, as if made by claws, and it came from a yellow birch sapling within the fire's glow. His eyes went up the sapling, up its golden bark that shone in the firelight, until they came to a dark, thick shape bigger around than the tree. The scratching came from there. It was a porcupine climbing backwards down the tree with the careful, ponderous slowness porcupines never varied from, no matter what.

Food. Here was food given to them. In the legends the Old People ate porcupines when they were hungry and out of food. They called the porcupine "grandfathers' meat." Anyone could catch them because they depended too much on their long quills for protection and never bothered to run very fast.

Arn got up and picked a club from among the branches on his woodpile. The porcupine kept coming down, scratching the bark with his nails, slowly coming down toward the ground. When he got down even with Arn's head he stopped and turned his snout toward Arn, his black eyes knowing. His quills rose along his back, shiny black spears with white bands on them.

"I'm sorry, porcupine," Arn said. He'd never said anything like that before and didn't know why he said it. Then he went on, hearing the words but not knowing where they came from. "I need your fat and meat. Nothing of you will be wasted."

He hit the porcupine as hard as he could on the end of its black nose, and it dropped with a thud to the ground, bounced and quivered. Some of its quills stuck in the ground and were held there by their barbed tips. It lay on its back, dead now, the soft dark gray fur of its belly exposed.

Jen had been watching without making a sound. She had heard the porcupine and had been the first to see it as it came down the tree. She heard its dull wish to leave the tree where it had been eating the rich inner bark. It was full and didn't understand the fire nearby but was protected by its quills, so it just came down. She heard its alarm, then its resignation when it saw the boy with the club.

Now Arn worked over it with his knife, slicing into its center through the soft belly, peeling away its skin so that finally the skin came off inside out, the quills covered. One quill did stick into his wrist, but he just pulled it straight out, with care that it didn't break off. He put the liver and heart on the flat stone next to the fire, cut the yellow fat from the meat and put pieces of it into the iron pot, then cut off the porcupine's naked head. He was making food. He looked expert, busy, knowing exactly what he was doing. He left the firelight for a while and came back with some long green maple branches. Two of these had forks in them, and these he cut shorter, sharpened and pushed into the ground on each side of the fire. A longer, thicker branch he sharpened on one end and ran it through the porcupine's empty body, then cut off some of the narrow rope and bound the body to the branch, which he placed in the forked sticks so the meat would roast over the fire. On another notched stick propped over the fire he hung the iron pot with the fat in it, and it began to hiss and fry. On a narrower stick he impaled the liver and heart and set them to cook.

Soon the liver and heart were done, and he let them cool a little before offering them to her. She had wondered at first if she could eat that meat, but now her body told her that she must have it, that it was life itself she was being offered. Arn cut both liver and heart in two and put half of each into her hand. As she ate the meat she could feel warmth and strength gathering in her. This food was good beyond preference or taste, good beyond good.

After a while Arn turned the roasting meat on its spit and poured some of the melted fat on it. Drops fell from the dark red meat to the fire, where they burned with orange flashes. Arn had let the fire die down to coals, and he fed it on one side, just enough and not too much, so the meat browned without burning. He turned the spit, basted the meat with fat and tested it every once in a while with the point of his knife. Finally, when he thought it was done, he propped the spit next to the fire, cut off a haunch for each of them and served hers to her on a stick. Then they ate the dark meat, each thanking the porcupine for this gift of strength.

Jen's mind changed, gradually, with this bounty, toward hopefulness once again. No longer was she about to cry or to feel lost or lonely. She would find Oka, with Arn's help. He wasn't like her brother any more, her brother who was just a little boy whom she had known to cry and to be spiteful at times, but more like her father, with her father's certainty and confidence in what he knew how to do.

"Thank you, Arn," she said.

He turned away, a little embarrassed by her admiration, to build up the fire again. "Your clothes are dry now," he said. "Your boots aren't yet, but they will be by morning if it doesn't snow or rain." He tossed her her buckskin trousers and shirt, and her fur parka, which were warm and soft again as she put them on.

"If it weren't for you I'd be dead," she said, handing him his own parka.

"I guess so," he said.

He went to the brook to wash out the pot and get water to make some more tea from the powders.

Before they were ready to go to sleep he built the fire up high again. It would burn down in the night and the cold would wake him so he could build it up again. He took off his inner shirt and wrapped it around Jen's feet, then put his parka back on. They lay on the soft boughs, other boughs surrounding them on three sides, the sweet scent of the drying balsam all around them.

"It's cozy here," Jen said. "I'm not afraid of the boars any more. I was, because I couldn't tell what that one thought of me. I just couldn't tell."

"How can you tell what an animal thinks?"

"I don't know. I just seem to."

"Could you tell what the porcupine thought?"

"Yes. And he knew what you thought. He knew what you were going to do."

"Did he know that I didn't want to kill him, but I had to?"

"All he knew was that you were going to kill him."

Arn was silent.

"We had to eat," Jen said.

"Yes."

"And now I'm warm and I feel more hopeful."

"But it's not like home," he said, and all at once they thought of Tim Hemlock and Eugenia alone in the cabin, the cabin locked in ice, and how they would be worrying about their children. Arn told Jen about how their mother went behind the waterfall but couldn't find the passage through the mountain, and how it was right there, wide open, for him.

"Do you think it's Tsuga's black gate?" she said.

"I don't know. It scares me to think about that."

"It's all so strange, Arn. Poor Mother and Dad. They'll think something awful's happened to us. Maybe that we're dead. If we can only find Oka and go home again."

Before Arn went to sleep he thought about the words that had come into his mouth without his thinking. He had echoes in his mind, deep inside him, as if things were trying to be remembered there.

And Jen, staring up at the balsam boughs Arn had made into a shelter for them, with the firelight flickering, then looking out into the woods where the firelight brought out the standing trunks of trees from the deeper dark where all the night wilderness was—she suddenly trembled with fear of their aloneness here. It was wrong of them to have left their home, wrong of her to have run away without telling anyone. And now she and Arn were so small in this strange night within the mountain.

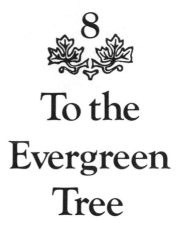

8

To the Evergreen Tree

Back at the Hemlocks' small farm, through the mountain and over the miles of ice, the cabin creaked in the cold. Eugenia had gone out with an ax and though it exhausted her, chopped the rails from the pig's pen, dragged them inside and was building up the fire in order to make some potato soup from the precious seed potatoes. She looked old, now, pale and tired. She went through the motions of keeping the small fire going, but much of her reasons for living had gone with her children. After getting the fire blazing under the kettle she looked down at her sleeping husband to find that he was twisting his head, straining his shoulders and neck as if trying to escape from bonds. She put her hand on his cheek, which calmed him, and then was startled by his open eyes. They were not the eyes of hallucination he had opened before, those staring eyes that saw whatever they saw far beyond the room, even beyond the earth. These were her husband's dark brown eyes looking right at her.

"Eugenia," he said in a dry, unused voice.

He had been gone so long. He had not really been here with her, and now she knew how lonely and near despair she had been.

"Eugenia, you must tell Jen and Arn . . ." His face turned perplexed. "You must tell Jen and Arn . . ."

"But they're gone, Tim. They're gone!"

He didn't seem to understand. "You must," he said weakly. "You must." Then he slept, but later as she raised a cup of soup to his lips he drank and his eyes opened upon her face again.

"How long have I been sick?" he asked in his dry, unused voice.

"For a long time. For weeks."

"Where are the children?"

She had to tell him they were gone, how Jen had followed Oka and Arn followed Jen, about the falls and the narrow trail along the cliff, and how the trail ended behind the falling water. He made her tell him everything that had happened, how Arn had learned the old lady's sign language and made the medicine for him, and how it had seemed to make him breathe easier.

"What did they take with them?" he asked.

"I don't know. All I know is they're gone. Our children are gone!"

"You must look carefully and tell me." He tried to get up, but hadn't the strength in his arms to push the bearskin robe aside. He sank back with a groan. "I can't help them. But please, Eugenia, you must tell me what they took with them."

"Jen wore her warmest clothes and her crampons. She took Oka's bridle, but nothing else."

Tim Hemlock groaned. "And what did Arn take?"

Eugenia looked through Arn's things, at the clothespegs near the door, everywhere in the cabin. He, too, had worn his warmest clothes and his crampons. He had also taken flint and tinder, a coil of narrow rope, his pack, his knife, a piece of bannock and one of the birch-bark boxes from the mantel.

"He could make fire, then," Tim Hemlock said.

"But, Tim . . . I went to the end of the trail. They didn't come back, so they must have . . ."

"We can't be sure. And the old lady? She never came back?"

"Yes, she's gone. They're all gone. Arn and Jen fell into the chasm! My poor children!"

"I know that place," Tim Hemlock said.

"But I thought you never went to the mountain!"

"I've gone farther than I've told you." He struggled to get up, but he had no strength. "My arms are like lead. Where is my strength? But I *must* find them!" He lay back, his eyes staring, his face slack with despair because he could not go to find his children.

Morning came to the strange valley—cold, gray, with a mean wind and a mist that swirled over the ashes of the fire and up Arn's legs and into the spaces between his mittens and his sleeves. He wanted to sleep but the wind teased him cruelly. If he pulled up his legs, it got in around his ankles; if he rolled up in a ball, it laid its icy touch on his back. Finally he knew he had to get up and build up the fire again, as he had twice in the night. Then he and Jen would at least be warm on the side they turned to the fire.

His maple spit was gone, and with it the roasted carcase of the porcupine. The head was missing too, as were the innards and the skin; only the quills still lay there in a ragged pile. Something had come in the night—and there were the tracks, one of them very clear in the blown ashes at the edge of the fire—the wide, fuzzy, clawless paw print of a lynx.

He built up the fire, and when Jen woke up he told her that a lynx had taken the rest of their food. Then he went to the brook with the iron pot to get water so they could at least have tea from the powders for their breakfast. There was strength in the tea; he had felt it the night before and seen the change in Jen, how the hot tea had brought her back from the cold. It had given him the energy to skin and roast the porcupine. No, more than that, it had given him the will to do it.

He knelt by a pool of the brook to dip water into his pot. Something below the moving surface took his eye, just beyond the rim of the ice he'd had to break, and made his eyes go deeper, into the water depths. A long dark green thing moved away from his shore, deeper, then disappeared. The wind paused for a moment, and as the ripples lessened he saw it again, down by a boulder, lying in its moving element behind its holding stone, its fins barely pulsing for balance. He could just make out the red, green, blue and yellow spots on its sides, dimmed of color by the water. It was a brook trout, a squaretail at least a foot long. There would be others, too, alive down there, waiting for the current to bring their food to them.

He took the pot of water back and hung it over the fire on its propped, forked stick. If only he had a fishhook, some line and bait. But he didn't, so that was that. Then, later, as they drank the tea made from purselane, dock, dried red mushroom and the brown powder from the box marked with the curved hand, he began to get ideas. He had his knife; what couldn't a man do with a knife, a sharp, tempered blade he kept always by his side? His knife was his faithful tool, all he needed in the wilderness if he knew how to use what was there to use. If he kept his wits about him and didn't get scared and turn into a baby, he ought to be able to survive and to provide for his little sister as well.

So he began to think. Jen sat with the pot of tea in her hands, pensively staring at the fire.

As he thought, he took the piece of flint from his pack and with one of its facets carefully honed the cutting edge of his knife where the edge had touched porcupine bone. His knife wasn't really dull, but he could just make out along its edge the slightest burr. After lightly honing it he stropped the blade on the side of his boot until it was so sharp it faded at its very edge into invisibility.

He would make a hook and line. He might make a spear

out of a thin maple wand, but the brook was too deep
where he'd seen the trout, and if he got wet his clothes
would be a long time drying. So he must let his bait go
alone across those depths, counting on the hunger of the
trout to fasten themselves to his line so he could pull them
out onto the bank. He went over in his mind every possible thing he and Jen had between them that he might use.
The hemp rope, though narrow, was too large. He might
possibly untwist some of its strands and use only a few of
them, but that seemed too lengthy a job. Then he noticed
the decorative border at the bottom of Jen's parka, a strip
of red fox fur that had been sewn on by her mother, either
with thin buckskin rawhide or with the linen thread the
Traveler brought.

"Jen," he said, "I saw trout in the brook and I'm going
to catch enough for breakfast."

"How?" she asked. "Did you bring fishing gear?"

"No, we're going to make some. But I need some line."
He wondered how she'd feel about unstitching part of the
band of red fox fur from her parka because he knew how
proud she'd been of it. "Would you mind taking the bottom stitches out of the fox fur on your parka?"

She thought about it for just a second. "No," she said,
looking at it. "It's just decoration, so it doesn't matter."
She took his knife and started the thread loose on the end,
and he whittled her a sharp stick she could use as an awl
to loosen each stitch in turn. The thread was the strong,
waxed kind the Traveler brought, which would make
good line.

Now he had to have a hook. As he considered this,
strange visions and alternatives began to come into his
mind, pictures of hooks quite unlike the steel ones his
father made, with their curved shanks and small barbs.
One he thought was just a straight piece of bone or wood
sharpened on both ends, with a hole in the center for the
line. Sticky bait of some kind kept the hook parallel to the
line until the fish swallowed it, and then a pull on the line
caused the sharpened ends to go crossways in the fish's

throat or stomach. He seemed to see a man in brown buckskin peering into the water, watching this device with patient eyes. But then other hooks appeared, carved from jawbones, from the spines of animals and fish.

He had been looking at the porcupine quills the lynx had left scattered on the ground. "Nothing of you will be wasted," he'd said to the grandfather, the porcupine, not knowing why he'd said it. Gingerly he went through the piles of quills and picked out some of the strongest, sharpest ones. Then he found a piece of dry, unrotted pine and carved out a small shank, tapering it at the bottom so that the porcupine quills, cut off short at their tips and lashed with thread to the wooden shank, would stick back up at an angle. At the top of the shank he carved a groove all the way around to tie the line to. It was close, careful work because the hook had to be quite small, less than an inch long. He made several of the shanks. Jen had freed a long piece of thread by now, and he took enough of it to wind and tie two quill barbs to each shank.

It was Jen who suggested that he try a small fluff of fox fur, stuck with spruce gum and then tied, on each hook. She remembered what some of her father's trout and salmon flies looked like.

"But what will the trout think they are?" Arn said.

"I don't know, but I think they'll try to eat them. They'll think they're some kind of a bug," Jen said with such conviction he knew it was that strange talent she had for knowing deeper things than he about the thoughts of animals.

Jen managed to free a good six feet of the strong thread, and while he looked for a straight pole among the hardwood brush at the edge of the field, she found a spruce that was leaking gum. They finished the trout flies, which did look like a strange sort of insect. Arn tied on one of the flies, then tied the line to the end of a good pole, and they went to the brook, keeping low and quiet as they crept up to the head of the pool.

"Charr, charr, you will eat," Arn whispered. Charr? he

thought. Why did he say that? He remembered then that his father had once used the word for trout.

He and Jen hid behind a boulder and Arn let the fly down on the water with hardly a ripple. It floated a few feet, turning slowly in the eddies of the pool, before something swirled excitedly down in the water, then shot up toward the fly and took it with a rounded swirl of water and a splash. Then came the tug on the line, that wild thing turning away toward safety, but caught, struggling, zigzagging, pulling with its water strength. Though his arms were shaking from the surprise of his sudden connection with that desperate creature of the water, Arn held the pole as steadily as he could and backed away from the boulder to the more gradual bank of the pool. Then, with a smooth motion because he wasn't sure of the strength of his hook and line, he pulled the trout out over the thin rim of ice to the dry pebbles and grabbed him with both hands.

The trout was beautiful in his dark green and bright jewels of red, blue and yellow along his sides. He was about a foot long, plump and muscular. "Charr," Arn said, "nothing of you will be wasted," then took his knife and hit the trout just behind its head with the back of the blade. The trout quivered and was dead. He took the hook from its mouth to find that one of the porcupine quills was bent over, so he tied on a new fly.

He got three more good fish from the pool before the trout grew suspicious of the red-fox fly and would try to eat it no more. "We've got all we need for breakfast anyway," Arn said. He cleaned the fish beside the brook and they took them back to the fire, where they roasted them lightly over the coals, the fish impaled on green sticks. They ate the trout down to their pearly skeletons. They ate the crisp fins and even the round buttons of muscle in their cheeks, the muscles that closed the trout's jaws upon their prey. Then, full and feeling the borrowed strength coming into their arms and legs, they had some more of the tea made from the powders.

Arn drowned the fire down to its last hiss with water from the brook, coiled his narrow hemp rope and arranged everything in his pack, and they were ready to resume their search for Oka.

Arn had put the line and the hooks carefully away in his pack. They might need them again, of course, but what he wanted so badly to do was to show them to his father. His father would be proud of him, and of Jen for thinking of the fox-fur dressing on the hooks. But there was sadness and uncertainty in that feeling because he didn't know how his father was, if he was getting better or worse. He worried about his mother, too, knowing how little food was left at home—except for the animals and the seeds they would need to get through another year.

But how proud he would be to show the clever hooks to his father, and see his father's big, craftsman's hands holding the tiny hooks and admiring them!

As they crossed the meadow toward the big evergreen tree, Jen saw in her mind only that far animal she had seen, or thought she'd seen, the day before. The one that was stockier than the deer, with the white spot on its neck. It had to be Oka.

"If we don't see Oka from the height of the land, or find her tracks, we're going to go home," Arn said.

"We must find Oka!" Jen cried.

"Look, Jen, I'm worried about Mother and Dad. They'll think we're lost."

Jen heard in his voice that he had made a decision. She didn't know how to change his mind. He seemed bigger and more decisive than he ever had at home. He'd stopped, and looked at her sternly as he spoke. "We haven't seen one of Oka's tracks in this valley."

"She went along the ledge to the falls! You saw her tracks there!"

"Oka and a deer," Arn said. "Maybe the deer led her away. How do you know she'd even want to come back?"

"We have to find Oka!" Jen heard tears in her voice, knowing with just a little shame that she was using them to try to change Arn's mind. In the past her tears hadn't always affected him that much, but she felt that he had changed.

"Think of Mother and Dad," he said. "Think how they must feel."

Arn was right, and he knew it. He didn't have to listen to Jen at all because if he started back for home she would have to follow, and it didn't matter how much she cried, either. He was in charge and he'd saved her life and that was that. "We'll go up where the big tree is and look around, but that's all. Then we start for home." He felt his power, one her tears could not change.

But he looked at her tears, and as he did he remembered something he had done, once, something powerful and shameful. His father had made him a bow of ash, with a waxed string, and four spruce arrows. While alone near the river he saw a toad upon a clay bank, where the clay would receive and not break his arrow. A brown toad. No matter how he tried, and tried afterwards, he could find no harm in a toad. Yes, it had been a lucky shot, but that was no excuse for the harmless toad impaled and in agony. He had withdrawn the bloodied arrow from the clay and the dying toad and shot it away, across the river where he would never find it. He told no one what he'd done.

"Arn!" Jen was crying. "Please, Arn!"

"We'll look for a while," he said. "But if we don't find any sign of her, we'll go home."

"Thank you," Jen said, rubbing her eyes with the backs of her mittens. "Thank you, Arn."

Then Arn seemed to be fading out before Jen's eyes. Everything about him whitened, faded. He seemed distant from her even though he hadn't moved. "Arn!" she called.

He moved toward her and took her hand. "It's fog," he said.

The air had grown moist and warm. They looked around them, but beyond the crisp brown grass stems at their feet the whole valley had faded out until everything was as white as paper. They could move their hands into the white and it didn't resist them, but it was blank, quietly opaque. Its warm dampness was already beading on their skin and clothes. They could just make out each other. Even their feet were almost lost down in the whiteness.

"Now we can't move at all," Arn said.

"But we have to," Jen said. The silent fog made them keep their voices low, as if it were a presence they must not disturb.

"We'll just get lost," Arn said.

"You don't care about Oka!"

"Well . . ." he said, listening as if to the fog. There was a distant thrumming, felt through the ground, through their feet. Arn said, "We belong at home, Jen. I don't understand this place."

The thrumming grew louder, but seemed to come from no one direction. For a moment the fog around them lifted as a space of clear air the size of a room opened upon them and passed, moving swiftly though they felt no wind. Jen saw how Arn's face was shiny with the beads of warm water, as were the arms of her parka and the backs of her mittens. She took off her mittens and put them in her pocket, feeling the damp warmth on her hands. The ground began to shudder with the drumming sounds.

"The boars," she said, taking Arn's hand again. "It sounds like the boars!"

"Stand still," he said.

The fog passed them in white waves with openings in between, so they felt hidden and then not hidden, though the fog's blankness was ominous because in it everything else was hidden from them. The drumming grew louder. The earth shook beneath them until they were certain they would be run over by the power that came toward them. The fog still moved, fading and thickening. When the drumming grew so loud they knew they must be caught beneath a thousand hooves, they held their breaths and saw dark hunched shapes go by them, several yards away. The dark shapes, made gray and insubstantial by the fog, drove on by and faded in the fog as the rumbling lessened.

"It was the boars," Jen whispered. "It was the boars."

"If we could find the tree, we might climb up in it," Arn whispered back. He was shivering. "We were downwind, so they didn't get our scent."

"Yes, they didn't know we were here," Jen said.

"Could you feel them thinking?"

"About other things, maybe."

The rolls of fog, according to Arn's memory, came from the direction of the tree, so they went forward carefully into the unfelt but moving air, trying as best they could not to stumble. After a long while the fog began to thin, and finally they found themselves just at the edge of it, where it swirled from a lake or pond of hot water, rising up in whirls from the water's surface. On their right the field was clear in colder air, but down to their left was the water from which the warm steam boiled soundlessly. An odor came from the water, the same odor that had been barely evident in the fog that had surrounded them. Arn recognized it now as something like a faint whiff of gunpowder, or the way his father's rifle smelled after having been shot, before his father cleaned it. The stony edges of the pond were stained bright red, yellow and a mineralgreen. The winter sun, just now coming out from behind high clouds, made the swirling mist pure white. To their right the winter meadow turned from green grass near the heat of the pond to sere brown hay as it rose to the northwest. The great evergreen tree was nowhere in sight, though halfway up the slope of the meadow were some piles of granite stones, some as regular and angular as walls.

Without a word Arn and Jen climbed the slope toward the piles of stones. They would have to reach the height of the land in order to see the whole meadow and find the tree. Arn wanted to see the stones, too, in spite of his desire to get home as quickly as possible. He thought of the dream he'd had the first night in the valley, of all the people together among log huts, and tents made of animal skins. Those people all together had seemed, in the way of dreams, to have a powerful meaning; they had caused a yearning in him. The dream had been of this valley, he was certain now as they came up to the stones. Though they had been tumbled by time and weather, there was a regularity in their patterns that nothing in nature could have caused. There were four squares, each several yards across, each about the size of his father's stone-walled forge house.

"People lived here," he said to Jen.

Nothing was left but the tumbled walls. The brown meadow hay was as smooth as a lake up to the stones and between them, just the lonely walls keeping nothing in or out. The people who had lived among the walls were gone, all traces of their pathways gone, yet Arn felt their presence in this valley as if his own eyes, seeing the white snow fields and the far stone cliffs, made their eyes alive again. The valley was once their world, familiar to their eyes.

He and Jen climbed on toward the top of the slope. All the meadow they could see was deserted. Not even a bird flew. Near the height of the land they began to see the top of the great tree, first its highest green branches, then more and more of it as it grew up into their sight. They were still far from the tree; they'd had no idea of its great size. As they approached, it loomed above them, its gray-brown trunk ascending, its long branches and short green needles like great wands extending to a hundred feet over their heads. The trunk grew out of jumbled gray rocks and an outcropping of granite, the muscular brown roots extending like huge clenching fingers over the ledge and down into the earth. They had never seen a tree like this one. It was an evergreen and bore small cones, but its great trunk and random branches had the clean separateness and strength of hardwood. The bark was grooved in random patterns, dry to the touch. The trunk was at least six feet in diameter and the first broad branches were far above their heads, much too high for them to climb.

A light wind sighed through the tree, or the tree itself used the wind as its voice. They could hear no words but they felt at once another presence, a calm, distant strength that almost seemed to be aware of them.

Suddenly Jen went to the tree and put her arms around one of its great arched roots. "I love this tree," she said.

Arn stood looking up into the tree. Thin winter clouds passed over the valley; the sturdy tree in its height seemed to stabilize the earth itself against their passing, keeping the ground where they stood firm against the turning of the sky. He had not been surprised by Jen's sudden feeling for the tree, yet he wondered why she hadn't surprised him. She nearly always came to such sudden conclusions, skipping whatever steps he might have to take. She always leapt into new things, attitudes, actions like her mad journey to rescue Oka. It was up to him to look carefully, to figure out what had to be done.

Around the ledges from which the tree grew, tall thin stones were set at intervals, making a circle on the meadow with the tree as its center. The gray stones were all about the same size, each about as tall as his father. Carved designs, worn by time, circled the waists of the squared stones. He climbed down from the ledge and went to one of the stones.

"Arn!" Jen called.

"Come here," he said, "but be careful getting down from the ledge."

The stone was mute, an unmoving sentry. It was headless, but around its middle was a carved band, like a wide belt, with what was obviously a sheath hanging from it, all in deep relief in the gray granite.

The sheath was exactly like his own; the knife handle that protruded from it, though worn smooth, resembled the final curve of his own knife's stag handle. He undid the bone buttons of his parka and drew his knife from his sheath to look at it. Jen had gone to the next stone in the circle. "Look, Arn," she called. He went to her. This stone sentry's sheath was empty, but his arm, carved in relief across his chest, held a stone knife whose curved blade, choil, hilt and pommel were exactly the same design as Arn's. He held the smaller knife against the stone one and they were just alike, one in ancient worn stone, the other bright and sharp. His living hand grasped his own knife's handle just as the rugged stone hand grasped its stone one.

They could only wonder. The sentry stones, mute in their grainy age, ringed the great tree.

"Look!" Jen said. She had turned back toward the tree, and now pointed to the ledges.

At first Arn saw only tumbled rocks and granite with the tree's brown roots arching down across them. But then he saw that here, too, was a design that could not have been accidental. At one place the roots formed an arch above a platform of smoothed stones, and behind the living arch was another, made of stone, surrounding darkness.

"Come on," Jen said, but Arn held back.

"Let's be careful," he said, knowing they would go there, to the center. Jen, not listening to him, ran back toward the tree. From the corners of Arn's eyes the stone sentries seemed to stand straighter as he followed Jen.

They climbed up to the level place, where each stone was smoothed and fitted to the next. It was like an altar, or a place to be watched by people standing like the sentries, within the sentries' circle. Thin echoes of their own footsteps sang in their ears, as if the small sounds rebounded from the walls of the whole valley.

"This place is very old," Jen whispered. "There's no end

to it. I can feel it going back and back, like there's no bottom or end to it."

They both thought of the old stories but neither wanted to say so out loud. The valley had been neither kind nor unkind to them so far.

The roots, thicker than the trunks of most trees, came down like the fingers of a giant hand on either side of the dark entrance, which was much larger than they'd first thought. It was an arch of fitted stones, higher and wider than their home cabin back in the frozen world.

It had turned cold. Light snow sifted past the high column of the tree, coming from a graying sky where the pale sun was only a lighter gray place beyond the mountains to the southwest. As they looked, shivering, the mountains faded into the gray-white of swirling snow.

They held hands as they moved slowly toward the entrance, each of them in dread but as if in a dream unaware of any other thing to do. At the living arch Jen stopped to put her hand to the thick root. She started, then took Arn's hand and placed it where hers had been.

"Do you feel it?" she asked.

"I feel the bark," Arn said.

"It moved," Jen said. "It moved, Arn."

"It was the wind moving the tree," he said.

"No, it wasn't like that."

The dense flesh of the tree had moved under her hand, in response to her touch. She knew it had moved, but she didn't know what that strange convulsion of the wood had meant, whether it was a welcome or a warning.

9

The

Sacrifice

They turned to the dark entrance beneath the tree where the gray stones arched against the black. Something moved in the half-light—a small brown figure glided toward them and stopped at the edge of daylight. It was the old lady, one arm held up, the fringes of her tattered buckskin blouse hanging down. The wrinkled brown hand was palm-forward, telling them to stop, to not enter. Her ancient face was stern, her small eyes glittering. For a moment no one moved or spoke.

Jen gave a little cry, and said to Arn, "Ask her where Oka is!"

Arn's hands moved in the language. For "cow" he made the gestures of milking; the question part was his open hands, palms up, empty and asking.

The old lady's arm came down and pointed behind them, so they turned away from her, toward the east.

At the eastern edge of the meadow several large animals grazed, moving together slowly, one or two raising their stocky heads to look around. They were dark, heavy beasts.

"What are they, Arn?" Jen asked, but he didn't know.

Suddenly the animals were in alarm. They jumped and came down with all four hooves together, then ran on a curving course toward the center of the meadow. Jen and Arn felt the heavy thudding of hooves before they heard it. Behind the large animals smaller gray ones bounded through the winter grass, gray backs appearing and disappearing like the backs of salmon going upstream.

"Wolves!" Arn said, with an excitement in his voice not all caused by fear. Jen was frightened; Arn's excitement seemed wrong, strange to her.

The large animals were driven closer to the ledge, running side by side, touching each other as if for comfort in their fear, their eyes showing white and their mouths slobbering. They had short horns and looked like cows except for their long shaggy hair. One of them had dropped behind, an older, slower one. It turned desperately, fighting its own great weight, and tried to hook the following wolf with its horn. A white spot flashed on its sweating neck.

"Oka!" Jen cried. "Oka!"

But it couldn't be Oka, with that long shaggy coat now suddenly flecked with blood as a wolf's fangs raked it. Silently running, the other wolves caught up. One bounded in from the rear and cut a hamstring with one audible clack of its white teeth. The cow thudded down on its side and the wolves went in to its belly, slashing and ripping until they had pulled its insides out in long ropes while it was still dying, groaning out its last sounds in the deep grass.

The other cattle had formed a ring, back to back, with their heads down and horns menacing the wolves that circled them. After a few feints toward the closed circle of horns the wolves went back to feed upon the dead cow.

Jen and Arn stood absolutely still, Jen crying silently, while the wolves snarled and tore at their meat. After a long while the wolves, gorged, lay down in the last light of the winter sun, their bellies plump. The other cattle had gone quietly back to grazing, tails swinging, their muzzles methodically wrenching the brown grass loose from the roots before they slowly chewed. Red and white ribs arched over the carcase of the dead cow, its torn coat folded back over the grass like a shaggy robe with a red and yellow lining.

Arn stared at the carcase of the cow and the sated wolves, full after their hunting. He turned to Jen and she saw their triumph in his face. She thought only of the cow that had been taken from life and brutally changed into meat, but Arn had been running with the hunters all the while.

She moved away from him, feeling alone. At her movement the cattle raised their heads and stamped nervously, their large eyes upon her. Some of the wolves raised their heads, their ears straight up, staring directly at her with an alert curiosity that was neither fear nor aggression.

Arn watched the wolves, his eager curiosity matching theirs.

"Arn," she called to him as if he were far away. For a long time he didn't answer, and when he did speak, he said, "Did you see that? Did you see the wolves hunting?"

"She said Oka was out there!" Jen cried.

Arn turned, the excitement of the hunting fading from his face. "She pointed that way, that's all we know, Jen."

They turned back to the archway, but the old lady was no longer there. The sun had gone down, the earlier snow flurries had ceased, and the moon was a bent sliver among thin clouds that moved silently across the sky. Darkness had begun to settle in. The black archway now seemed as palpable as a wall. They peered into that blackness, but it was like a curtain of fur, something they might reach out and touch, and they were both struck again by the old lady's admonition not to enter. Never, when she had stayed at their cabin, had she seemed so stern, powerful and unfriendly.

They had to find a place to spend the cold night, and it

was Jen who found a protected place beneath a whorl of the great tree's roots. Arn went to gather fallen twigs and branches so they could have a fire, while Jen gathered together the fallen needles of the tree and heaped them beneath the sheltering roots.

When Arn returned with an armload of wood he put it down and said, "Listen!"

They held their breaths, hearing a distant sighing, at first the wind in the high branches of the tree, but changing, coming now from the meadow. They crept over to the edge of the stones. The sighing, or chanting, came from across the meadow, where many flickering lights, small moving fires, came toward them.

"Those are people," Arn whispered.

The stone of the ledge and archway, and the gray trunk of the tree, became visible in the flickering orange light. Several of the dark approaching figures carried bundles of branches. Crouching down, Jen and Arn watched while several bonfires grew at once in a half-ring around the central ledge. As the fires ate brightly through their kindling and branches, figures stood or crouched around them, strange shapes half men, half animal. A chant, dry and toneless as the wind, came from the figures behind the fires. "Hey-yeh, hey-yeh, hey-yeh, hey-yeh," the chant went on, neither rising nor falling.

"Those *are* people!" Arn whispered.

As the fires grew higher they saw that the figures were human, but the heads and upper bodies, all shaking up and down in a dance to the rhythm of the chant, were animal. The men wore animal skins with the masks of animals. There were the shoulders and head of a black bear, the fangs gleaming white in the gaping mouth, and there was the huge head of a boar with its ivory tusks. Other figures wore deer heads, antlered and without antlers, others the heavy heads of shaggy cattle, or the sharp muzzles and stiff ears of wolves. One figure was half the tawny head and cape of a lynx that grinned in the flicker-

ing light as all cats grin. Firelight glinted on fangs and hair
as the creatures danced in place.

Just below the stone platform on which Jen and Arn
crouched, a long stone, high and flat as a table, was set in
the ground, the higher flames of the fires reflecting across
it. It was toward this stone that all the animal heads gaped
and nodded as the chant went on. The fires made a great
room out of the darkness, so that the thin moon glimmered faintly high above. Behind the dancers were the
dark silent shapes of others who didn't move. Their human faces shone as dimly as the moon.

The chant ended all at once, so quickly and simultane-
ously Jen and Arn were startled, as if the steady noise had
hidden them and now they were about to be discovered.

From the darkness at the side came a figure whose arms
were long black wings, whose head was that of a giant
crow. It approached the table rock. Following the crow
came a stooped figure wearing a cape of long needles and
quills, with a stubby, furred face—a giant porcupine.
These stood silently beside a stone, waiting. From the
people in the darkness of the meadow rose a high, faint
humming that changed into the sad keening of women.
It was not so much a moan of immediate sorrow as a
formal imitation of that long, hopeless wail. It rose and fell
in slow waves. Jen felt the sound within her as if she had
been born to hear that song of infinite loss. She thought
of her mother, who might be uttering just those mourning
sounds over her lost children. She felt that she, too, was
born to someday feel that same intensity of grief. As the
keening rose and fell she became Eugenia, bereft of her
children. Her own throat sang with the strange women on
the meadow.

Two men dressed in cattle skins, with cattle heads, appeared at the edge of the dark. Each held a child by the
hand, the children dressed in buckskin with bright designs made of dyed porcupine quill beads sewn all over
their clothes. Their dark hair was braided and oiled. Jen

and Arn could see that one was a girl, the other a boy, the two children about their own ages. The mourning song rose higher as the cattle men led them toward the stone.

The little girl's face was rigid with fear, though she walked steadily, the cattle man's hand on her arm. Jen trembled with her and couldn't breathe. She had never known a girl her age but she knew this girl in the deepest possible way, fearing for her as if she herself were approaching the unknown ceremony.

Arn saw the fear and bravery of the boy, who walked erect, his dark face set against any weakness. He would never cry or try to run away from what he had to do, though whatever it was caused hidden terror. Arn felt it in his bones like a chill.

Without a sound a deer—a man wearing the head and coat of a great antlered buck—appeared at the head of the stone. The cattle men, still holding the children's arms, took their places next to the crow and the porcupine. To the foot of the stone came a figure all in long white fur, with a white animal face, bearded in white, with narrow curved horns. This one wore the skin of a mountain goat.

The fires grew tall, their orange flames, higher than the men, wavering as their highest wands burned out in the upper air. The keening grew as a man came forward, naked to the waist except for a long necklace of polished teeth, holding in his right hand a knife that shone copper or bronze. The knife was short, like the sticking knife at home, with a sturdy broad blade. The man's dark hair was pulled back and tied with rawhide behind his stretched, grim face.

The cattle man who held the girl lifted her to the stone, where she lay on her back. Her chest and arms trembled but she made no sound. The cattle man holding the boy lifted him up and placed him beside the girl, where he, too, trembled but his stern young face didn't change. The man with the knife stepped forward and raised it over the children, point down.

Jen started up, ready to cry out and run to the stone, but Arn held her arm, whispering, "Quiet, quiet!"

Just then a tree, moving on human legs, came out of the darkness and stood between the man and the children. It was really a man holding a young evergreen, the soft needles and branches hiding his upper body. The small cones and short needles of the tree were like those of the great evergreen of the ledges, though this tree was so young and soft it was hard to compare them. The tree stood quietly, not moving, hiding the children from the knife. The mourning song faded, but underneath was still a low hum of sadness, muted but not gone.

The goat and the deer raised their heads to the night sky, their front hooves out over the children on the stone. All was quiet except for the low humming of the women and the windy crackling of the fires. Black clouds moved past the thin moon without changing shape, silent in a wind that was far above this place.

With a harsh cry like a cough the knife man hacked a branch from the tree, then another, the soft boughs falling lightly to the ground. The keening song rose again with each falling branch until the tree was naked and the women's song was a cry that filled the night. The knife rose high above the children. As it began its swift plunge Jen cried out but could not be heard above the rising chant of grief that came from the men and women on the meadow. The men in animal masks had surrounded the stone so that the two children could not be seen. The waning fires flickered orange and red, staining the moving edges of the animal heads as if their light were blood.

Then several of the animal men lifted the two bodies to their shoulders. The people, now silent, followed the bearers of the children back across the meadow into the darkness. The embering fires glowed in a wide half-circle around the stone.

Arn and Jen crouched side by side behind the jagged rim of the stone platform. A cool mist moved over them, coating the stones and their faces with moisture. In the soft dimness of the mist and ember light, they were still, staring at each other, feeling small and abandoned. "The children," Jen whispered. "The children."

Arn could not make his feelings clear to himself. Those had been people. He didn't know, yet he must know, what had happened to the children. The children were still with him though ages seemed to have passed since he watched their fear and trembling. It was their acquiescence that filled him with doubts about his own judgement and made his feelings hurtful and deep. What had happened did not seem all wrong, but how could it not be wrong? He himself had killed, stopped life and revealed, with the sharp blade of his own knife, those inner parts of animals that made them live. Killed them and eaten them. He, too, was an animal, alive and seeing, as was Jen. They, too, could die as easily as he had killed. And it was not easy for those people. To the animals they pretended to be on that dark night, whose skins and meat they had taken, they would prove their kinship by sacrificing two of their own kind. But it was wrong. The brave boy and the brave and fearful girl, willing to die. He felt deep hurt, a round, swelling hurt inside because of feelings he could not understand.

Jen thought of that boy who would not show any fear in his face. She admired his bravery but she wanted to shout that it was wrong, all of it was wrong. And the girl —if only she could have known her and had her as a friend. But even in her loss she felt responsible, as if she had something to do with the ceremonies she had only observed. The girl had not cried out that it was wrong. Though the women mourned, no one tried to stop it. It seemed Jen's own failure too. Then there was Oka, whose presence in this world, or in this valley, now seemed to fade, as if the wolves' kill she had seen was Oka, and that death natural and inevitable, unlike the deaths she had just witnessed, done by her own kind to her own kind.

10

Old
Snaggletooth

Though the mist was damp and uncomfortable, it was much warmer than the night before. The valley seemed, perhaps because of the lake of warm water, to vary a whole season in its temperatures. Arn took Jen, who was sobbing and shuddering, to the protected place they had found beneath the great tree's root. He didn't dare light a fire, so they lay down next to each other, for warmth, and shut their eyes.

It seemed a long time, but it was no more than minutes before they were asleep. Then, sometime before dawn, they were taken, slowly and easily, by a dream in which a calm, dry voice, neither kind nor cruel, spoke to them. They were high in the air, with the meadow spread below them, the grasses moving in swathes that changed from green to gold in rolling movements of the wind as the grass bent in warm sunlight a hundred feet below. They were cradled in soft green arms, though in the dream this did not seem strange. "What you have seen and are seeing and will see is true," the voice told them. The language was not theirs, though it did not seem strange that they could understand it.

"The people, after they understood what they had done, went away," the voice said in the whispery tones of the wind.

Each child, without speaking, asked what the people had done.

"They changed in their hearts," the voice said. "They came to believe they owned the valley and all its creatures."

I'd never do that, each child thought. The green arms were strong and soft around them.

"In the other world they forgot what they had done, and lost each other. They remembered nothing."

Are the Old People all gone?

"The world is merciless yet not cruel. All living things must die. Change is the law. It is the law that gave you birth and what joy you have had."

We want to go home.

"All you will be given is knowledge."

But we want to go home.

"They held the creatures prisoners in pens, fed them and gained their trust, only to betray them at the end. Others they changed through generations until their only desire was to kill their own kind. They made of the wild a slaughterhouse. They became worse than what they most feared."

Home. We want to go home.

The green arms that held them faded with the voice, became a coolness that was the damp needles and the gray rock where they lay. They were cold, and as they woke they felt mean in their discomfort, angry without anyone to blame. Jen felt a pout upon her face. Arn felt that he had had enough; he shouldn't have followed Jen in the first place. He got to his knees, shrugging off his old feeling of responsibility. He had to get out of here. He must get up and look, be careful, hide, escape. Dawn was just breaking.

As he rose cautiously to peer into the mist, Jen watched

him. He moved slowly, silently, like a hunter, his eyes alert and cold. While he looked out into the mist he was so still he might have been taken for a stone. His eyes were simple, instruments as pure as the eyes of a bird. He reminded her of her father at those times in the woods when he would freeze to look and listen. He seemed not to exist, then, as her father, not even to exist as a person, just as eyes that observed. In his immobility Arn seemed more a part of the horror they had witnessed than the brother she knew, who had saved her life from the cold and built shelter and a fire to warm her.

Arn climbed down the stones at the edge of the platform to the wet meadow grass.

"Don't, Arn," Jen called. "Come back." But she seemed so far away, her voice so whispery and thin he could barely hear it.

The sentry stones were dim figures out on the meadow. As he left the ledges he felt as though he were floating out upon a broad lake, leaving the land behind. Mist and fog surrounded him as the ledges receded. The stone figure he approached grew more substantial. It turned from mist-gray to a darker color and had a sharper outline. It grew in height and width. In its immobility it was a presence that beckoned to him, half against his will. To his left and right other sentries faded into the mist in a wide circle. He had started toward this one and he would go right up to it and examine it. He would go straight up to it and look at it where it loomed, ancient and inscrutable in the half-light. It seemed to approach him as he walked toward it. Now he saw that it was different from the other stone sentries. It was not squared off at the shoulders, but had a head. Would there be carved stone eyes to look at him? He didn't want to see their frozen expression, but still he approached. Then he saw, with a chill of fear, that this one was not all made of stone. Upon its granite shoulders sat the head of a boar, its red eyes gummy and spoiled. A wrinkled tongue hung out over the yellow tusks on one side, and along the black lips was the glint of somnolent maggots. He turned away from the sudden cold stench of carrion and ran back to Jen.

"What is it?" she asked.

"We must stay together," he said.

They sat down side by side on the needles where they had slept. "We've got to go home," Arn said.

"I had a dream," Jen said, looking up into the ascending boughs of the tree, so high they seemed to be in another world where all was gray and green.

"So did I!" Arn said. "There was a voice . . ."

And then they heard a voice, a cracked, cackling old man's voice, and looked around to see a bent, bony old man watching them and laughing, nodding and shaking his gnarled old face. Sparse silver hair stuck up above his ears, and his mouth was all black when open, except for one crooked yellow tooth at one side. They were afraid, and got up to run, but the old man shook his head and put his wrinkled hands out to reassure them, as if to say, "Now, now. How could I hurt you?" So their fear receded and they noticed how his buckskin tunic was ragged and split in places, his buckskin trousers stained with grease and dirt and worn clear through at the knees. His back was so bent that his head seemed at first to be growing out of his chest. Even looking down at them he seemed to have to raise his head. He leaned on a short, crooked, unstrung bow, and at his belt hung a quiver of arrows, some of their feathers missing.

But his eyes were bright, and the wrinkles at their edges were friendly.

He spoke to them in a strange language that at first sounded harsh, most of the words clipped and guttural, though others were longer, smooth as the words of a song.

Arn sat cross-legged, and so did Jen. The old man put down his bow, pushed his leather quiver aside on his belt, and sat cross-legged in front of them.

"Ah nee ah, no ah nee," he said. When they shook their

heads he raised his old hands and made them into pictures and actions as had the old lady so long a time ago, it seemed, when she sat on the bench by the hearth at home.

Arn answered with his hands, saying that they were Arn and Jen, pointing to himself and to Jen as he spoke their names out loud.

"Arn to Jen nee ah," the old man said, nodding.

"Jen nee ah," Jen said.

The old man smiled, pleased, but shook his head. "Jen ah nee," he said, pointing to her.

"Jen ah nee," she said, and he nodded, smiling so hard the bottom half of his face shortened and widened.

"Ganonoot ah nee," the old man said, pointing to his chest, then to his one long yellow tooth. He made more signs with his hands.

"Snaggletooth," Arn said.

"Ganonoot," the old man said, smiling and pointing proudly at his tooth.

Arn asked him in hand language what this valley was called, and was he one of the Old People? As Arn moved his hands he spoke the words aloud so Jen could understand, and Jen found her own hands following Arn's, learning each word as it was formed.

As the old man answered with his hands he spoke the words of his own language. "Nee a no notomanay ... This is the world," he said. "Have you been elsewhere? Yes, I am certainly old!"

Arn and Jen found that they learned each word of the new language as soon as they heard it once, that the rhythms of meaning grew deep into them.

"But we've heard stories about the Old People, and about Tsuga Wanders-too-far, and the Black Gate," Arn said.

The old man's eyes were still for a moment as he looked straight at Arn's eyes, then he smiled and giggled, his dark gums clicking together. He told them he was so old, all he

could do was tell stories. His bow, that once had the reach
of a hundred paces, was as crippled as his back, and his
arrows were warped and their fletching ragged.

"Only the old stories now, mind you!" he said. "These
new stories, you can't trust them at all. I mean you can
listen to them, but you can't trust them the way you can
the old stories. I don't know the new stories and I don't
care if I don't remember the new stories. They can have
the new stories, for all I care!"

He seemed to be getting so upset, Jen put her hand on
his arm and patted him.

"I'm hungry," the old man said. A tear followed a complicated track down beside his nose, out along a wrinkle
to the corner of his mouth, back across another wrinkle to
the middle of his chin, where it stayed.

"So are we," Arn said. "We had porcupine the night
before last but a lynx stole the rest of it."

"And trout yesterday morning," Jen said.

"But nothing since then?" Snaggletooth asked. "Your
people didn't give you food?" He got slowly to his feet,
leaning on his bow, which by its worn places seemed more
of a walking staff than a bow. "I thought," he said in a
whiny voice, "you might have a little bread, or bannock,
or maybe a little smoked venison, or some dried apples,
or some beef jerky, or some pemmican in your pack."

"No, nothing to eat at all," Arn said, "except for some
powders to make tea." He looked at Jen, and they exchanged a glance of dismay that the old man was so childish.

"Well!" Snaggletooth said. "I'm only an old man and
don't deserve respect like the others. When I lose my last
two teeth I won't be able to eat and that's the end of it.
Then they can forget the old stories, for all I care!" With
that, tears came to his old eyes again and found various
channels down his wrinkles.

"But what about your people?" Jen asked.

"People, people, they're all the same. They don't care
about an old man."

"If we had some food we'd give it to you," Jen said, "but we just don't have anything to eat."

"Ha!" Snaggletooth said. "Have you eaten rotten boar head? I can smell one now. Have you licked the rim of the winter moon? Chewed on your own leather? I can tell you about hunger—that's an old story if you want one."

"We just want to go home," Jen said.

Then something seemed to change, to harden in Snaggletooth, as if he remembered an old responsibility or maturity, and he said, "You're just children. You won't hurt anyone, will you?"

"No, we won't," Arn said.

"But you came with *them* last night, didn't you?" He seemed shy as he pointed to the east, smiling without any mirth. "You came with the Chigai, didn't you?"

"Chigai?" Arn said.

Snaggletooth spoke with his hands as he explained, though his eyes slyly doubted the necessity of explaining. "Chigai ah nee nonomen . . . The makers of prisons, the slave-keepers. You came with them last night, didn't you?"

"No," Arn said. "We were already here when those people came. We hid over there and watched them."

"Did they really kill the boy and girl?" Jen asked.

"Kill? Kill? Do you call it kill when one can't run away?"

Half mumbling to himself, his long tooth pushing his thin lip down, he said that there was a word for that kind of death, but no one could say it. None of the hunters could say it, so they had another word, and even that one was hard to say: murder. Snaggletooth shuddered as he said it, his hands quivering like oak leaves on a winter tree.

"Cold and hungry, cold and hungry," he said. "Well, come with me, then. We've got a way to go. Can you walk, can you jump, can you crawl and creep and slip and slide? Hungry, hungry makes the feet go!"

"We want to go home," Jen said.

"Home? This is home," Snaggletooth said, pointing as

he turned all the way around. "And the Tree is the center. Don't you know anything at all? Didn't Ahneeah give you any brains?"

In spite of his fear and hunger and lostness, Arn grew irritated. This old man seemed always to be talking about something beside the point. They were weak from hunger, and in danger; death seemed all around them. "We've never heard of Ahneeah and this is *not* our home!" he said, raising his voice and getting to his feet. Because of the old man's stoop Arn was nearly as tall as Snaggletooth, who backed up in surprise and nearly tripped over his bow.

Then a deep voice from above called, "Over here, Bren. I've found him." The voice was firm, with a calm authority in it that reassured Arn and Jen even before they knew who it might be. It was a grown-up voice, with no fear or craziness in it, and they were so exhausted and hungry they were ready to be children again.

A sturdy man in buckskin jumped down the ledges and stood looking at them in surprise. "Chigai nee ah?" he said. "Are you Chigai? I can see by the blood on the altar that they were here last night." He carried a short, thick-handled bow, and at his waist hung a quiver of arrows and a stag-handled knife in a sheath. "Ganonoot—Snaggletooth—if you have your brains together, who are these children? How did you find them?"

"I'm hungry, Amu, hungry!" Snaggletooth said in a whining, quavering voice.

A boy Arn's age came jumping down, rock to rock. He, too, was dressed in buckskin, and carried a strung bow. He had a fierce look, and when he saw Arn he strode forward aggressively and stared him in the face. "What have we here—Chigai?" he said. He seemed to be measuring Arn for a fight.

"We're not Chigai," Arn said. "We never heard of Chigai until this old man told us the word." Arn stared back at the boy. He understood the fierce challenge he saw in

the other's bright brown eyes, but he had never seen a
boy his own age and he was so curious he didn't answer
that expression at all.

"Come, Bren," the man said. "Let's sit and talk." He
reached into a pouch in the lining of his tunic and brought
out several long brown pieces of smoked venison. Snaggletooth took one and immediately wet it with his tongue
and lips, then hooked at it busily with his long tooth. Jen
and Arn each received a piece and thanked the man.

"Go ahead and eat; I can see you're hungry. I am Amu,
and this is Bren, my brother's son. You can tell us your
names when you've eaten," Amu said. They all sat cross-
legged, Amu and Bren watching Jen and Arn. "The Chigai are rarely hungry," Amu said, "and they are of the
People and don't speak strangely, with strange rhythms,
the way you do. No, go ahead and eat before you talk. We
will wait."

Snaggletooth, working on his venison, drooled out of
one corner of his mouth. He had another tooth, a flat one,
on his lower jaw, about an inch to the right of his long one,
so to make them meet his jaw slid over so far that he
drooled on his shirt. Occasionally he would gather up that
place on his shirt, bring the buckskin to his mouth and
suck the juices from it.

"Waste not," Amu said, smiling at Jen, who had been
watching this as she chewed.

When they had finished their meat, its strength growing warm in their blood, Jen said, "Thank you, Amu. That
meat reminds us of home, and my father's smokehouse."

"You are very sad," Amu said. "But who are you?"

"I'm Arn, and this is my sister, Jen," Arn said. "We came
here past a waterfall and through a long cave." He
pointed toward the northern mountains, now hidden in
the cold mist.

"Ah!" Snaggletooth said. "There is an old story, *Ahneeah and the People Who Left the World*. I will tell it
now!"

"Wait, Snaggletooth," Amu said, smiling and putting a hand on the old man's hunched back. "Eat your meat. It's not time for the telling of stories."

"It has a waterfall and a cave!" Snaggletooth said. "It's got bats and time and sorrow, and the longing of men to find out who they are!"

"I'm sure it has, old Clown, old Ganonoot," Amu said affectionately. "And sometime you must tell it at the evening fire. But now I think we must go. The world is uneasy, and Tsuga will want to speak to Jen and Arn."

"Tsuga!" Jen and Arn said at the same time.

"He is coming here in three days, for the meeting of the People and Council."

"Here?" Arn said, remembering what they had seen in this place.

Amu looked at him for a moment, his wide face open and calm with its brown eyes and high, ruddy cheekbones. "Don't worry, Arn, we don't leave blood on the stone altar. That is something new with the People—with the Chigai. But you don't have to stay if you don't want to; we do not have prisoners."

"We should go home," Jen said.

"But why did you come past the waterfall and through the cave?" Amu asked. "If your father lives through the mountains and beyond, why did you come here?"

"I almost can't remember," Jen said. "I thought it was to follow Oka, our cow, but now I don't know why. And Arn followed me, to bring me back."

"You must be brave, then, both of you."

Arn saw that the boy, Bren, in spite of his challenging look, was impressed by Amu's statement.

"Your father keeps cattle, then," Amu said. The word "keeps" was a new one, and Jen and Arn saw that it was a polite word for holding prisoners.

"Just Oka, for her milk, and Brin to pull the sledge and plow," Jen said.

"Ah," Amu said.

"You don't even have a bow with you," Bren said to Arn. "Do you have a knife?"

Arn reached beneath his parka and pulled his knife from its sheath. The smooth steel blade shone.

Bren unsheathed his own knife and handed it, hilt first, to Arn, who did the same with his. Each examined the other's knife. Bren's was sharp, though more crudely made—some of the hammer marks of its forging and shaping were visible along the blade, and the tang was just wrapped with rawhide.

Bren tested Arn's blade on his thumbnail. "That's a knife," he said. "How it fits the hand!" Bren's hand was the size of Arn's own, the first Arn had ever seen that was the size of his own. It was as if he sat across from himself; yet this boy was another person.

Bren handed Arn's knife back, hilt first. "That is a beautiful knife," he said, the word for beautiful, "yodehna," sounding hard, really meant, like steel in his young voice. Arn felt the same about the spareness and usefulness of a good tool.

"And yours is sharp and strong," he said. "I'll bet it can clean a deer without spilling guts."

Bren nodded seriously. "It has. Only one, though, so far."

"Mine has cleaned only small game," Arn said, "so far."

"Ha," Bren said appraisingly; there was approval there, for that honesty. Bren was dark and sturdy, like his uncle, Amu, but his brows came down closer to his eyes, as though he looked at the world with more judgement and suspicion.

"Well," Amu said. "Will you come to our winter camp while we wait for Tsuga, or will you try to find your way back through the northern mountains?"

Arn and Jen looked at each other. In the fair and kind words of Amu they had found, after what had seemed an age of lostness, authority and reason. Here was this strong, big person whose presence, though he was shorter and heavier, reminded them of their father. And Tsuga, of whom their father always spoke with reverence—could the Tsuga Amu spoke of be that same man? And what might he tell them? Both had seen, all their lives, their father's yearning for something beyond where he could go. And now maybe they were there, and Tsuga might tell them more than how to get home again.

And there was the old lady, who had spent so many days sitting so quietly before their fire at home. They had seen her once, just for a moment, in the black archway.

"The old lady," Jen said, puzzled by something she thought she ought to know.

"An old lady?" Amu asked.

"Yes, in the arch, there. We saw her."

"In the Cave of Forgetfulness? You saw Ahneeah?" Now there was wonder and awe in Amu's voice. "Then my best advice for you is to come to our winter camp and wait with us until Tsuga comes, Jen and Arn. Yes, that is my best advice for you."

"Ahneeah . . ." Bren said, and in his voice was a long sigh of mystery and reverence.

Old Snaggletooth had finally finished his smoked venison. He licked his lips, scraped juices from his chin with a finger, then licked the finger clean, a lick for each side and a lick for the bottom.

"Only Tsuga has seen Ahneeah as an old woman," he said. "We hear her voice in the wind and thunder, feel her tears in the winter rain that freezes on our shoulders. The People are not allowed to see Ahneeah as an old woman."

"Maybe it wasn't Ahneeah," Jen said, "but just the old lady who stayed at our cabin."

"A story! A story!" Snaggletooth said. "There is an old, *old* story! Tell me, children—did she take her moccasins with her when she left? Did she? Did she? Tell me, now!"

"No," Jen said. "She left them there. And it was so cold the woods were all ice."

"Ice like a knife! Ice of iron, ice of steel! And a cave of many passages, in and back, and only Ahneeah knows the way! Yes, that is a story!"

11

The Winter Camp

Without saying anything more to each other, Jen and Arn knew that they would go to the winter camp. Before they left, Amu, Bren and Snaggletooth climbed the ledges to the great evergreen's massive trunk. Each pressed his right hand to the tree for a moment, in silence, and then they were ready.

They walked to the south across the meadow, west through deep woods, then around to the south again, then toward the east for a long time until they came to another, smaller meadow. Here the air was warmer, the grass not as frost-burned. As they came over a rise, the roofs of hogans rose into their vision—square log houses, their rafters covered with sewn skins. Jen and Arn had never seen so many buildings, so many people. The cold mist had disappeared, and the winter sun slanted across field and hogan, lighting with gold the southern edges of grass, buildings and the people, who, seeing Amu's party approach, stopped their errands and tasks to watch. Beyond the hogans was a river not quite as broad as the one at home, flowing more shallowly, with white water in stony places along its banks.

"The winter camp of the People," Amu said. "It is not our only winter camp, but we are here for the running of the shandeh." Glancing at Arn, he evidently saw that the word meant nothing to him, so he spoke with his hands: "Little winter fish." South of the hogans were tall racks of saplings slanted to catch the sun's light, and on the racks were impaled hundreds of small fish about the length of a man's hand, each split so it looked like two fish, the flesh open to the light and air.

At the riverbank the fishermen had set their nets in semicircles, some men on the far bank pulling the lines taut against the current. At tables made of hewn logs, others cleaned, filleted and salted the little fish. But as Amu's party came into the camp, all the people except the net-holders left their tasks and gathered in front of the largest hogan.

"What have you there, Amu?" asked a stocky gray-haired woman. Putting her thin filleting knife in a leather holster at her waist, she wiped her hands on her cloth apron as she came forward from the rest of the people.

"Two children from beyond the mountains," Amu said. "They do not seem to be Chigai."

The stocky old woman came closer and looked at Arn and Jen. She smelled of fish, and when she wiped her wiry gray hair away from her forehead with the backs of her hands, her palms sparkled with small silver fish scales. "Where are their people, then?" Her voice was deep for a woman's, as if it came from a barrel.

"They say they came alone, past a waterfall and through a cave, and they say they saw Ahneeah as an old woman."

The stocky woman blinked, but showed no other emotion. "See how the girl's eyes are the color of the sky," she said. "Yes, they are strange children. Tsuga will want to talk to them when he comes. Will they stay with us?"

"Yes, I think they have agreed to stay."

Such was the authority and power of the woman, Arn

and Jen felt they shouldn't speak directly to her at all.

But even as he listened, Arn was trying to decide just how many people stood there in the yard before the hogan. He remembered his dream when he had first entered this valley, but there were even more people here —real people. A hundred? And each looked different—in age, in height, in complexion. Each was a whole other person, part of this camp, of this people. In the dream he had been outside, just looking on, and he had felt lonely then.

"Bren," the woman said, "you will stay with these children and be their host." She turned to the people. "Now we must go back to work. The shandeh will tell us when we may stop to rest."

She looked at Snaggletooth, and he, bent over so far he had to cock his head to look up at her, smiled rather guiltily. She said, "So, Ganonoot, you wandered off again. Where shall we find you next? In the Cave of Forgetfulness?"

He laughed, like the cackling of a bird. Several of the people laughed with him, or at him. "I'll be there soon enough, and when that time comes I won't have to walk!" he said.

"Unless you fall into a woodchuck hole and disappear, you'll live to tell us more stories." The people laughed at this, and Snaggletooth did a little shuffling dance and bowed to them.

As the woman turned away she drew her filleting knife and a thin sharpening stone from her sheath. Others did the same, and the musical ringing of many stones against knives sounded as the people went back to their work.

Bren didn't seem too happy with his new responsibility. "Come on," he said gruffly, and they followed him to the edge of the camp, past the drying racks, to a hogan set somewhat apart from the others. Jen had noticed a girl following them, a girl about her age, and when Bren pulled the bearskin away from the door the girl had caught up with them.

"Hello," the girl said. She wanted to smile, but the smile flickered on and off, as though she didn't dare.

Bren sighed and shrugged his shoulders. "This," he said, "is my cousin, Arel, who is a pest."

"Bren thinks he's grown up already," Arel said, laughing. She was a thin little girl with a pale, almost sickly color in her face. Her hair was cut short, like Bren's, and she wore the same kind of buckskin tunic and trousers Bren wore, but fine beadwork, in black and white, checkered the cuffs and lower edge of her tunic. She turned toward Jen. "My father told me your name is Jen, and your brother's name is Arn, and I could stop working, which was scraping fish guts and bones off the tables (ugh!), and be company for you, if you want." She scowled out of worry. All her expressions seemed to flicker on and off.

Jen was thinking, This is a girl. Like me. She couldn't stop looking at Arel, but then knew Arel really needed to know if she was welcome, and said, "Yes, yes! I've never talked to a girl before. I've never even seen a girl before today."

"You've never? You're the only one among your people?" Arel was perplexed, scowling again in that strange way that contained no anger. "You've never seen a girl before?" she asked, her curiosity now beaming out of her pale face.

They went inside the hogan and sat on skin rugs around the embering fire pit in the center. The smoke rose slowly to a round opening in the ceiling. Around the walls were hewn shelves holding bundles of clothing, wooden canisters of food, and racks where clothing dried.

"I don't want to just sit around," Bren said. "If we don't have to work, we ought to *do* something."

"Arn, have you ever seen a boy before?" Arel asked, and Arn shook his head.

Even Bren was curious about this, so in turn Jen and Arn told them about their cabin, their mother and father, and the farm in the wilderness so far from any other people. Occasionally they would have to use hand language when they didn't know a word, but this happened less and less as they spoke with Arel and Bren.

It was the animals that excited Arel. "You kept animals? Were they prisoners?" she asked.

Jen was surprised to have to answer that she guessed they were. They were kept in pens, or harnessed, in Brin's case, to the plough or sledge. But she'd never thought of Oka as a prisoner.

"But she escaped!" Arel said.

In turn, and Bren became more interested in the telling, they told Arn and Jen about their own lives, how in the spring they planted corn in the south-sloping fields, pruned the fruit and nut trees, gathered the wild food and hunted game. They could never keep anything that could move, and know that it wanted to move, as a prisoner. But once an animal was killed, then it became food and skin and bone for them to use.

"Except the Chigai," Bren said. "They have prisoners."

Arel shuddered at the word, but Bren seemed more curious than anything else about the Chigai.

"We saw them come to the place where the tree is," Arn said. "We think they killed two children."

"You *saw* it?" Arel said.

"We saw the children on the stone, and the knife. And they carried them away."

"Amu and I saw blood on the stone," Bren said. "And the ashes of their fires." The Chigai, Bren told them, kept the shaggy cattle in great pens, and were never hungry. No one was sure whether they actually killed children on the altar, but some said they did kill the children to pacify the spirits of the cattle they imprisoned and slaughtered.

"How could they do that?" Arel whispered, shivering, her face drawn down as if she had been crying.

They were all silent. Jen was hurt by it, by that reality. The brave children; it was an ache, a bone ache so deep she couldn't find the place to touch it.

"There are many among the People who want to live like the Chigai and never be hungry," Bren said.

Arel looked at him quickly and was silent. Jen saw that this was important to them both. Bren, too, was silent and thoughtful for a long time.

And in that silence both Jen and Arn had time to think of home. They thought of Christmas and the tree, their father so gravely acting the part of the Stag, then his smile as he divided the maple-sugar doll among them. They thought of their mother, so warm and happy in the light from the hearth. Then they saw the small cabin locked in ice, their mother's eyes full of tears, their father sleeping the sleep of his sickness. Would they ever hear their voices again?

Arel saw this sadness and took Jen's hand, her thin hand pale against Jen's. "Tsuga might help you," she said. She squeezed Jen's hand, a shy little squeeze like the flutter of a bird's wing.

Bren shook himself and jumped to his feet. "Let's *do* something," he said. He looked at Arn in the speculative, challenging way he had before. "Can you run?" he said. "Can you shoot and throw? Can you wrestle?"

Arn knew he could run, shoot an arrow from a bow and throw a stone, but he'd never wrestled. He knew he could do some of these things, but not how well because he'd never been able to compare himself to anyone like himself. And while he was worried about how he might do, he was suddenly so full of joyful anticipation his thoughts of home faded.

Bren looked at Arel and then at Jen. Arel said, "It's all right, Bren. I'll keep Jen company. You can go play."

"Play!" Bren said. Arel was laughing at him again, and his dark eyebrows went even lower. "Play!" he said. He couldn't think of anything to say, so he turned and left the hogan, Arn following.

Outside in the winter sun, Bren said, "Leave your pack there, inside the door. And you won't need your parka as long as the wind holds from the west. Then we'll see if you can run."

Without his pack and parka Arn felt light and free, though his boots were much heavier than Bren's moccasins. Carrying his unstrung bow in his left hand, Bren ran. Arn followed, running behind easily, even thinking with great pleasure that if he knew where Bren was leading him, he might pass him. They ran around the perimeter of the camp, past the fishermen and the fish cleaners, circling over the meadow, the hogans always on their left. Soon the thought of passing Bren had gone. Arn gasped through his mouth. His throat hurt; each breath felt as though he were being jabbed in the throat by a stick. But still he followed. When they came back around to Bren's hogan Arn was afraid Bren would start around again. He would follow, but he saw himself having to stop, even to drop to his knees. But Bren did stop, breathing hard himself, and said, "Your boots are too heavy for running and you haven't eaten enough in the last few days." He took several long breaths. "But you can run."

Arn's face was warm, from the running but also from pride in what Bren had said—that he could run.

"Now we'll go to the bowyer and see if we can find you a bow. Here, can you pull mine?" Bren put the end of his bow in his instep and bent it as he pushed the loop of the string into the nock, then handed it to Arn.

The bow was carved of hickory, thin but wide in its limbs, thick enough at the grip to feel secure in the hand. Arn placed three fingers on the string, as his father had taught him, and drew to his cheek. The pull was heavier than the one his father had made him, but he could hold the string against his cheekbone for a few seconds without his arms shaking. Then he let the string slowly back.

Bren nodded as he took his bow. "I draw to the ear," he said, "but some say it's better to draw to the cheek." He turned as abruptly as before, and Arn followed him.

*   *   *

Jen and Arel went to Arel's family's hogan, which was much like Bren's. Amu and Arel's mother, whose name was Runa, were working with the others, so the hogan was empty. The dirt floor had been swept smooth and there was no fire in the large hearth. Two small windows were bright but not transparent because they were made out of animal skins scraped so thin the light came through. Arel had noticed where the stitching had been removed from the red fox fur border on Jen's parka, so she went to a wooden chest with leather hinges and found needles and thread. The needles were much thicker than the ones the Traveler brought at home. Then they went outside where it was brighter and worked on the sewing. It was hard because the stitching holes were smaller than the needles, so they had to press each stitch through with a bone palm thimble.

"The animals," Arel said as they took turns pushing the needle through. "I know an animal, like you said you know Oka. I've never told anyone because we're not supposed to know them."

"Not supposed to know an animal?" Jen said.

"I knew it was wrong but I couldn't help it. His name is Mask, and he's a raccoon. His legs were broken and he didn't want to die." Arel was shaking as she spoke, in fear at having done what was not supposed to be done. "Can I show him to you, Jen, and you won't tell? I've always wanted to tell somebody about Mask."

They put away the needles and thread, and Arel led Jen across the meadow toward the southern forest. They ran and then walked. A brown rabbit ran ahead of them in panic before it veered off and hid in the taller grass of a gully.

At the edge of the forest Arel stopped and looked guiltily back. No one was in sight. She led Jen into the green shade of the pines. "Mask!" she called. "Mask, I'm here!" She sat down on the moss. "He'll come if he heard me.

Sometimes he's so far into the woods he can't hear me, but if he hears he'll come."

They waited quietly. Jen felt there was no hurry to ask or tell anything, that they would in their understanding of each other get around to all the things she wanted to tell or to find out. Then Jen said, "He's nearby."

Arel said, "I know that. How did you know?"

"I can feel him thinking. He's worried about me being with you. I'll bet he's so close we could see him if we looked carefully."

"I know that too, Jen! I didn't think anyone else could do that!"

They looked very carefully into the shadows, into the low bushes that grew between the trees, then higher into the trees. Arel said, "I see him, Jen. Look."

And there he was, a young raccoon with his masked face still, his bright black eyes observing them. He sat on the limb of a pine, ten feet from the ground, peering quietly at them through the needles.

"It's all right, Mask," Arel said.

The young raccoon watched them, thinking of old dangers that spoke to him in his bones, then of Arel, who had touched him without hurting him. Finally he moved and came down the other side of the tree where they couldn't see him. Halfway down his masked face peered around the tree trunk to see if they had moved. When he saw they hadn't, he came all the way down, then came toward them, looking from one to the other. Finally he came up to Arel and let her touch him. After a while he let Jen touch him too.

"I don't know how he broke his legs. They seemed bitten," Arel said. "His front legs—maybe a wildcat or a lynx. But I tied on wooden splints, like we do for people, and brought him food. He hid over there beneath that rock. What he liked best was corn, fish and bread. Then in a week he could get around by himself, and now he's as good as new."

"But you said it was wrong," Jen said.

"Tsuga says it is wrong to change the animals. He says the animals belong to themselves and we should never interfere, but I don't know why it was wrong to help Mask."

The raccoon rolled over on his back so Arel could scratch its belly. "He's grateful, I think," Arel said.

Jen remembered a windy voice she had heard in a dream: *They held the creatures prisoners in pens, fed them and gained their trust, only to betray them in the end . . . They became worse than what they most feared.* She shivered at the belief she had felt in that strange, gentle voice.

"Goodby, Mask," Arel said, getting up. "We've got to go home now."

The young raccoon watched them from its wild black eyes, its thoughts, too, masked from Jen and Arel as they left the forest for the afternoon light of the meadow.

"Arel," Jen said as they walked back toward the houses, "if we ever get back home I wish you could come and visit us."

But then she remembered the blackness of the cold cave beneath the mountain, a cold, unearthly black so absolute it had seemed to dissolve her eyes, and she heard old Snaggletooth's gleeful voice: *A cave of many passages, in and back, and only Ahneeah knows the way!*

On the way to the bowyer's Arn and Bren stopped to watch the fishermen, who waited with their nets in loose curves pulled by the current. Downstream a watcher suddenly shouted, "Shandeh! Shandeh!" and in a moment they saw a dark shadow approaching along the river bed, a long, sinuous shadow that appeared below the smooth swirls of water, then disappeared beneath the rapids' froth, only to appear again, always moving swiftly upstream. When the moving shadow reached the nets, they were drawn tight, then as suddenly loosened by the men on the far bank. On the near bank men with lines ran away from the river, pulling the nets around in a circle to capture the shadow and pull up on the shoreline hundreds of small fish that now, in air, billowed all silver in their desperate tries to swim in air and among the teeming bodies of their fellows. But the nets were drawn away from the water and the fish were soon gathered in wooden sieves to be prepared for drying.

"We will have fresh shandeh for the evening meal," Bren said. "This is called the month of the shandeh. All the rest of the year they stay deep in the warm lake."

The bowyer, who, by his glowing forge and bellows, many hammers and tongs, was also the smith, greeted Bren. "Bren who will not remain a child!" he said. He was a tall, muscular man, his hair turning gray in a fringe around his face, as if the heat from his forge had faded it. When he left his forge for the woodworking part of his hogan he put a buckskin shirt on over his sweat-gleaming arms and chest. He spoke to Arn. "He's the best bowman of his age, and better than many twice his age."

Bren found it difficult to conceal his pride.

They looked through the rough bows stacked at the rear of the hogan, trying to find one to fit Arn, and finally they did find one that seemed right in pull and length. The grip was unfinished, however. "But you can finish it; I've heard you have a good knife," the bowyer said.

"A knife!" Bren said. "Show him your knife!"

The bowyer gently took Arn's knife in his big hand, as if it were something precious he might accidentally drop. He looked at it carefully—pommel, hilt, choil, guard, and finally the blade, which he sighted down, turned in the light, and rubbed with his thumb.

"I heard that your father forged this blade," he said. "He is one of us, a master of his craft. Also, I sense by color and brightness that this blade is harder than ours—a bit brittle, perhaps, but very strong. When you see him, tell him that Rindu, the artisan, greets him as a brother."

Arn's thoughts went again across the miles of forest and darkness to the world of ice where his father lay silent in the small cabin. The bow his father had made for him had seemed more like a toy than the one he now held, yet his father hadn't treated it that way. "This weapon fed a thousand generations of the Old People," he'd said, looking seriously into Arn's eyes. "Treat it with care and respect." And then came the shameful memory of the impaled toad; he had used his bow as a toy, and the result had been a cruel and needless death.

Gradually, as he carved the bow's grip to fit his left hand, these thoughts faded. Bren and Rindu twisted and waxed a bowstring for him and found an old, repaired leather quiver for him. Then he was given ten arrows, five with bladed hunting points, five with blunt points for practice and small game. This was, Arn learned, a ceremony in which he must take each cedar arrow in his hands and memorize its grain and other small differences of detail so that he would always know each arrow as his own.

"Arn's arrows," Rindu said. "May they give death without pain."

Then, until the sun was low in the southwest, Bren and Arn practiced with their bows. They went to a clay bank, where spring freshets had cut a gully in the meadow. Bren took a stick and drew the rough outline of a deer in the clay, and they shot their arrows from twenty, thirty and forty paces. Bren's arrows, released the moment his string touched his ear, flew with such straight tension and authority, Arn didn't think he could ever come close to matching their flight with his own. He did improve, though, after many tries. Bren finally lost his initial impatience with him, and when Arn learned, as if in his fingers themselves, to release his arrows smoothly, with little wobble, Bren said he might someday make an archer.

Before the first haze of dusk they walked back toward the winter camp, where cooking fires had been lit. Blue-gray woodsmoke rose from the central openings of the hogans to form a soft mist that drifted slowly, in smooth layers, across the river toward the east. Arn was thinking of his hunger, after this day, and of the warm hogans where the people would be hungry after their long day of work. He felt himself part of them now.

Bren stopped and looked toward the east, where the light from the western sky still made the trees glow a dim orange. "See!" he said, excitement in his lowered voice. "See, by the trunk of that tallest pine! Do you see?"

Three deer—a doe and two yearlings, their backs fading into black, their chest and belly markings white, fading into the dusky orange of the evening light, browsed silently at the edge of the forest.

"See?" Bren said. "We were not playing. When you learn, that is not play." He gazed, as motionless and watchful as the deer, who had seen them stop and knew across all that distance the quick intensity of hunters. "They know," Bren said with reverence in his voice for those lives and minds far across the river, those free animals who were of the wilderness that gave sustenance to his people.

12

An
Interrupted
Tale

That evening Jen and Arn met Fannu and Dona, grand-
son and granddaughter of Aguma, the stocky gray-haired
woman who was Chief Councillor, whose palms had glit-
tered with the silver scales. They met other children,
some younger and some older than they, each different
from them and from all the others. At the evening meal
they saw two nursing babies held across their mothers'
laps, heard their small noises as they fed at their mothers'
breasts.

Because of the constant work of the month of the
shandeh, the people ate in communal hogans, some having been assigned to prepare the food for others. Jen and
Arn sat at a long table in Aguma's hogan, the largest in the
winter camp. Huge pottery tureens of shandeh stew
steamed upon the table. Plates piled high with hot yellow
cornbread were passed from end to end, with plenty for
everyone. Each took his bowl and with a wooden ladle
dipped out as much of the rich stew as he wanted. Among
the vegetables—Arn recognized cattail tubers, arrowroot,
corn, beans and small wild carrots—thick flakes of the
white meat of the shandeh swirled in the rich yellow
broth.

The people, young and old, were tired but friendly with each other. The shandeh had run well this year, and they foresaw less hunger in the hard months of the false spring when the sun would be high but the earth still cold and fallow.

After the meal were the evening fires, most of the people returning to their own hogans.

Amu and Runa, Arel's parents, stayed for a while with them by Aguma's fire after the dishes and bowls had been collected and taken to the river for washing. As they sat in the warm firelight Bren kept looking toward the door of the hogan, obviously worried about something, and finally Runa came to kneel behind him and put her hands on his shoulders. "Bren is worried," she said in a voice in which they heard a smile of affection. Her round face was bronze, her black hair glowing with fine threads of reddish gold in the firelight. Arel had told Jen and Arn that Bren's mother was dead, and that after her death Bren's father had changed. He would go away sometimes for weeks at a time, no one knew where. And now he had been away again for several days.

Bren seemed to gain some comfort from Runa's concern, but still he was silent, seeming very small among the adults, his brows down over his eyes like dark awnings.

When the bearskin curtain over the door began to move, Bren looked up eagerly. The bearskin was pushed aside and what looked like half a man—all legs—came through the doorway. It was old Ganonoot, all bent over, his head tilted up in order to see. He cackled when he saw Arn and Jen, Bren and Arel, Fannu and Dona and the other children by the fire. "Here are my little ones who like stories!" he said as he came swiftly over to them, moving smoothly like some kind of insect that had more legs than it ought to have.

Bren's face went dark and still again; he had been expecting someone else. But Ganonoot, smiling so wide his dark gums shone in the firelight, sat down among them, took his yellow fang in his fingers and moved his head up and down as if that tooth were a handle.

"Don't you think I know you, my little ones?" Ganonoot said, looking quickly with his bright little berry eyes at each child in turn. "I know what you want to hear and do! And some will get their wishes and some won't; that is the way it is in the world. Bren wants to grow up too fast and be a great hunter, Arel wants to hear all the small thoughts of meadow and forest, Fannu is vain of his running and jumping, Dona wants to dress in ermine and wolverine, Jen and Arn are sad for their home, and search for the answer to a question they don't know how to ask. Now, can I give each of you what you desire? What story would you like to hear?"

Fannu, who was tall for his age, and thin, just the opposite of his grandmother, said, "Tell about the boy who rode the deer."

Ganonoot said, "Ah, that was a smooth ride with a big bump at the end, for he's still flying toward the morning star."

"Tell about the Queen of the West," Dona said.

"When she grew too beautiful she turned into wind," Ganonoot said, "and the snow is her ermine cloak."

"Tell about the white-footed mouse who spoke to Ahneeah," Arel said.

"He was the only mouse who dared complain of the weasels," Ganonoot said, "and the only thing Ahneeah granted was that the weasel kill swiftly, with one clean bite."

They looked to Bren, who was silent, staring at the embers. Ganonoot said, "Come, Bren. What story would you choose?"

"That my father return," Bren said. He looked up, his face closed and stern against showing his feelings. "But that's not a story." He looked down again.

"There is a story that is old and sad, but noble in places. I will tell you the tale of Ahneeah and the People Who

Left the World." Ganonoot's voice changed as he began the story; it grew deeper and clearer.

"Long ago, so long ago the Great Tree was a sprout no higher than a rabbit's eyes, the People lived among orchards and meadows and gardens, groves of sugar maples, hills and valleys of the trees who give of their meat—hickory, beech, butternut, chestnut and oak. Each plant had a purpose—to live and grow. Each animal had a purpose—to live and grow, and the People knew this, deep beyond all questions, for they knew their own purpose and saw that it was the same. They ate only plants, and the plants they ate could not feel pain because plants have no need of pain, and the People knew this without asking. But we ask, 'Why do the plants have no need of pain?' It is because they cannot run away, and pain is to tell you to run away, and after you have run away, to rest and heal.

"Ahneeah is of the sun and moon, fire and ice; her voice is the wind and thunder, her glance is the lightning, her tears are the rain. But the earth is older even than Ahneeah, and we are all made of the earth we till and walk upon and sweep from the floors of our hogans.

"Now, of the animals who were not men, certain of them chased and killed and ate each other. Certain of them ate only the plants, who felt no pain, but others killed the creatures who could run, and be hurt, and cry out in agony as they died. The men saw this, and being hungry for flesh they invented the sling, the spear, the snare, the trap and the bow. Ahneeah said to them in her voices, 'All right, you have chosen to give death to those who swim and fly and run from it. But when you kill you must be present in order to see death, and hear its cry; therefore you may not use the snare, the poison, the toothed trap or the trap which holds a prisoner. It is the right of all prey to be free to escape if they can, and if a kill is made, the red blood of your prey must flow over your hands, as your own red blood flows through your hands, and every man and woman who would eat meat must kill and clean the body of the kill. No one who has not killed, or helped to kill, may eat flesh, for knowledge of the agony of death is the price of flesh.'

"But there were men who could not hear Ahneeah's voices, or would not hear them, or who were mistaken and confused. They thought that what they could do justified the doing of it. And now I will tell you how this confusion led to the murder of prisoners and finally to the killing of men by men. It is a story of heroes lost, of brave children and men and women, and of the sad people who, with Ahneeah's guidance, left the world for alien lands, only to yearn through generations for Ahneeah's justice, though they had long forgotten from whence it came, or from whence they came."

As Ganonoot spoke the formal words of the story he seemed to them less and less the childish old man he had been. He was just a voice saying words that rang in the air solemn and clear.

"Ahneeah planted the Great Tree when the People first came into the world, but that tree was destroyed during the time of greed and war. The second tree grew in the shade of the first. The second tree is the Great Tree we know, but it was a sprout no higher than a rabbit's eye when Ahneeah . . ."

At this moment the bearskin across the hogan door was pulled violently aside, so that its skin side slapped against the doorpost like a whip. Everyone looked and saw a tall, thickset man who stood with his legs apart, his hands on his hips. His dark hair was ruffled as if he had been running, and his eyes gleamed with red flashes in the firelight. "It's Bren's father," Arel whispered.

"Bren!" the man said. "So you are wasting your time listening to the old idiot tell children's tales!"

Bren got up, apprehensive about his father's anger, yet there was relief and joy in his face.

"Andaru, my brother," Amu said. "Bren has been here with us."

"Yes, listening to the whimsy of this dodderer!"

"While you've been who knows where?" Runa said, matching Andaru's anger.

Andaru turned to Amu. "Brother, tell your woman to speak more softly!" His face was strained with his anger; like Bren's, his brows came low over his eyes.

Then the old woman, Aguma, stepped out of the shadows to face Andaru. "Andaru, where have you learned such manners? And why do you bring your sourceless anger to my hogan?"

Andaru looked at her steadily for a moment, then shrugged as if she and her hogan were not important. "I'll take my anger with me, then," he said in a calmer voice. "Come, Bren." He turned and went past the bearskin into the darkness. Bren seemed embarrassed, and kept his eyes away from them all as he followed his father from the hogan.

Ganonoot said, "The story was for Bren, the hunter, and now it will have to wait." He said the words solemnly, but then, with his silly cackling laughter, he rose to his feet and scuttled like an insect to the doorway. "Goodnight, goodnight, goodnight, children! We will have to wait and see! Goodnight!" And with that he turned and glided swiftly past the bearskin into the night.

The people murmured among themselves, giving their opinions of Andaru's behavior. Arel said to Jen and Arn, "Some people say that my uncle Andaru has been with the Chigai." She whispered the last word.

Jen and Arn looked at each other, feeling the uneasiness all around them. Because of all the things they didn't know, they seemed to be among strangers, though earlier they had begun to feel almost at home with the people of the winter camp. Arel took Jen's hand, and put her other hand on Arn's arm. "You'll stay with us tonight, in our hogan," she said. "My mother has made up beds for you."

That night they slept on shelf beds in Amu and Runa's hogan, on mattresses of aromatic balsam covered with supple skins. They went to sleep hearing the muted voices of the adults around the fire.

In the morning Bren and Arel woke them shortly after dawn. "The net men say the shandeh have stopped running," Bren said, "so we can do what we want today." He said nothing about what had happened the night before.

"And tomorrow we go to the council fire," Arel said.

For breakfast they had cornbread and honey, and tea brewed from a dark ground powder like the powder Arn carried in his pack. After breakfast Fannu came in, tall and lanky for his age, and Dona, dressed in her bead-decorated parka trimmed with the fur of fox, rabbit and squirrel.

"Dona doesn't want to, but we've decided to show you how to play our game with the ball," Fannu said. "You have to run. Do you like to run?"

"Arn runs pretty well," Bren said.

"You'll get your clothes all dirty," Dona said. But when they went out on the meadow to the place where they played the game, Dona put her parka carefully to the side on the grass and played with them.

The ball was sewn leather, as big as an acorn squash, stuffed with leather scraps. At each end of the grassy space a bent hoop made of a thin sapling had been placed in the ground, forming an arch about five feet high. The object was to kick the ball through the other team's hoop. Fannu and Bren chose sides and agreed that Bren's team would be Dona and Arel, and Fannu's, Jen and Arn. The ground was still frozen from the night's frost, and the sun was rising at a flat angle that just brought it over the southeastern mountains.

Fannu was very good; he could run and turn while still playing the ball between his flickering feet. He passed it over to Jen, who kicked it by accident to Arel, who kicked it to Dona, who kicked it ahead of her as she ran until Bren could get into position by Fannu's hoop. She passed it to him and he quickly kicked it through for a point. Arel, who looked sickly and pale, could still run as well as anyone.

The hard ground and frosty grass passed beneath their feet as they played. Jen and Arn were beginning to understand the game, and how to keep the ball rolling as they ran. Fannu made the next point, after a pass from Arn. They were all breathing hard in the cold air, their breaths white plumes, their feet dashing and dancing through the worn grass, their voices calling happily yet seriously across the meadow.

When the score was three for Fannu's team and two for Bren's, Arn got the ball near Bren's hoop and dribbled it forward to give it its final kick. Bren was between him and the hoop, and he was about to sidestep Bren when suddenly the sky whirled above him and he was on the ground, numb, unable to breathe. Bren had run right over him and taken the ball. At first all Arn could do was try to get his wind back, to make air come into his lungs. His chest was paralyzed by the blow he had taken; he couldn't understand the hardness, the violence of Bren's action. It was as if Bren wanted to hurt him very badly, as if Bren really hated him. He lay there in the icy dust struggling for breath.

Jen and Arel stood over him. "Are you all right?" Jen asked. "Arn! Are you all right?"

He couldn't get enough breath to speak, but as the moments passed he began to get more air. He was perplexed. Anger flirted around the edge of his feelings, and also a sadness that hinted at tears. But he didn't cry. Finally he could breathe again, and got to his feet. Fannu, Bren and Dona were playing out the point near the opposite hoop. When Bren made the point they came back.

"Did you mean to hurt him?" Jen said to Bren, anger in her voice.

"That's part of the game," Fannu said. "If there's only you between the hoop and the player with the ball, you can hit him as hard as you want to."

"Bren wanted to hurt him, then," Jen said. "Did you, Bren?"

"Can he take it?" was all Bren said.

"I can take it," Arn said. He looked at Bren, feeling cold and calm now. Bren's look was as cool as his own.

They played the game for a while longer, but the exhilaration they had felt was gone. The coolness between Arn and Bren remained, as though everyone couldn't help thinking about it.

As they walked back toward the hogans, Fannu told Arn and Jen that they would make good players, and that they had done very well at a game they had never played before. Both Jen and Arn were pleased by this, and by Arel's and Dona's saying the same thing. In spite of the small cloud caused by Bren's silence—he walked ahead of them, not speaking—they were so pleased, Jen felt herself blushing. Arn thought, This was just a game. Why should it have pleased him so much? He was still sore in places. That was real, and the game was real, as real as anything he had ever done.

That day they took a long hike through the western woods—Bren, Arel, Fannu and Dona, Arn and Jen. Their lunches in their packs or pockets, they walked westward toward a knob of stone from which they would get a view of most of the valley. They walked through the quiet green woods on an easy trail of moss and evergreen needles, dead winter ferns and the leaves of the summer before. After a mile or two they came to the rising slopes of the lookout knob, then climbed around and around the knob itself, always going upward, until they came out into the sunlight and the wind upon the rounded stone, with the valley spread out below them. To the east was the meadow, where the hogans were just little dark or green squares. The hot lake was to the north of the meadow, its rainbow shores dimmed by the distance. Nearer, the tops of the forest trees pushed up below them, a green depth that changed and became more solid in the distance. Far away in every direction rose the sharp mountain walls of the valley.

They found comfortable places in the sun and got out their lunches of smoked boar ham slices, cucumber pickles, bread and dried apples. Bren had brought a skin bag of water in his pack, and the brook water was clear and good.

Arel saw that Jen was looking to the far north, where she and Arn had entered the valley. "Tsuga will be back tomorrow, for the council fire," she said. "Maybe you can ask him how to get home again."

"Can you talk to him?" Jen asked. "Who is Tsuga? What's he like?"

"He's older than the mountains," Fannu said. "At least that's what they told us when we were little."

"Bren's talked to him," Arel said. "What do you think, Bren?"

Bren was quiet and sad, unsmiling. He glanced at Arel and away, as if he were not going to answer. Then he said in a low voice, "My father says he is only a man. He's old and maybe he does know a lot, but he's just a man."

"He's the oldest of all," Dona said. "They say he remembers when he could raise his arm higher than the top of the Great Tree."

"He smiled at me once," Arel said. "He looked right at me and smiled."

Bren was watching Jen, his eyes more alive than they had been all day, as if he were looking out of his head rather than at some dark problem within it. Then he said, "Are you homesick, Jen?"

Jen knew how hard it must be for Bren to say anything like that, so she knew she had been looking very sad. She had been thinking of the way through the mountain, then the frozen forest, then the small cabin; and then she remembered a time that seemed so long ago, when she and her mother were making butter in the churn and her mother sang the butter song in her clear and happy voice:

Out of night comes daylight,
Out of thin comes thick.
Oka knows how butter grows,
So turn the paddles quick.

Jen turned her face away from Bren's dark eyes. "But I like it here, too," she said.

Arel said, "If you can't find your way back, we'd like you to stay here with us."

Fannu said, "Arn can play on my side anytime he wants."

Dona came over and sat on the other side of Jen, and the six children were quiet in the warm sun. They knew they were only children and could not decide things beyond their powers, but they could by their closeness make real for a while their separate world.

13

The
Council Fire

The next morning all the people—men, women, children and babies—made ready to travel to the Great Tree, where the council fire would be held. After the council fire they would camp by the warm lake and return to the winter camp the day after. Aguma herself had predicted that the next day would be clear, though it would be cold on the evening of the fire. Each family distributed food, arrows and necessary gear among its members, and each person would have a sleeping skin to roll up in on the cold ground, the fur inside.

Bren's father had left early that morning, alone, so Bren went with Amu and Runa, Arn, Jen and Arel. Fannu and Dona went with Aguma's party. It was a long walk across meadow, around swamps and through the woods, and they stopped only once, toward late afternoon, to rest and eat. Bren, who had been silent all the way, took his food and sat apart from them, his unstrung bow across his lap, his back against a spruce.

Arel looked at him worriedly and spoke in a low voice to Jen and Arn. "Bren is upset because he couldn't go with Andaru. It doesn't seem right to him."

"But everybody seems worried," Jen said. "I can feel it."

"So can I," Arel said. Her pale, delicate face was sad. "I heard my mother and father talking last night when we were all supposed to be asleep. It's the Chigai. The people don't know what to think about them and their ways, because it is said that the Chigai are never hungry, and the people don't want to be hungry."

Soon they rose and continued their journey to the Great Tree. Arn carried his unstrung bow in his left hand, his quiver tied to his pack, in which he carried both his and Jen's food. Jen carried her sleeping-skin rolled and tied across her shoulders. It was a long walk, but finally they came to the meadow and climbed up the slope to the ledges and the tree. The sun had set behind the western mountains and a half-moon had risen in the southeast. Far above, a few thin coins of clouds still caught the light of the sun and lent a golden light to the valley. The Great Tree rose above the ledges, branch above branch, the sturdy trunk finally disappearing into green. At its base, behind the stone platform, was the black archway of the Cave of Forgetfulness.

The people gathered at the ledges, taking their places on the winter-brown grass around a large pile of branches that would be the council fire. On the stone platform in front of the archway, Aguma and several older people sat waiting for darkness and the lighting of the fire. Bren and Arel, with Fannu and Dona, took Jen and Arn to the front, where all the children sat. The grass was soft, the earth still warm from the departed sun, and all the people waited, speaking to each other in low voices.

Fannu and Dona had heard rumors that the council would be an important one. They were to have visitors from a settlement on the eastern edge of the valley, where some of their own people had visited in the fall. There were rumors of discontent with Tsuga's teachings. Some people had left early that morning, as had Andaru, and actually visited the camp of the Chigai on the eastern edge of the meadow. It was said that the Chigai had wolves as servants, or as slaves, though that was hard to believe.

"Is Tsuga up there?" Arn asked. They could just make out the outlines of the people on the stone platform.

"He's there," Arel said. "He sits on Aguma's left. You'll see him when the fire is lighted."

Bren, who had been silent, spoke to Jen and Arn. "But you had a 'cow,'" he said. "Was that your servant? And the 'ox' and the 'pig' and the goats? Was that wrong?"

"They served us, I guess," Arn said. "But they weren't wild animals. Without us to protect them and feed them in the winter, they would have died."

"Then how could they be animals?" Fannu wondered. "Tsuga says the animals live in the world, but we live in our clothes and hogans."

"And we have fire," Arel said.

As the light died the people grew silent and tense, and the children felt it. When Jen shivered, Arel reached for her hand and took it in hers.

A dim figure rose from among the people on the right and came to the base of the pile of wood. A few flickers from flint and steel, then a small red flame from within the pile, showed that the fire-lighter was Amu, Arel's father. He stood silently in his buckskin clothes as the fire grew and began to crackle as it climbed within the black branches, turning the inner ones gold and red. Then Amu returned to his place. The crackling turned to a roar as the fire rose through its fuel. The ledges, the faces of the elders, and above them the high green branches of the Great Tree were lighted as if by daylight for a while until the fire fell back within itself to feed quietly on the larger wood. Faces, hot from the fire's first surge, cooled in the new embering silence.

Jen and Arn had been watching the person sitting on Aguma's left. They saw an ancient, wrinkled face below pure-white hair. The face was thin; the skin over the sharp cheekbones shone red. Now that person rose to his feet, and he was tall and wide-shouldered, like their father, though thin with age. His collarbones stood out at the neck of his deerskin tunic, angular and shiny. His black eyes were sunken, yet they reflected the firelight like shiny black stones.

"Let the council begin," he said. His voice was sad and old, penetrating yet dry as a dying wind. "I am Tsuga Wanders-too-far, and what I know I will tell you." He sat down again, waiting with an expressionless face.

From the left, out of the darkness, came a man in a deer mask with great antlers. Jen was afraid, and squeezed Arel's hand.

"It's all right," Arel whispered in her ear. "It's just the beginning of the council. Now they'll choose who's to make the gift to the stag."

On the platform, Aguma rose to her feet. She held a loaf of bread in her hands. When she spoke she almost sang the words in a deep voice. "Arel and Bren have been chosen."

Jen looked at Arel, who was nothing but proud and excited at having been chosen. Bren was proud, too, though he tried not to show it. They both got up and went to the old woman, who broke the loaf in two and handed half to each. Arel and Bren turned and went solemnly to the man in the deer mask, who nodded his great antlers as he received the bread. Then Arel and Bren turned and came back to take their places before the fire.

Jen wanted to ask Arel about this ceremony, which was almost like the one they had at home on Christmas Eve, but so much unlike the horrors she and Arn had witnessed here before.

Tsuga rose to his feet again. He stood leaning on his long, unstrung bow as if he were very tired. The people were silent, waiting for him to speak.

"I am old enough to call you my children," Tsuga began.

"Too old!" someone shouted from the darkness beyond the firelight. There were gasps of dismay from the people, who turned their heads to search for whoever had spoken so rudely.

Aguma stood up heavily and spoke in her deep voice: "Who speaks to the council? Come into the light; only liars shout from the dark."

"Come forward! Come forward!" the people said.

Soon a flustered though angry young man made his way to the council fire. He wore a long knife and carried an unstrung bow, his buckskin tunic decorated at neck and cuffs with wolf fur. "All right!" he said. "Here I am!"

"What do you want to say to the council, Lado?" the old woman said.

"The people of the eastern foothills have meat, while we nearly starved last winter!"

"We were hungry, but we did not starve," Tsuga said.

"But they had all the meat they wanted!"

Tsuga sighed before he spoke again. "Yes, I know. And you would also have us keep these strange wolves, these creatures who kill their own kind . . ."

"The Chigai have shaggy cattle they can kill whenever they are hungry!"

"Prisoners," Tsuga said.

Some of the people groaned at that word, in horror of it, but at the back, in the darkness, a different sound arose. It was a harsh murmur of defiance against Tsuga and the councillors. Someone shouted, "That's what *you* say, but the Chigai increase!"

"They increase in numbers," Tsuga said. "But why do they need numbers? Does it make their councillors feel more important?"

"They *are* more important!" Lado said.

"I cannot stop you from emulating them," Tsuga said. "Knowledge is all I can give you. I have lived a long time and I will tell you what I know."

"You're a doddering old fool!" came a shout from the

dark. "You and your tree! Can we eat wood in the iron month?"

Another of the councillors, a man of middle age who wore a cape of white mountain-goat fur, stood up and motioned for silence.

"I, too, have visited the Chigai," he said, "and I am of mixed mind. I was taught to cultivate the earth and to hunt. But the hunting is harder than it was in my youth. We, too, grow in numbers; to have meat that is always available, and even the half-wolves to help us hunt . . . how can that be bad?"

Cheers came from many of the people. Those sitting around the children spoke excitedly to themselves.

"We must take a vote!" the young man shouted. "Let the Chigai show us how to fill our bellies!"

Another man came from the darkness to stand next to the young man. He was much more sure of himself, and when he spoke his voice was steady and his hands made reasonable gestures.

"I, too, have studied the Chigai and their ways," he said. "They are numerous and wonderfully large and strong. They keep their cattle in wide fields and in long covered pens made of wood. The cattle are fed on grass and grain; they are protected, and multiply. Only a certain few of the people do the killing; the others never have to soil their hands with blood and fat, but partake of the meat and are never hungry. Others have taught the half-wolves to protect the herds and also to hunt down boar, bear and deer. The people are warm and fat in the coldest winters."

Amid the resulting shouts and cheers, Tsuga stood, his arm in the air, asking to be heard. From his belt he took a small green branch and held it out before him. Finally the people grew silent, watching.

He spoke slowly, in his sad old voice. "I will not tell you the future because it is not mine, but yours—for better or for worse. All my life I have been a tiller of the earth, a caretaker of the fruit trees, and a hunter. We know each other and are equals, the creatures and I. They know my need and I know theirs. That is neither good nor bad; it has been my life.

"But before I go into the silence I will tell you what I know: it is evil to own another; it is evil to kill a prisoner; it is evil to teach betrayal; it is evil to have clean hands and eat meat, for ignorance of death is the greatest evil of all."

When Tsuga had finished, the people, who were used to believing his words, were confused. Low murmurs arose as they asked questions among themselves. "What does Tsuga mean?" "Is it not necessary to wash your hands?" "Can anyone be owned?" "No one is taught to betray us." "What did he mean?" "What did he mean?"

The young man, Lado, and the man who had made the reasonable gestures climbed to the stone platform next to the councillors.

"People!" said the man of the reasonable gestures. "Let us show you what man may do with a wolf, whom you now fear!" He signaled to the darkness, and a large man came to the platform leading something low and gray on a thong.

The man was a stranger, taller and more muscled than anyone else. His broad arms shone red in the firelight; his nose and mouth seemed small in his wide, oiled-looking face. He wore a broad shirt made from the glossy black skin of the shaggy cattle. He led a wolf, its white teeth and wide eyes gleaming with fear and hatred. "Now," the big man said. "This is how we have our wolves." He jerked the thong until the wolf, its gray fur ruffled, the hairs along its back stiffly rigid like a brush, came to the man's feet and sat trembling, at one moment lowering its head in submission, at the next snarling defiance that was all white teeth and show.

The big man took a short, thick leather whip, or knout, from his belt and held it above the wolf, which cowered, grinning and snarling and fawning. "Are you my servant, animal?" the man demanded.

The wolf cowered yet snapped its long wet ivory teeth as if at an insect that had appeared in front of its jaws.

"That is not good enough!" the man said. He shortened the noose until the wolf choked and gagged, then beat it with the stubby knotted whip. The animal rolled over on its back to expose its tender underside to the hissing blows of the whip. It cried, whining and barking in short sharp chirps, almost like a bird, before the man stopped. Then the half-wolf, still submissive on its back, licked the man's moccasined feet and ankles, whining and salivating, its tail tucked along its belly.

From the people came expressions of fear and wonder; even, from some of them, cries of satisfaction that a man could so dominate the feared wolf. "*That* one won't steal our meat!" someone shouted.

"Nor ever chase a man up a tree," the big stranger said. "Our people own the earth they walk upon. Everything is ours. We own the forests and the meadows and all the creatures who live in them. Our servants hunt for us. We have no need to run, or to use our noses and eyes and ears like animals, or to freeze silently in the chill before dawn. We are the masters!"

The people were in awe of the big man. They murmured to each other, questioning. Tsuga, who was still standing, said to the big man over the murmuring of the people, "And you, Morl, are you master of the masters?"

"I am!" Morl drew himself up and stood with his feet apart and his arms akimbo.

The young man who had first spoken against Tsuga said, "We must say whether we will prosper under the new ways or follow old Tsuga, who keeps us too lean and hungry."

"Lado," Tsuga said, "would you like to be treated as that wolf is treated?"

"I would be master of the animals!"

"It is evil to own another."

Lado reached out and took the green branch from Tsuga's hand. "Did this ever fill our bellies?" he said, and tossed it like a spear into the fire. It crackled and blazed up with a flash of yellow light.

This act of impropriety amazed the people again. They were silent, looking from Tsuga to the young Lado, to big Morl with his subservient wolf groveling at his feet.

Tsuga said, "I have told you what I know. Express your will now, my people. It is part of freedom that you are free to give it up."

The people still didn't know what Tsuga meant. They asked themselves questions and shook their heads. From farther back came shouts of anger against Tsuga's words, and from others demands for quiet.

Aguma stood and raised her thick arms out to her sides until the noise quieted. "The council will recommend and the people will judge," she said, "but first we must have quiet. Those who shout cannot listen. We will hear from the council."

The councillor who wore the cape of white mountain-goat fur stood first, a small smile on his face that Arn, for one, didn't trust. It was not a smile of pleasure or friendliness, and what other kind was there? It reminded him of the expressions of the goats at home. From their rigid masks no one could tell what they were going to do next. They seemed only alert and interested, yet at any moment, with no change of expression at all, they might butt you or run away. They were born to wear that look, but this man's face was made up by him. As he spoke, Arn knew what he was going to say. He wanted to find out what most of the people thought and he was going to think that way too. So he had nothing to say except that the new ideas were very interesting. And also that they must remember the traditions they had always lived by. But, he suggested, probably something as good and helpful as the smelting of iron and the making of steel was objected to by someone when it was first proposed. "We must be careful to examine and not to discard all new ideas."

Then the small smile broadened just slightly because he had come to the tentative conclusion that most of the people wanted all the meat they could get and didn't care how they got it. So he said that he was inclined to go along with Lado, Morl and the others who wanted to keep cattle and make servants of the wolves.

Many of the people cheered him, but Arn saw that their cheers were partly ironic because they knew he hadn't made his choice out of his own beliefs.

Another councillor, an older man whose face had been clawed on one side and had healed long ago into deep red furrows, rose to speak for Tsuga. As he spoke, those who agreed with him nodded but didn't cheer. He held out his left arm and Arn saw that his right one was missing. "Listen well to Tsuga," the man said. "He is saying that anyone who calls one creature his servant will in turn be a servant. Morl has already said that he is the master of the masters. When he wants to he will turn his craven wolves upon men, upon you. When the real wolves run they kill only what they need, as we do. That is not dishonorable. But for a man to be master of a man or of a creature is to be cruel beyond need. I have no hatred for the bear who took my arm. How could I have? We were both doing what we had to do to live. The reason for life is to live. But this craven of a half-wolf has in him hatred, as you can see. It is a disease given to him by his master."

At these words Morl, who stood on the platform with his wolf at his feet, pointed to the one-armed man and jerked the wolf's thong. The wolf leaped, snarling and slashing, only to be jerked short by the thong. The one-armed man drew his knife and held it before him, its point toward the wolf, but didn't flinch.

"So," he said. "Does the half-wolf need me for food?"

Many of the people sighed with disapproval of Morl and the wolf. Morl said, "This man's fine thoughts will mean little when your bellies are empty in the iron month. Perhaps we will come by then and give you some red meat." He laughed and turned, dragging the wolf on the thong until it found its feet and followed at heel, its tail curled up under its belly.

"Wait!" Lado said. "Let the people say!"

Aguma stood and said to Lado, "You want the people to choose because you think you know how they will choose. Tell me, Lado, would you want them to vote now if you had doubts about what they would say?"

Lado was silent, and the old woman went on. "You would have them vote before they have heard from all of the council? Your thought is sick with your hunger for red meat. You do not believe in freedom any more. You would rather be the master of slaughter than be free."

"Free to starve," Lado mumbled. "What kind of freedom is that?"

"No one has starved, not in your memory."

Tsuga said, "To be hungry is to live and be quick. To starve is to die. There's a great difference, Lado."

"Why should we be hungry at all?"

"Why should winter come before spring? Why should night come before day? Why should fasting come before a feast? Would you live your whole life at table? You are a good hunter, Lado. You know more than you think you do of what the woods, the meadows and the water can give to us. But when you have grown slow and thick upon a glut of slaughter, and when the cattle die of the sickness that comes to all prisons, then you will starve."

Lado laughed at the idea of his ever becoming slow and thick and forgetting how to live from the woods, the meadows and the water.

Tsuga spoke once again to the people. "All I can give you is knowledge," he said in his sad old voice. He paused for a while, an old man with thin white hair falling like mist to his shoulders. He was still wiry and strong, but he was wrinkled and old. "No matter what you decide at this council fire, I am afraid it is too late. We are all one people in the valley and what happens to one settlement happens to all." He turned away from the people and looked to the tree that grew above the ledges.

"See!" Morl shouted as he dragged his leashed wolf back up to the stone platform. "He is powerless, as he has always been powerless!" Morl took a short broadax from his belt and tossed it to Lado. "Here, Lado. Show them what a man should respect!"

Lado caught the ax in the air and swiftly climbed up the ledges to the tree. The ax blade gleamed red in the firelight as he drew it up and back, then sank it, with the deep quick sound of steel cleaving wood, into the living trunk of the tree.

A moan rose from the people, not of outrage at this new act of brutality so much as sorrow and resignation at the passing of respect. Tsuga didn't speak or move; the tree accepted the blade without a tremble and was silent. Lado wrenched the ax from the tree and struck again. A thick wedge of wood and bark tumbled into the light and to the ground. The tree's white wound remained as Lado came back down and returned the broadax to Morl.

"No lightning?" Morl said. "No thunder from the gods of wood?" He laughed, his coarse laughter the only sound in the night except for the quiet hissing of the fire. When his laughter stopped, he grinned at the people, at the councillors on the stone platform. "You haven't yet tasted the power we have, the dark powers we do not hesitate to use. There are other gods besides your meek ones— your tree and your Abneeah and your stag." He looked to the tree and then, with contempt, to the man in the stag mask who sat quietly at his place by the fire. "Let me show you a more powerful rite!"

With that he raised his broadax, jerked the wolf's head up with the rawhide thong, and with one quick blow severed the head from the screaming animal. He picked up the still-quivering head by an ear and threw it to the stag man, the teeth and eyes turning and glowing over the fire, blood and cut wolf hair falling over the people and the children. The stag man jumped away from the cruel gift, which rolled past him into the darkness.

There was silence then. Soon after, when the voting came, the people were subdued and divided. Most wanted to know more, and spoke of their love and respect for Tsuga. But that love was muted and sad, as if they spoke at a funeral. Some were afraid of change, and said that their granaries and root cellars were not yet empty, and the shandeh had run well. Others saw, even though they had doubts and fears about them, the power of the new ways and knew, as did Tsuga, that they would probably come to pass. Only a few, like Lado, spoke with anger toward what they would destroy, needing their hatred to disguise whatever doubts they had.

A smaller few stood firm with Tsuga, saying that his wisdom must not be ignored. Amu spoke and held the attention of all. He was the lighter of the fire and was respected. He stood, sturdy and dark beside the embering fire.

"We have made no clear decision tonight," he said. "All the councillors have not spoken because two of them have not yet returned from hunting in the western mountains. I say we should study these matters for seven days and vote at the next council fire.

"For myself I will think also of the actions of Lado and of Morl. One wounds the Great Tree with a stranger's broadax; the other kills his helpless prisoner. Are these the new ways, my people? Are the dark powers those of cruelty and murder? If so, what price must we pay for all this promised meat?"

The people murmured among themselves. Many nodded. Lado and Morl stared darkly at Arel's father, not daring to challenge him.

When the murmurs died away Aguma, who was the speaker of the council, rose tiredly to her feet and said, "What the lighter of the fire says is true. We will meet again on the seventh day, here at the entrance to the

Cave of Forgetfulness, below the Great Tree, with our guest the stag. This council fire is over."

The people began to rise and move off into the meadow that was dimly lit by the falling half-moon. Many were thoughtful and silent, though others spoke heatedly in low voices as they stood in groups before moving away. Morl, Lado, the councillor dressed in goatskin and some others laughed and spoke in louder voices as they went off to the eastern edge of the meadow toward the camp of the Chigai.

The children were silent and afraid. Many were pale, their round faces like small moons. Bren, Arel, Jen and Arn stood together waiting for Amu and Runa, who were talking with some of the councillors. Only Bren looked angry at what had happened. He spoke in a voice harsh for his years. "The way they treated Tsuga!" But he was disappointed in Tsuga, too. Things had been done that should not have been done; the council fire he had revered all his life had been disrupted so easily, without punishment. "How could they do it? Lado! I never trusted him." But Bren was still a child and his world was changing all around him. He didn't know where his father was, or what his father would have thought about what had happened. Arn saw all this and went to his side, but Bren turned furious and pushed him roughly away, then strode off into the darkness.

Jen said, "He's upset, Arn." They both knew that Bren could not take sympathy, that it was not his way. Jen thought of her father and mother, wanting them. "Arn, are we going to ask Tsuga . . . ?"

They looked around, then, for the tall, wiry old man with the long bow. Amu and Runa were there on the stone platform, and Aguma, and the councillor with the one arm and the scarred face—but Tsuga was gone.

14

Strung Bows

Tsuga was gone. They looked everywhere for him—all around the ledges, among the people who were leaving to make their camps down by the hot lake, out as far as the stone sentries that made their silent, headless circle around the ledges and the tree. No one knew where Tsuga had gone, or why he had left so quickly. Arel tried to comfort them, saying that surely Tsuga would return, but Jen and Arn were worried and sad as they went with Amu and Runa to the shore of the lake, where Amu made a small fire of brush and dead branches. In the distance other fires glimmered upon the faces of the people, who seemed to sit in little rooms of fire scattered along the shore of the lake.

It was a cold night, chill but windless, and the fire's warmth drew them close.

"Where is Bren?" Amu asked. "Didn't he come with you?"

Before anyone could answer, a young man came quietly out of the darkness and sat on his haunches by Amu's side. He was a thin young man with a dark, lined face that looked weathered. He was quick and nervous in his gestures. He and Amu went away from the fire, where they spoke for a long time in voices inaudible to the others. Then the young man left and Amu came back to the fire.

"We have heard from Tsuga," he said in a low voice. "We must go back to the winter camp tonight, in the darkness with no moon."

"But why?" Runa asked.

"Bad things are happening with the people. Tsuga thinks it would be best if we went away until the next council fire. If we can return to the winter camp tonight and get food and arrows, we can go toward the western mountains, where the Chigai never hunt."

"What about Jen and Arn?" Arel asked.

"We will meet Aguma as soon as the moon has set, at the Cave of Forgetfulness. Maybe she will answer more of our questions." Amu looked at each of them in turn, his wide face serious. "But where is Bren? Has anyone seen him?"

"After the council fire he went off by himself," Arn said.

"He was angry and upset," Arel said.

Runa said, "Well, no one can blame him for that." She was angry; her dark eyes glinted. "Where is his father? Has he gone over to the Chigai, as people say?"

"Andaru is my brother," Amu said. "Now be calm, Runa, my wife. We will see what we will see." And then Amu, with a look to the western sky where the half-moon fell slowly toward the mountains, was silent.

Jen and Arn looked at each other, wanting to ask about Tsuga, and if they could find him, whether he might help them find their way back through the mountain. But Amu, Runa and Arel were so quiet, so solemn now, that they didn't ask.

Soon the thin young man came back, and he and Amu went away from the fire again to talk. When Amu returned he told them Bren had been seen earlier, standing alone near the stone sentry with the rotting boar's head on it, and no one could make him leave that place. "He may have heard from Andaru," Amu said.

The hot lake beside them breathed mist, which rose from its surface and slowly moved eastward as it rose and folded in the waning moonlight. It was as if somewhere deep within the lake a great silent fire burned, and the mist was its voluminous smoke.

Along the lakeshore came what looked like a big spider, but then they heard its giggle and it was Ganonoot. "Amu, Amu," he whined, "Ganonoot is hungry and his tooth is coming loose. What shall he do when it falls out? Then the story will be over, the long story over." Ganonoot sniffled in self-pity, like a little child.

They gave him food and he sat down by the fire, worrying a piece of smoked fish with his fang and drooling onto his tunic. When he finished the dark meat of the fish he picked a little bone out of his mouth and threw it into the fire, then folded the fish skin and tucked it into his cheek. He wiped his face on his tunic, but they could still see shiny lines of grease deep in the wrinkles of his face. Only then did he seem to notice the children. He smiled so broadly his whole lower face seemed to fold, so that his chin nearly touched his nose.

"Brave Jen, sturdy Arn and delicate Arel!" he said. "But where is Bren, who should be here at Amu's fire? Without Bren the story will have an unhappy ending!" He looked at Arn, his dark little eyes glittering from the cracks between his many-folded lids. "No, I can't tell the rest of the story without Bren, so if you want to hear it you must find him, find him, find him!" He giggled as he got his legs under him and glided, in that strange half-shuffling, half-smooth gait of his, off into the night.

"His stories are harmless," Amu said. "And some even say they are true." He looked at the half-moon, which just now touched the sharp rim of a mountain. "We must go to the Great Tree and meet Aguma and her party. We will leave our fire burning, and each will get up separately and wait in the darkness for the others. We must go quietly. Arn and I will string our bows. Runa, have your knife unthonged in its sheath. It's not the free animals we have to fear tonight; there is murder in the world."

Amu spoke the words slowly, in a low voice. The fire hissed. Runa got up, as if casually, and moved into the darkness that fell over the meadow and the misty lake as the moon slid out of sight.

When they had assembled in the darkness, they walked single file up through the whispering stalks of grass toward the Great Tree. Runa went first, then Arel, then Arn with his small bow strung and a bladed arrow nocked, then Jen, and in the rear Amu, his thick-winged bow strung and a long arrow nocked on the taut string. The stars gave them a gray half-light that their eyes, as the fire faded behind them, could just barely use. They passed a headless sentry stone and soon could feel the presence of the Tree above the ledges.

"Hello," a voice called softly from the darkness.

"Hello," Runa answered.

"By the Stag and the Wounded Tree," the voice called back.

"Amu," Amu said, and they went on toward the ledges from which the voice had come. They passed the embers of the council fire, avoiding a dark lump that was the severed head of the half-wolf.

Aguma and her party waited for them in front of the Cave of Forgetfulness. They spoke in low voices. Aguma said, "Tsuga believes that the Chigai, or those who favor them, might try to kill you, Amu, or take your family hostage. They saw how you made the people think."

"Lado?" Amu said. "I can't believe it. Morl-the-Chigai, maybe . . ."

"Lado has gone over to them. Did you see his face as he wounded the Tree? And so has Goat Skins, who once had more sense than avarice. There are many gone over."

"Andaru?" Amu said, his voice controlled and low.

Aguma didn't answer for a moment. "We don't know for sure about your brother, Amu."

"Yes. But you think . . ."

"We don't know."

Jen stepped on something bladdery and soft, and jumped back with a small cry.

"Hush, now," Aguma said. "What is it?"

They looked closely, to find that it was the headless body of the half-wolf. A man of Aguma's party picked it up by two legs and heaved it from the stone platform out into the meadow, where it landed with a rustling thud. "The Chigai murder their own," he said. On the stones a black pool of blood was visible in the starlight.

"Now you must go," Aguma said. She came forward until she stood over Jen and Arn. "I told Tsuga about you, Jen and Arn, and how you came through the mountain into the world. All he said in answer was, 'Yes, they have come.' He did not seem displeased by what I told him, and that is all I have to tell you."

"Will you come with us, Jen and Arn?" Runa said. "We will be safe in the western mountains, and in seven days we will see Tsuga again."

Arel said, "Come with us."

Fannu and Dona were there in the darkness too. Dona said, "Stay with Arel, and we'll see you in seven days."

Fannu said, "And we'll run the ball again."

The moonless night spread over the dark valley. Around them was the dim grayness of the meadow and the dark woods, and all the strange shapes they would not be sure of in the dark. A chill winter wind had come up, which pierced them at the edges of their clothes. Again without a word between them Jen and Arn knew that they would stay with the warmth of these people they knew.

They climbed the ledges with Amu, Runa and Arel, who put their hands on the Great Tree, whose new wound gleamed. "The Tree will grow over its wound," Amu said. Jen put her hands on the Tree, one on each side of the ax-wound. She felt the slow movement of the great trunk, the heart-wood flexing deep within to the movements of the wind and even of the earth. Arn did the same, but with him the pale wound caused an unfamiliar sadness, tinged with the possibility of anger. The anger felt strange to him because he knew how young and weak he was compared to the adults whose terrible arguments and passions had caused this wound as well as all the black blood on the stones below. He had seen Bren put his hands on this tree, right here where the tree's cambium and sap-blood was exposed to the chill air. He thought of Bren. In spite of Bren's anger and violence, he felt he could trust him as a friend. Where was he now?

Runa went first, and they took a wide circle across the meadow to avoid any of the campfires of the people. Amu told them they would stop just once, in the deep woods, to rest and have something to eat and drink. They must reach the winter camp before dawn.

Runa's were the best eyes for seeing in the night. She told Jen and Arn how to look, in the darkness of the woods, not directly at what they wanted to see, but just to the side of it, where the eyes perceived more light. Then the looming bole of a tree would come to their eyes in a ghostly shimmer. "In the dark you cannot look at what you want to see," she said.

After they had walked, as silently as they could, for what seemed hours, Amu softly called for them to stop. By the way the Big Dipper lay across the sky, it was midnight. He took them many yards off the trail into the evergreen woods, where they rested quietly and ate bannock and dried apples, passing the water skin around by feel in the dense darkness. Here only an occasional star winked through the covering branches.

"The Chigai are not good hunters," Amu said, "and the half-wolves are not dangerous unless their masters are within sight. We must be away from the winter camp before first light."

With that they rearranged their packs and burdens and continued their journey. Because they had to walk more slowly than they had in daylight, and their caution slowed them, they reached the meadow of the winter camp just before dawn, with the eastern sky lightening behind the sharp mountains. In the open now, they hurried down the slope to the deserted hogans, hoping no unfriendly eyes observed them. Fortunately, with the pale easterly light came a bank of clouds which slowly overcame the sky; in a short time the clouds would temporarily erase the dawn.

They went to the bowyer's first, for arrows and extra bowstrings. Runa chose a bow and a quiver for herself, and small knives were found for Jen and Arel—short blades as yet unfitted with handles, so that Jen and Arel were busy wrapping the tangs with wet rawhide, which would harden into useful handles. For sheaths, each folded a piece of leather around her blade and tied it with rawhide. Then they went to Amu and Runa's hogan, where they took the supplies and tools they knew would be needed—awls, a broad-bladed ax, a packbasket for the carrying and gathering of food, a scraper to clean hides of flesh, pots and pans and a crooked knife for carving wood and bone. The packbasket, carried by Amu, was filled with food, though each now carried a small leather water bottle and a rucksack with enough food for two days.

It didn't take them long. When they emerged from the hogan dark gray snowclouds had covered the sky. The light of the wintry day was beginning to grow in spite of the clouds and the thin snow that now fell.

"Let us hope the snow continues long enough to cover our trail," Amu said. "Though the half-wolves could follow our scent for half a day in spite of it."

They passed the high shandeh racks, where the thousands of small splayed fish, offered to the sun, now turned white in the gently falling snow. They were about to pass the outermost hogan, Andaru's, before taking the western trail, when Amu stopped. "Heh!" he said softly, and they all stopped. Arn's nocked arrow tapped against his bow as he turned to where Amu looked.

A wisp of blue smoke rose from the hogan's roof, then rose higher to dissipate in the falling snow. Amu motioned to Arn to come close. "Bren told me you could shoot pretty well," he whispered. "Could you shoot a man if you had to, or a half-wolf?"

Arn thought. He had shot an innocent toad; he had shot at targets. He knew that even his small arrow could pierce a man or a wolf. "I don't know," he said, trembling so much his arrow tapped again against his bow.

Amu merely placed his hand upon Arn's shoulder and squeezed, as if he approved of Arn's answer. Then, with a nod to Runa, whose strung bow was armed with a broad-headed arrow, he motioned to Jen and Arel to stay close to the wall of the hogan. With his own arrow half drawn he shouldered away the bearskin door flap and went quickly inside. Soon he came back out. "Someone spent the night here. Maybe Andaru," he said. "Someone cooked shandeh and corn."

The snow grew thicker around them until it was a white silence, a white nothing when they looked back toward where the hogans had been. It fell straight down, wide flakes that gave a feeling of warmth as they descended from the white sky and landed silently. "Well, we must go," Amu said.

They crossed the meadow toward the southwest, on the same trail, now white and silent, that the children had taken on their walk to the bald knob. Soon the trees loomed up before them, tall pines growing heavy with snow, and they passed beneath the sheltering branches into the softwood forest where the fallen needles were brown and quiet. It was like a great room, where they could see down the aisles of trees. But then they heard in the distance a long howl, choked off at the end. It came from ahead of them, from somewhere down the long dim corridors beyond their sight.

They all stopped. Amu said in a low voice, "It might be a wolf. But it might be a half-wolf. We'll have to leave the trail and circle downwind." He picked up a handful of dry needles and dust, held them at eye level and let them fall. There was hardly any wind, but the dust and needles seemed to be carried in their falling slightly toward the south. They knew the trail ran east and west, but when they left it for the almost windless twilight of the forest, with the snowclouds above masking the sun, it would be hard to keep on their course.

They hadn't gone more than a quarter of a mile in an angle to the southwest, when three wolves came running toward them through the dark trunks of the pines. The wolves were silent, leaping forward smoothly, their eyes observant but obviously not seeing Amu and his party. Short thongs were attached to the wolves' leather collars, proving that they were half-wolves of the Chigai. Then they stopped, sliding forward in a flurry of snow and pine needles. Their eyes opened to the whites in their surprise at seeing five people in their path. They stopped for a second too long, for Amu's and Runa's arrows whicked from their bows and two of the half-wolves grew arrows from their gray bodies. One fell to its side with Amu's feathers at its chest. The other gave a short scream and ran several yards before it fell kicking to its side, the random kicking of death throes. The third half-wolf had disappeared into the trees.

Arn stood with his arrow half drawn. He knew that if he had shot he wouldn't have aimed, would have in panic simply let his arrow fly in the direction of the half-wolves. He would have missed. But as it was he had been too surprised even to draw his arrow to the full. His bow seemed only a toy, his arrow only a fragile little stick.

Amu put down his packbasket, went forward and with both hands pulled his arrow from the body of the wolf. Runa's arrow had been broken by the other half-wolf's kicking and thrashing, so she broke off the bladed arrowhead and stripped off the feathers to save them for another arrow. Amu took out his knife and cut the collars free. "It was not their fault they were slaves," he said. He left the severed collars next to the gray bodies. "No time to skin them now," he said. "Their masters will be near." Then he coughed and looked around, surprised. The fletching of an arrow had appeared below his right shoulder blade, the head and shaft protruding from his chest. He went slowly to his knees.

Runa gave a long cry that continued as she turned and drew her arrow to the full. "Lado!" she cried. She had recognized the fletching of the arrow, which was Lado's. Several men and a half-wolf appeared from close behind the trees and ran toward them. When the men saw that Runa held a drawn bow, they were surprised and tried to run to the side, but her arrow was already in the air. It caught one of the men just above the hip, and he fell. This time Arn had his bow fully drawn. The half-wolf had run right over Jen, knocking her down with its shoulder. For a moment it shied away from Runa and her bow, dancing in place with frantic energy as it clicked its long teeth, wanting to attack. Arn was no more than ten feet from the half-wolf, his arrow drawn. He put the arrowhead upon the hairy gray side with his eye, and his fingers loosened smoothly. He saw the arrow jump from his bow across his left hand, flex in the air and straighten before it disappeared between the half-wolf's gaunt ribs. The half-wolf screamed and turned to bite the arrow's shaft where it emerged from its side. Arn heard the clash of teeth on wood and the snapping of the arrow. But then he was knocked to the ground, his breath taken from him as it had been before in play. An arm roughly grabbed him up and held him. All around were grunts and screams. A bowstring twanged, and there was another scream much like the half-wolf's. He was pressed cruelly against a man's body, trying to breathe, when his hand found the hilt of his knife, his fingers from long habit loosening the thong before he drew the small blade and stabbed, stabbed wherever he could through the leather clothes of his captor. With a yell the man dropped him to the ground, where he could try again to breathe.

When the sweet air came again into his lungs, all was quiet except for a low, musical sound that softly repeated itself over and over. He raised his head and looked cautiously around him. The sounds came from Runa and Arel, who sat cross-legged on each side of Amu, their heads nodding together, almost touching as they hummed and moaned.

Lado's arrow, now broken and pulled from Amu's chest, lay beside them, its shaft smeared lightly with Amu's blood.

Nearby lay the third half-wolf, killed by Arn. Blood was bright everywhere on the snow and needles. Arn himself was sticky with it. The man transfixed above the hips by Runa's first arrow lay slumped against a tree, his open eyes sightless, his bow caught beneath his leg. Lado lay near him on his back, his dead hands still seeming to try to pull Runa's second arrow from his own neck. A trail of blood and footprints led away to the east and disappeared among the trees.

Arn looked all around this enclosed place within the forest, this forest room that had been so violent and was now so calm. The dead men were so still; they were like stone. His eyes seemed to see the point of every needle, the texture of the bark of every tree. But something was wrong even beyond the horror of the blood and the dead. Jen should be here for him to see and to speak to; he should hear her voice. She would be frightened.

Amu groaned; he was still alive. Air bubbled in a light red froth from the hole in his chest as Runa rebound it with a coarse woven cloth. Arn came nearer. Arel saw him and cried out in fear before she recognized who he was. Her face was paler than the skeins of snow that shaded the ground.

Amu's eyes were open. His skin was a dull iron color, but his eyes were clear. "They have taken Jen," he said.

"I could only watch. She was alive." Then he was out of breath. A fine rim of blood encircled his lips. He breathed several short, quick breaths, then wanted to say more. "Runa, your arrows made them fear Ahneeah in their hearts. They ran away."

"Arn killed the half-wolf," Runa said.

Amu's dark eyes sought Arn's, and he nodded, as if to say yes, good. He tried to speak again, but blood caught in his throat, so he used his hands to say that he would soon be dead and they must go on. The Chigai, even without Lado, might grow brave and return for them.

"I will not leave you," Runa said.

They all knew that there was no other meaning in her mind or heart, so they said no more about it.

Arn thought of Jen, carried away by the Chigai. Maybe she was hurt, her small bones broken. The arm that had held him had been cruelly hard. He must follow their trail, at a distance. What else he might do he couldn't think of; what could he do against them, or against the half-wolves who would surely get his scent? He looked off into the dim forest, where the snow sifted down through the branches of the pines, thinking, *Should I follow the Chigai? I am only a boy, but I have good eyes, a good knife, a good bow and nineteen arrows.*

Then he thought he saw, off in the dimness where the corridors of the trees narrowed, a small figure dressed all in brown. Its arms were crossed. Some smooth, quick thing about the way it stood there, or had appeared there just at the moment he first saw it, told him that it was the old lady; it was Ahneeah. One of her arms unfolded from her breast and pointed to the east. Then she was gone, leaving only darkness and a mist of snow where she had stood. But had anyone stood there? In the swirls of snow were shadows, changing and fading, that even now suggested a small brown figure to him, but were in the next moment only snow and shadows.

15

The Village
of the Chigai

Arn and Arel gathered wood so that Runa could make a
fire to warm Amu, whose breath came in short, shivery
gasps. Runa had made him a bed of pine needles covered
with his sleeping-skin, then her own sleeping-skin over
him to keep him as warm as possible, though he shivered
badly whenever he awoke. The arrow had pierced his
lung without having cut any of the major veins or arteries,
so there was one chance in a thousand that he might live.

When Arn and Arel had gathered a large pile of dry
pine branches, the only wood there was in that part of the
forest, Arn said, "I must follow the Chigai and find Jen."

Runa looked at him gravely, for a long time, before she
nodded her head. She was a person who was hard to
please, Arn knew. She would think and then give her
judgement, and now she had judged that his course,
though it might seem impossible, was the right one.

"Arel will go with you," Runa said.

Arn could not understand that at all. He was fairly certain he would be scented by the half-wolves as he followed
downwind.

"Arel knows where they will cross the river of the

shandeh, so you can make a circle and not be upwind. And she has the forbidden gift, which might help you."

Arel gasped when her mother said this.

"I knew it when you were a baby, Arel, when birds spoke to you in your crib. And though you seem pale and weak, you are not weak."

"I'll help find Jen," Arel said.

After they had eaten at midday, Arn and Arel left Runa and Amu and began a circuitous journey toward the northeast. Amu had awakened enough to take some hot soup and to say goodby to them. Arel was crying as they left, but quietly, to herself. Amu had thought they were going toward the western mountains and safety. Now she turned again and again to see the small camp in the forest grow smaller and then, after a hundred yards, disappear behind them.

All afternoon they made their circle, coming finally to what they hoped was the edge of the meadow not far from the winter camp. The snow had thinned; occasionally in an opening where a tall tree had fallen they had been able to perceive a faint shadow to tell them where the sun was, and their direction. They followed the edge of the meadow then, going directly east until they could see the hogans and drying racks of the winter camp. No smoke rose from the hogans, but they didn't dare go near. They followed the river upstream until, just before dark, they found the crossing place—a series of stepping stones across a wide, shallow place in the river.

The stones were covered with unbroken snow; either the Chigai had not yet come to the crossing or they had crossed somewhere else. Darkness was falling quickly. Then Arn had a thought: Runa might have guessed that the Chigai would come back to finish what they had started, and that was why she had sent Arel with him. Amu could not be moved, and she would stay with him to meet whatever fate would come.

Although the fight in the forest had been confusing, Arn

thought there had been three other Chigai beside Lado and the one Runa had killed. Then there was the one who had picked him up and whom he had stabbed deeply with his knife. That one would be sore. There were four of them left, one wounded; even so, they might have gone back.

But as darkness fell, shade by shade across the snow and the dark moving river, they heard voices coming from the forest. Quickly they went back on their tracks until they found some low junipers to hide in. Three large men came tramping out of the forest, all armed with bows, axes hanging from their belts. One carried a bundle over his shoulder which might have been Jen. They stopped on the riverbank, brushed away the snow and sat down. No half-wolves were with them. Arn and Arel could just hear their words.

"You *sure* Lado got him?" one said. He was the one with the bundle, which he had roughly dumped in the snow.

"Stop asking that, will you?" another said. "I saw the arrow hit him in the back. I even heard it hit. I saw him go down."

"Lado was a good shot," the third one said.

"Not as good as that woman."

"Now it's dark and we'll have to sleep in the snow; we shouldn't have waited for Gort," the third one said.

Then a fourth man came slowly along the trail, limping badly and using his bow as a crutch. He mumbled and cursed as he limped up to the others, one leg stiff and his pants dark and shiny with what looked, even in the dim light, like blood.

"Teach you to pick up strange little kids, Gort!" one of the others said, laughing.

"I just want to live long enough to get my hands on that kid again," Gort said as he lowered himself to the ground with a moan of pain and anger. "I should have stayed long enough to finish him off."

"Except the woman had you scared blue with that quick bow of hers."

"Did you see her center Lado in the neck?"

"Listen," the first Chigai said. "We'll have to tell Morl we got both of them or he'll flay us alive. He'll hang our pelts on the hide stretchers. We'll say we killed the other two kids, Amu and his woman, all right?"

"If he finds out, we'll pay for it later."

"Well, we got one live kid anyway."

"And we lost three wolves, Lado and Tromo, and Gort's all chewed up. If those people fight like that . . ."

"Shut up," Gort said. "Just shut up and build a fire. I've got a chill. He stuck me deep." Then Gort gave a hard low moan of pain that chilled Arn because he was responsible for such hurt.

But Jen was alive, and the Chigai had been told, evidently, to keep her alive.

The men went to the edge of the trees to gather wood for a fire, then brought their branches and sticks back to where another chopped and split them with his ax. Arn knew they must have crossed his and Arel's tracks several times, but none of them took notice. They were not good hunters. The way they clumped and stumbled around, they seemed not to care about the earth beneath them and what it might tell them. They had lost all of their half-wolves, too, so they would have no sentries who could read the wind.

Soon a large fire was blazing on the riverbank. Arn saw that in order to keep it going, the men would be scouring wider for wood. He tapped Arel on the shoulder and motioned for her to follow. In the dark they went back down the river until they found a depression in the bank covered with a roof of junipers. From here they could just see the fire and the men's shadowy forms as they crossed in front of it.

Once they settled into their little cavelike place and felt around them to see what room they had, they undid their packs and got out their sleeping-skins of wolf fur, then had something to eat—jerky and dried fruit, washed down with water from the river.

"We'll wait until they go to sleep," Arn said. "I'll stay awake and you can sleep, Arel." She was shivering, so he wrapped both their sleeping-skins around them. Arel's arms slipped around him and her head lay against his chest. Her dark hair smelled of woodsmoke. As his hand smoothed her hair down into her collar he felt a surge of care and tenderness for this young girl who had so bravely agreed to leave her father and mother and come with him. Her arms squeezed him, as if to thank him for smoothing her hair, and soon she had stopped shivering and was asleep.

He woke, not remembering how he had fallen asleep. He had the heavy feeling in his eyes that meant much time had passed, though he didn't know how much. He was no longer sitting up, but had fallen back against the sandy bank. Arel murmured in her sleep as he sat back up again; then she made a small whimper at an unhappy event in her dream.

"Arel," he said softly. "Wake up."

Her arms squeezed him and her head snuggled down, wanting more sleep. The clouds had thinned, he noticed, and a moon rode faintly behind them.

"Arel," he said. "I think it's near morning. Wake up."

"What?" she said in a small voice that was submerged in the skins and the fur of his parka. "Yes," she said, coming awake. "It's Arn," she said, as if she were talking to someone else. "Warm Arn." Her dark eyes, now wide awake, looked up at him. He could just make them out, black in her face that was as pale as the moon.

"I'm going to see if they're all asleep," he said. "Maybe I can cut Jen loose."

"I'll come with you," Arel said.

"No," he said, thinking only that Arel was so small and pale.

"I have a knife, and I can run, too," Arel said. "I can move without making any noise, and I came to help you and Jen."

Arn realized how little he wanted to approach the Chigai alone on this cold night. His feet were damp in his boots, and that small chill seemed to go all through him. "All right," he said, "but let's be slow and quiet. We've got to make sure they're all asleep."

They covered their packs and Arn's bow and quiver with the sleeping-skins and crept out into the snow, going up the riverbank. The soft gurgling of the moving water would help mask whatever noises they did happen to make. The snow was still fluffy and quiet, but it hid stones and sticks that they might kick or step on. They tested each step with a tentative pressure before putting their full weight down.

The fire had embered but still threw enough heat to let the Chigai sleep. The four men lay around the fire on mattresses of evergreen boughs. Near one of the men was a bundle that might be Jen, so they made a circle around to that place, listening to the sleeping breaths, then crawled slowly up to the skin-covered bundle. Breath had frosted an opening at one end. In the diffused moonlight Arn could see the leather thongs that bound it. He put his mouth to the frosted breath hole and whispered, "Jen, is that you?"

The bundle moved convulsively and a soft sound came from it, a sob that was Jen's.

"Don't make any noise at all now," Arn whispered. "I'm going to cut you loose." His knife slit the thongs, from top to bottom, without a sound. Then, as he was trying to unroll the stiff skin in order to free Jen, there was a ragged, triumphant shout and big hands grabbed him and threw him over on his stomach.

"Did you think I could sleep with all the holes you put in me? I've got you now, you little rattlesnake, so enter the blackness!" It was Gort's voice. One hand pressed Arn's back, squashing him against Jen, while the other reached for ax or knife.

But then Gort gave a cry of pain and let him loose. *"Ow!*

Another one!" Gort yelled. He had Arel by the ankle and pulled her roughly into the pile made by Jen and Arn. "I'll skewer the whole mess of 'em!" Gort yelled, his knife raised. But Arn still had his knife in hand, and he stabbed Gort just above the knee. The point of his knife stopped on bone. Gort howled. Before he could stab down with his long knife the other Chigai pulled him, screaming and bleeding from his new wounds, over onto his back.

"Enough!" said the one who was evidently the leader of the group. He turned to the three children, his broadax raised, and said, "Put your weapons at my feet."

Arn and Arel gave up their knives, then were searched and tied together on a three-foot thong with loops around their necks.

"So," the leader said. "We're in luck—all except Gort, that is!" The three unwounded men laughed loudly.

"I'll kill them!" Gort said in a voice tight and husky with pain.

"Morl wants them alive," the leader said.

"I'll kill them before we get back!"

"You do, and Morl will have our hides drying on the racks," the leader said. He looked to the east, where the sky had begun to show the cold light of a winter day. "We've nearly a day's journey home. Morl will be pleased, now. We didn't kill the woman, but we can say we did. Better one lie than three!"

"I'll kill them!" Gort howled as he tried to get to his feet.

The leader knocked him back down with the flat of his ax. "We can't wait for you this time, Gort. The way you're bleeding, I doubt if you'll make it anyway."

The light had grown. Gort stared at the three men, who looked back at him indifferently. His rough face grew pale and gray as he understood. Hatred seemed to run in waves across his forehead and eyes and jaw. He looked colder than the eastern sky. But he said no more.

Jen had got herself loose, but before she could move, one of the men had tied a loop around her neck. He tied the three children on one thong, so that he had them on a leash.

"Are you all right?" Arn asked Jen, but heard no answer because he was slapped so hard he fell to his knees and could hardly see.

The men ate breakfast, each with a hot chunk of broiled meat impaled on his knife. Juice dripped down their chins and cheeks as they gnawed. The children were offered no food, but the man who held their leash allowed them to drink from the river as they began to cross it on the stepping stones. Jen had time to nod to Arn and Arel, to signal that she wasn't hurt. But when Arel began to speak to her the man raised his hand threateningly and she remained silent.

Back at the fire, Gort sat alone, tilted to one side from the pain of his wounds, and watched them go.

All that day they walked toward the east, through forest and swamp and meadow, until they stopped on a small rise and looked down across a wide field at the village of the Chigai. The field was crisscrossed by fences made of saplings and stones, some of the enclosures trampled into mud, others still white with snow. The village itself, which looked huge, endless in its buildings and pens to Arn and Jen, gave off a steady and distant sound that grew louder as they approached. Before they knew what the sound was, it made them tremble. It was not human, but contained in its hoarse breathiness an emotion that humans could feel, and that was the fear of death.

"An east wind tells them the news," one of the men said. "They can smell the blood of their own kind."

"Roasts and ribs," another said. "That's all it means to me."

"You can smell the stench of the slaughterhouse, can't you?" the leader said.

Then they began to breathe it in the air, the sweet odor of carrion that seemed to coat their mouths and nostrils with a syrup, it was so smooth and pervasive.

"I get used to it in about a minute," one of the men said.
"I still prefer a west wind," the leader said.

As they came closer to the village, the lowing of fear and the stench of rotting flesh grew. The sun was setting, its rays red upon the poles of the stockades and the roofs of the wooden buildings. Beneath their feet the earth turned into deep, silky mud as they came up to the first tall gate in the barricade of vertical logs that surrounded the village.

As they approached the gate they saw a flurry of movement through the cracks in the barricade—gray fur, dark eyes and white teeth as the nearly hysterical howling of the half-wolves began. The fat red face of a man peered over the top of the gate. His mouth opened and closed upon yellow teeth, but nothing could be heard but the howling. The face disappeared and the wolves' howls turned to cries of pain and fear as a whip cracked and thudded among them. The face reappeared. "Now," it said. "What do you want?"

"We're a patrol and we have prisoners for Morl," the leader said.

"If you're a patrol of Chigai, where are your wolves?"

"Dead, all three of them."

"To catch three children?"

"Never mind your stupid jokes, sentry. Just open the gate and keep your wolves back," the leader said.

The sentry sneered and climbed back down from his perch, and the gate swung open. The cowed half-wolves snapped their teeth and whined at them as they passed on into the village. The lowing of the cattle was like a harsh wind. Both Jen and Arel put their hands over their ears to try to keep out that long moan of helplessness. The mud of the streets sucked at the children's boots as they walked. From doorways and windows people stared out at them, their expressions closed and fearful, though their eyes seemed to widen slightly at the sight of children on a leash. But then their faces closed again, as if to say it was none of their business.

The moaning of the distant animals was a pall over the village, and the heavy odor of blood seemed almost a cause of the dimming of the light as the sun went down. They passed many buildings that were shuttered, many that stood touching each other, as if crowding together, crouching in the dark, walled village against some enemy from outside. The houses stood in the trampled mud, their doorsills crusted with it. Reddish light from torches or fat-burning lamps shone from inside some of the houses.

They were taken to a large building in the center of the village. Logs had been placed in the mud in front of it to form a corduroy road for several guards to stand on. Torches flamed smokily on each side of the wooden doorway. The leader identified himself, and the thick doors opened on squeaky iron hinges to reveal a short hallway that led to another door guarded by two axmen who were so tall their heads nearly touched the ceiling. In the torchlight they seemed all hair, their own and that of the shaggy cattle skins they wore, all bound by leather belts and straps. The leader made a sign and one of the guards struck the door with the poll of his ax, a sound that rang of struck metal.

The door was opened from the inside by another guard. Inside was a large hall with a fire burning at its center, the smoke rising into a high ceiling gabled with log rafters. Around the hall on its dirt floor were stone benches and chairs where men sat, the highest chair a throne on which sat Morl in a cape of black cattle skin, his great arms gleaming. He motioned the party forward.

"So you've brought me three little yearlings, have you?" he said to the leader. "Now, that's well done, so I won't skin you alive. But where is Lado?"

The leader's voice was shaky as he addressed Morl. "Sir, Lado is dead with an arrow through his neck."

Morl's eyes widened. He seemed to hesitate and get his breath before he spoke again. "And I believe there were two other men with you, and three wolves."

"Tromo is dead of an arrow. Gort was wounded by this

one's knife." He pointed to Arn. "And this one stabbed him once, too." He pointed to Arel. "We had to leave him behind."

"And the wolves?"

"All dead of arrows."

"I trust you killed these expert bowmen?"

"Yes, sir. Except for this one." He pointed again to Arn. "He killed one of the wolves."

Morl looked down from his throne-chair at Arn. His eyes were hard and bright as he frowned. Arn was chilled by the power this one man seemed to have, yet he was surprised to feel so much fear in the air of the room, in its locked and guarded doors, and even in the muscular lean of Morl's great shoulders. Though Arn was afraid, the fear he felt was not all his own.

"This is the child that came from under the mountain," Morl said. "And that one is his sister." He looked at Jen. "And the other is the daughter of Amu. Now I have them all. But tell me once again: Amu and his woman are dead? Did you feel their still hearts? Did you look into their dead eyes?"

"Yes . . ." the leader began, but he was interrupted by a shout from a corner of the room.

"Amu! Runa!" It was a child's voice, and it was Bren's. As Bren came into the light his eyes were pouring tears. "Amu! Runa!" he cried.

Bren!" The command came from behind Bren, a deeper voice even than Morl's. Andaru came forward and pulled Bren back, his brow-hooded eyes so much like Bren's though they were stern and cold. Andaru wore the cattle-skin tunic now, and he was armed with the Chigai broadax.

16

Wolf, Boar, Bear and Man

At a signal from Morl, Jen, Arel and Arn were led from the room on their thong. As they were pulled away they all looked at Bren and Andaru, but in Bren's eyes they saw only grief, and in Andaru's a distant coldness.

They were taken down a narrow, muddy street toward the sounds of the fearful cattle. They began to hear other animal voices, too, all unhappy—the squeal of boar, the yapping of wolves, and a deep roar that could only be that of an angry bear. By torchlight they were led along, running and stumbling through the mud, trying to keep from falling and being dragged.

At a gate they were handed over to another man, this one wearing a grimy leather apron splotched with blood, new and old. His fingernails were caked with a dark sludge and he smelled of spoiled meat.

"Put these in an iron cage and see they don't die or escape, or Morl will have your gizzard for breakfast," the guard who had led them there said.

"Yes, Master! Yes! Yes!" the grimy man said. He cringed in fear; trying to smile, his mouth looked like the slash-mark of a wound. His eyes were round and simple-looking. Even his short-cropped hair and the bristles on his chin were stained with old gore.

"What's your name, so we'll know who to hang on the racks if they escape."

"Doro, Master, who always does what he's told, pardon me."

"I should pardon you for being alive, you greasy scum of a butcher," the guard said.

"Yes, Master!"

With an expression of disgust, the guard turned and went away. Doro led them inside the gate, then to a cage among other cages. Here the lowing, growling and moaning of the animals was all around them, for in all the cages and pens, large and small, were the prisoners of the Chigai. As Doro shut them in their cage he looked at them closely in the light of the torch he carried.

"Why, you're children!" he said. "Is Doro to butcher children now? Well, what does it matter? On the inside we all look alike. But," he added with a sly grin and a look over his shoulder, "only birds have gizzards. Doro knows what's in the insides!" With that he clanged the iron-barred door shut and secured the latch with an elaborate knot of chains. As soon as he left, Arn tried to undo the chains in the dark, but found that while his fingers could just touch them, his arm was so bent that his fingers hadn't the strength to move the chains at all.

They were weak from hunger and their long march, but they could at last talk as they untied the thongs from their necks, and they told each other what they knew. Amu was still alive when they left; the Chigai had lied to Morl when they said Runa was dead. Arn told Jen how Arel had stabbed Gort when Gort was about to kill him. But they didn't talk long because they were so tired they couldn't hold their heads up any more. Animals moved restlessly in cages all around them, and over all was the moaning of fear, now muted, as if the fear itself had grown exhausted. But they were so tired. The floor of their cage was covered with musty old straw, so they pushed it into a pile for a bed, then snuggled together as closely as they could, for warmth, and fell into deep sleep.

When the light came out of the east they awoke, shivering, and looked around them. Their cage was about six feet square, with a wooden floor beneath the straw. In a similar cage next to them a large gray wolf, quiet now, lay on its stomach, its head on its outstretched paws, and looked at them with bright yellow eyes. On the other side in its cage a great black-haired boar stood, moving its head back and forth, back and forth as it uttered short grunts or snarls of frustration. In back of their cage what at first looked like a black stump suddenly rose higher than the height of a man—a black bear. Its head, too, moved back and forth, back and forth, its paws on the bars of its cage. Other cages and pens contained shaggy cattle, still restless and moaning at the pervasive smell of blood, their eyes rolling in their broad faces, showing the whites all around.

Jen said, "I've got something for you, Arn, if you can use it." She pulled her leather-wrapped knife from her boot and gave it to him. He quickly hid it in his own boot. "They never thought to search me," she said. Then she thought how Arn and Arel had come after her to try to save her when they might have stayed with Amu and Runa, and how much more frightened and how lonely she would have been right now without them. Arn had saved her once before when she was freezing on the meadow; he was her brother, who seemed to have grown right out of childhood. But Arel, her friend . . . With that thought she began to cry because of gratitude and fear and hunger all mixed, and they tried to comfort her.

Doro came soon after with a bucket that he slid under the door of the boar's cage. The boar's eyes grew red as it stared at the bucket and then at Doro, but it didn't touch the food.

"Too proud to eat, eh?" Doro said. "Well, in six days when your head's fresh on the sentry stone you'll be beyond eating then! I'll have looked in your eating hole and out the other side, my friend, and the rest of you'll be food!"

Next he brought a joint of raw meat for the wolf, but the wolf merely stared at him. "Oh, Great Leader of the wild pack," Doro said sarcastically. "What a fine coat you have —to keep Morl warm in his cold house!"

For the children he brought a disc of hard bread and a bucket of water, which they accepted. Doro watched them eat and drink, his round eyes blinking once each time he looked from one to another of them.

When Arn had eaten his share of the bread and washed it down with water, he asked, "What does Morl want to do with us?"

"They look down on me and my kind," Doro said, "but we know what's inside. We cut the throats and watch the dying and then we slit the bellies open. We know all about that."

"But what's going to happen to us?" Arel asked.

"We get the grease and the bile in our fingernails and blood in our clothes and they say we don't smell good, so we can't go into the houses."

They saw that he was not talking to them, just talking as he talked to the boar, the wolf and the other prisoners. Soon, still complaining about how they treated him, he went away.

Jen watched the boar's long, hairy face with its yellow tusks and its small red eyes that peered through the black hair. It seemed evil, murderous; but then the red eyes caught hers and there was a recognition that contained no evil or murder. This was the boar who had stopped in the tunnel of juniper and looked so long and quietly up at her before he went on. She hadn't been able to read his thoughts then, but now, faint yet sure, a deep signal of intelligence came from the red eyes and the sudden stillness of his head. *The small human in the tree, not one who would trap me,* the boar thought, not in words, but that was what his recognition meant. *And now we are both trapped by a common enemy.*

A common enemy, Jen thought. She turned to Arel, who was staring at the great wolf in his cage. "Can you hear his thoughts?" she asked Arel.

"He's the leader of the wolves," Arel said. "And now he's been betrayed by the half-wolves. They led him into a trap."

Then they looked to the bear, who, as if he felt their probing of his mind, stopped moving his head and looked straight at them. He, too, had been free not long before. Now, sorely hurt from the wounds he received in a dead-fall trap, he would not eat the food his jailers offered him. *When you are trapped, you fight. You do not eat.*

None of the powerful animals was afraid. Each watched and waited for a chance at freedom.

"I wish they could understand us," Jen said.

Arel said thoughtfully, "I wonder if some of the animals have the forbidden gift, like us."

It was the wolf leader who replied. They both felt his mind and turned at once to see his yellow eyes regarding them calmly.

It is Ahneeah of the Deer who gives us our gifts, yours and mine. That is what his mind told them. He knew them to be afraid of his kind, as his kind was of theirs, but in the wild it was a different fear, not the kind that swept away all dignity, and dirtied the air of this prison.

Jen and Arel had a thought in common: *If we could set you free, we would.*

I know that, the deep yellow eyes told them. *We all know that now.*

"What are you looking at?" Arn said.

They told him what the wolf had told them.

"Well," Arn said, "I have Jen's knife now. All we can do is wait and watch for chances."

The wolf's wide eyes blinked in assent.

Over near the gate where they had been given over to

Doro by the guard, Doro sat in the doorway of his small hut, staring in his round-eyed, vacant way at the pens and cages. Then there was a noise at the gate, a rattling of the bars and a shrill, querulous voice. "Hey, Doro, hey! It's your old friend come to see you! At least you can open up and say hello!"

Through the bars of the gate they saw something low and brown jiggling and moving from side to side like a spider. Doro got up with a curse and opened the gate. It was old Ganonoot, his brown snaggletooth protruding from his face that was so squashed and creased they could hardly tell his mouth from the other wrinkles. He came scooting in, bent over, leaning on his bow, and sat right down in Doro's spot. Doro picked him up by the scruff of his neck and kicked him over to the side.

"That's my place, you filthy old beggar, so have a little respect for your betters!" Doro said.

Ganonoot ignored the kick. "If you please, Master Doro, Ganonoot is hungry! Hungry! Now, would you have a joint of roast beef, perhaps, with squash pudding and currant jam and a loaf of your excellent round bread for your old friend?"

"Old friend! You miserable wretch, you stringy piece of dried gut! I ought to feed you to the boar—maybe you'd be to his taste!" In spite of his words, Doro was enjoying himself, and soon he had given Ganonoot a piece of bread, which Ganonoot soaked with water from his leather water bottle before tearing off pieces of it and stuffing them into his mouth. Doro watched him eat, his round eyes blinking each time the long tusk tore into the bread. When Ganonoot had eaten all the bread, they talked in quieter voices. Ganonoot was evidently telling Doro a story, because he stood and sat down, gestured with his bow and his hands as Doro laughed or grew serious, wonder in his simple eyes.

When the story was finished, Ganonoot looked around the yard for the first time. "A wolf, a bear and a boar!" he said. "But what's this, Master Doro, master of the cleaver and bone-saw? Some small children in your cage?"

"Yes, and watch out you don't go too near. They say a soldier named Gort did and he thought he'd swallowed a porcupine."

Ganonoot came scooting over to their cage and squatted on his haunches.

"Don't get too close!" Doro called from his doorway, where he sat, his eyes droopy now in the winter sunlight.

"Ah, now!" Ganonoot said to them in a voice Doro wouldn't hear. "Arn and Jen and fair Arel, all in a cage!"

"Ganonoot," Arel said. "What are you doing with the Chigai?"

"Ganonoot, he comes and goes. Nobody cares about old Ganonoot except to give him a kick in the rear and maybe a moldy piece of bread. Ganonoot can go wherever he wants, because nobody cares." A tear came to his eye.

"Can you get us out of here?" Arn asked him.

"I can tell you a story, that's what Ganonoot can do. Do you want to hear a story, now? Ganonoot knows all the old stories, the best stories. Sometimes Ganonoot can't remember when he's eaten last, or what direction he ought to be going in, but he knows all the old stories, every one!"

"We just want to get away from here," Arn said. "We don't know what Morl wants with us . . ." Arn saw that Ganonoot wasn't bothering to understand, so he trailed off hopelessly.

"I will tell you more of the story of Ahneeah and the People Who Left the World," Ganonoot said in his storytelling voice, which was lower and less squeaky and crotchety, as if another person spoke through his lips. "Once upon a time, long ago, when the Tree was young . . ."

"Please, Ganonoot," Jen cried. "The Chigai shot Amu and caught me, and then Arn and Arel followed them and tried to cut me loose, but . . ."

". . . a man was made insane by power."

"Ganonoot!" Jen said. "Please listen!"

"The power of life and death was his, he thought, so he came to believe he owned the world. But he came to have small doubts, and the small doubts made him anxious and cruel. Now, we will call these small doubts children, and there were four . . ." Ganonoot stopped, seeming perplexed. He pointed a thin old finger at them and counted. "Didn't I say four? Yes, yes. But here are only three, and the story must have four, so the tale can't be told."

Behind Ganonoot, Doro lay slumped in his doorway, asleep. Suddenly their eyes caught a movement at the gate, and a small figure in brown buckskin quickly climbed the gate and jumped down, then looked around carefully before running toward them. It was Bren. He pressed himself against the bars of the cage and reached in to touch Arel's face. "I'm sorry," he said, his face tight, his lips quivering with tension, as if his face were about to break apart.

When they told him that Runa was not hurt, and that Amu, though shot through the lung, was not dead when they left, he put his hands over his face.

Ganonoot counted again. "One, two, three, four; now the story can be told."

"I'll find a way to get you out of here," Bren said. "Tonight Morl and all the Chigai start for the place of the Great Tree. I'll hide somewhere and when they've gone I'll come and get you out."

"That is not the way the story goes," Ganonoot said. "Perhaps you should listen to old Ganonoot's tale, for many lessons are learned by the ears, and old stories do not always have to repeat themselves."

"Ganonoot," Bren said, "we don't have time for stories now."

"But your father . . ." Arel said to Bren.

"Never mind my father now," Bren said. Anger and sorrow fought in him. "I will not see my friends in a cage. I will not." He clenched his fists. "I am myself."

"Yes," Ganonoot said. "That is in the story."

Bren said impatiently, "Be quiet, Ganonoot. We must make a plan for tonight."

"Wait, Bren," Arel said. "I want to hear more of Ganonoot's story. The wolf is speaking to me. Can you hear him, Jen?"

"Yes," Jen said. She felt the chords of a memory that was so old it went back through generations of paws and fangs and kills, moonlight on frigid snow and the fearful respect of wolf for man and man for wolf. The wolf leader had risen to his feet, the hair along his back rippling and erect. He stared at Ganonoot. Then they saw that the boar and the bear regarded Ganonoot with the same intensity. *We remember,* the fierce animals said. *Listen.*

Ganonoot's voice, calm and sad, seemed now the recalling of all the memories of animal and man. All of them listened; even the animals seemed to listen.

"And this man who was driven mad by power had once been a wise hunter and a good man, kind to his fellows, fair in the sharing of what he had, strong in the fields and orchards of his people, wise in council, and loved by children. When he was still sane, Ahneeah came to him in the form of an old woman and said to him, 'Great trials are coming for the animals and the people, and you will not be the least of their trials.' 'Me?' he said. 'A trial to my people? But I am a good man. I am respected and even loved. How could I cause trouble for my people?'

" 'You are a man,' Ahneeah said, 'and no man may take what you will be offered by your people. I give you a choice: do not take what they will offer you, even though it is offered freely.' But when trouble came, when a harsh winter, a winter of iron ice came, there was dissension among the people, and they asked him if he would lead them. He did take that gift, and it was the gift of absolute power, and it made him mad. In the name of the people, people were murdered. In the years that followed, always for the good of the people, the land was trampled by ten thousand slaves, and the lowing of death-fear was a pall across the world."

From the cattle pens that same lowing came back to their ears: *I am helpless, but I don't want to die.* Other caged animals added their own doleful voices, high and low, to the unending sound of fear.

"In his madness he changed; he was no longer loved, only feared, but at first he was unaware of the change. The people lived then in a large village on the meadow by the shores of the warm lake, below the Great Tree (which was a sapling then). The leader of the people grew afraid of anyone he thought opposed him, so the village was walled within and without. He was afraid of the leaders of the wild animals, so he trapped them and enslaved them."

From the wolf, bear and boar came the deep resonance of anger.

"Finally he became afraid of his own betrayal of Ahneeah's justice toward the animals, so he sacrificed the most handsome children, two by two, on the altar by the Great Tree, thinking that this would pacify the spirits of the cattle, the boar, the bear, the wolves and the other animals he had degraded.

"It was then that the pestilence came, and destroyed nearly all the animals in the world, slave and wild, so that the people began to starve.

"Then a young man called Tsuga gathered some of the people together in the forest and said to them, 'I know of a way to leave this world where the children cry in hunger, where the animals die for no reason. Come with me to the northern mountains, and we will leave this dying world for another.'

"Then Ahneeah appeared before them in the form of an old woman and said, 'You may leave the world if you wish, but you may never return, and ever after you and your children and your children's children will mourn the world you have lost and the justice of Ahneeah that cannot follow you.'

"And that is what happened, except that Tsuga Wanders-too-far did return through the Black Gate, and . . ."

Here the story was interrupted by a shout that startled them all, including Doro, who jumped up so quickly he banged his head on his doorframe and stumbled to one knee in the dirt. Andaru and several guards ran by him, one kicking him out of the way as they passed.

Andaru took Bren by the arm and pulled him back, shaking him in anger. "Are you my son? Haven't I told you not to come here? And never to listen to this old fool?"

Bren was silent.

One of the guards had raised an ax over Ganonoot's head. "No, leave him," Andaru said. "Get the animals trussed and ready to travel."

Loops were snaked through the bars of the cages of the boar, bear and wolf. Though they pushed, clawed and bit at the ropes, in time the loops found their marks and after all the roaring and snarling the animals were trussed and helpless on their sides. Once securely tied, they were dragged from their cages onto the dirt, where all three were muzzled, the thongs cruelly tight; but their eyes were open and alert. They were quiet, now, and watchful, dignified by their own silence.

The guards inserted poles between their tied legs, then carried them, hanging upside down, through the gate and down the street toward Morl's house. This sight brought from the other animals in the pens and cages a long groan of despair.

Why Jen
Was Chosen

As soon as the guards weren't looking, Ganonoot had scuttled off and disappeared.

Later, when Doro brought them their food, his cheek was turning green and blue where the guard had kicked him. His mouth was slanted down on that side and rimmed with dried blood. "Loss some my tees, too," he mumbled. "Kick my tees ow. I gone seep."

He left the bread and water with them and disappeared into his hut, but was soon hauled out of there by more guards, who had come for Arn and Arel. "Open up the cage, you scum," one of the guards said as he dragged Doro across the dirt. "We want that one and that one. The other you can keep."

The guard had pointed to Arn and Arel. The "other one" was Jen. The children huddled together in one corner of the cage as Doro, mumbling through his hurt jaw, undid the chains that secured the door latch. Jen felt something being pressed into her hand; it was her knife Arn was giving back to her. While she was shielded by Arn and Arel, she hid it again in her boot. "If you're going to be alone, you should have it," Arn whispered. "Maybe you can get away and find Tsuga."

The guards pulled Arn and Arel out of the cage. One of them had asked a question the children couldn't hear, but they did hear the reply: "Morl says they can't be brother and sister—it's an old law. Anyway, what business is it of yours?"

Again thongs were looped about Arn's and Arel's necks. Arel began to say goodby to Jen, but a guard said, "Quiet!" and threatened her with his fist. They tried to say goodby with their eyes; then Arn and Arel were led away.

Doro retrieved his water bucket from the cage. As he watched the departing guards he absent-mindedly shut the door and wound the chains around the latch.

But Jen, as he had looked away, had slipped out of the door and gone around behind the cage, so he shut the door on no one. He gave a cursory glance at her then, but didn't notice that there were two sets of bars between him and the small figure, who seemed to be still inside. Jen waited behind the cage until Doro had returned to his hut, then long enough after that to hope that he was asleep. She had read his inattention to her as he shut the door, and acted upon it at once. It was her way.

But now where to go to escape this unhappy village and find Tsuga? She felt so small, and the world so large.

Someone was watching her. She knew it all at once. She moved her head slowly, looking for the eyes she knew were bent upon her. In the cattle pens eyes would see her, from here and there through the bars, but they were terrified, unwondering eyes, not the one intelligence she felt directed solely upon her. Then she saw the two brown eyes, deep and luminous. They were the eyes of a deer, a large and handsome doe that stood inside the cattle pen. The presence of the doe made a place of calm and silent intent within the pen of frightened animals. Jen had seen no other deer in the pens or cages, nor heard a deer's whistle or blat. But here was the one doe within a fence it could easily jump, if unwounded. Then the doe did rise effortlessly into the air, with seeming slowness clearing the bars and coming down first on forelegs that bent gracefully, then on all four legs. Her white flag stood high; she was proud and unwounded. *Follow me,* the eyes commanded.

Jen followed as the doe walked slowly between the pens until they came to an empty shed. The doe entered. In the shadows of the dark shed the doe's message to her was *We will wait here until dark.* The doe lay down in the darkest corner, curled as deer lie. *Rest here, upon my side, and sleep.* Jen lay down within the curl of the doe's warm body, and put her head against her flank. Here was the warmth and strength she had known next to her mother, so long ago. She felt the deep rhythm of the doe's heart, and fell smoothly into a sleep like the sleep of home.

It was full dark when the doe's muzzle touched her face and woke her. *Come now,* the doe said without words, and they left the shed to find the sky strangely lighted, a flickering orange light reflected back downward by smoke and mist that hung over the village. They went past the pens, over a fence, and came to a street full of people, many carrying torches. The Chigai, men, women and children, were assembling now for a journey that would begin tonight. *They go in sorrow to the Tree,* the doe answered Jen's unspoken question. *Against their deepest will they go to witness the deaths of children.*

Arn and Arel! Jen turned to the doe.

All things must die, the doe's sad eyes told her. *When the columns move, you will walk among them in the shadows. You will do what you will do.* Then the doe turned and was gone into the dark.

That was how Jen left the village of the Chigai, walking silently among the people, her hood shading her eyes from the flickering torches. None of the subdued people spoke to her, and they spoke little to each other. From some of the older women came long sighs that were the beginnings of a chant of sorrow Jen had heard before.

The people traveled slowly, resting by day and, as befitted the dark purpose of their journey, moving only at

night. Before dawn Jen would lag behind, then hide during the days. At dusk she would rejoin them and eat the
evening meal, the food handed out freely to her as it was
to everyone.

After four nights of walking and four days of rest, the
Chigai came to the meadow of the Great Tree and set up
their tents on its southeastern border. Now, with the people not moving in the night, she had a chance to go among
them in search of Arn and Arel. She had thought to go
westward to try to find Tsuga and Aguma, but she had no
idea where they might be, and the next night would be
that of the seventh day, when the council fire would be
held again. No, she thought, she must find her brother and
her friend, who had followed and tried to rescue her.

Along the border of the meadow the dark forest rose,
the leafless winter underbrush thick at its edges. Here by
the warm lake the snow of the last storm had melted, so
the earth was soft and the going silent. She passed through
brush a larger person would have been caught in as if by
snares, and began her search along the eastern edge of the
camp. She knew when she had come near Morl's head-
quarters by the numbers of brawny guards in their cattle
skins, with their heavy bows and broadaxes. They stood
around fires, laughing and talking in raucous voices that
seemed to brag with every burst of sound. They were so
different from the people of the Chigai, who had offered
her food without question, and who were sad but resigned
about the coming sacrifice. She had heard them talking,
saying that Morl was the leader and knew best. They
might wish for this, and that, but there was nothing they
could do about it, and how sad it was, the necessity to
sacrifice children to the spirits of the animals. All this she
had heard in passing.

Ahead of her was a large tent surrounded by four
campfires, one at each compass point, two guards standing at each fire. These were huge men who stood stiffly,
not speaking to each other, with their strung bows held

upright before them. Although there were more than a hundred tents along the edge of the meadow, some as large as this one, she thought this must be Morl's. There was a chill here, a pervasive fear that she could almost smell. The air itself told her to go away, run away, don't come near.

She crouched by a jumble of stones, the grayish brush between her and the nearest guards at their fire. She saw no way to get closer. Arn and Arel might not be kept in this tent, even if it was Morl's, but how could she find out?

She hadn't been paying any attention at all to what was right in front of her—a small hole between two stones—but now she felt life here, and thoughts, small but intense ones. There was a small animal not two feet away from her, aware of her and worried about what she was and what she wanted so near his hole. Why had she stopped for so long right over his hole? Did she catch and eat his kind? Yes, he could smell that she had eaten meat. He saw now that she had two eyes close together on the front of her head; she couldn't see far around to the sides, or in back of her: she was a hunting animal, and he was afraid. See how intensely she crouched and waited, her hard eyes glittering.

No, she thought. No, little animal. What are you—a coney rabbit, a chipmunk, a white-footed mouse?

He was himself; he ate roots and grasses and the bark from stems and branches. He didn't have a name for himself or his kind, but they were warm together in their dry den, though always in danger, in danger. They harmed no one, they had many young in the right seasons, they were always listening and watching, nearly always hungry, but never for blood. Then he thought, Your thoughts confuse me and hurt my head.

I am not here to eat you, but I must use your mind and body for a little while. I'm sorry to force you, but I must: I have that gift and I must use it.

Already Jen was deep in his consciousness, seeing in a

ghostly light, half-whiskery feel, the labyrinths of moist
and dry tunnels, used and unused, whose turns and openings were the property of his mind. Several led beneath
the meadow, turning around or under submerged boulders, meeting with other tunnels and going on. She knew
now, by the size of those tunnels he could use, that he
must be a coney rabbit, too large for the passages of moles
or mice, terrified of the dens of foxes, neutrally aware of
the hibernating woodchucks in their long sleep.

There is a tunnel that leads beneath the tent, where the
tread of man frightens you; you will go there with a message from me, and if you are given a message in return,
you will bring it back to me.

Arel, she thought. Can you hear me through this small,
harmless, simple mind? I am below you now, in the
ground, but it is Jen, come to try to help you. Tell me what
it might help me to know.

Now go, little rabbit, and return to me.

She heard the faintest scurry, and he was gone. While
she waited the dampness of the earth came through her
clothes at knees and elbows. The guards were changed
with much stamping, marching and saluting with weapons, the watchfires heaped with fresh wood. The night
was moonless, the air still and cold.

After a long time she heard in the farthest part of her
mind the thoughts and feelings of the rabbit, even heard
his paws as he crept, frightened, back to the entrance of
the hole. He trembled at the faint old odors of carnivores
whose trails he had crossed—weasels, stoats and fishers,
their scents meaning death. But he had gone and come
back.

Jen, she heard now, faintly. Jen, we're here. We're tied
together and guarded. You can't come here. Don't try to
come here. Go find Tsuga and Aguma, Jen. Leave this
place. Morl knows you escaped, and he's in a rage. They
search for you everywhere. You must get away, get away.
Arn sends his love, and so do I. Goodby, brave Jen.

But Jen heard more; she heard what Arel didn't want her to know—that poor Doro had been flayed alive and pegged upon the hide-drying racks for the crows to eat; that tomorrow night Arel and Arn were to be killed upon the stone altar by the Tree.

Jen never took advice; she acted upon deeper, more hazily complicated information. She knew she couldn't go into Morl's tent, but there were unanswered questions she must think about. What were the wolf, the boar and the bear to Morl and his purposes? She would find them and see.

The little rabbit still trembled at the entrance to his hole, so she thought to him, Go back to your warm family now; I hope Ahneeah knows what you have done for me.

Then she crept back into the forest and continued along its edge. Soon she would have to leave it for the open meadow between the tents and fires, so she studied the lay of shadows out there, each tent causing shadows, each fire creating lanes of light.

With all her concentration she tried to hear the wolf, to visualize his yellow eyes, feel the horror of his bonds, wherever he might be. And the bear, hurt by the dead-fall trap and now bound with rope, and the boar whose ugliness could not mask his thoughts—she sent her concern out to them across the camp of the Chigai, wherever they might be.

But she heard nothing from them in reply, only the odd dream-thoughts of a ruffed grouse perched for the night in a nearby spruce, so she left the protection of the brushy edge and followed a shadow line across the meadow, between the looming tents. She saw a patrol of guards enter one tent without hail or warning and make the people come out into the light of torches. Any child near her size they took and held in the light to see the color of its eyes; they were searching for her. At one point she had to cross a band of light, but no one saw her. She moved and stopped, moved and stopped to listen and look the way a

robin stops and is suddenly quiet on the ground. Passing
one tent she felt a sense of forced immobility and bondage
that was so strong her own wrists seemed tied together.
Then she knew that something within the tent was bound
against the whole of its will. It was the wolf whose mind
reached out to her. She crouched against the side of the
tent and felt the thoughts of boar and bear, too. This was
the place.

In her boot she had the knife Amu had picked out for
her in the bowyer's hogan. She had never used it. Now she
took it out of her boot, out of its sheath of folded leather.
The rawhide thongs that made its handle had now dried
as hard as wood. No light came through the hides of the
tent; if there were guards, they would be at the fire
around on the other side, near the door flap. Carefully, as
quietly as she could, she cut a slit in the hide tent, down
then sideways, then back up to make a flap large enough
for her to enter.

Inside, the light of the guards' fire gave a dim glow
where it shone through the skins at the front. The trussed
animals lay on their sides, breathing thickly through their
muzzled mouths and noses. She felt the terrible frustration of their forced immobility, their muscles unable to
flex, the unnatural helplessness of wild strength that had
been free. Her first instinct, because she felt for them so
deeply, was to cut their bonds; but then she felt caution;
she must think with them first.

They knew her. The bear's thoughts came to her: *I
smelled you once, in the bog, but I was neither hungry nor
angry, so I moved away. Now set me free.*

You would set me free, the wolf thought. *In our cages
that was your intention if you could.*

The boar thought, *You have eaten my kind, but not in
cruelty; now we have a common enemy. Set me free.*

Their pain was too deep for thought. She knew that if
she cut their bonds, there would be a great alarm. Perhaps
they would escape, but she couldn't run in the night as an

animal could. But she could no longer stand their agony. She must act. Swiftly her hands found the thongs of the muzzles, the ropes that bound their feet and legs. Her knife slid smoothly through thong and rope. The bear was loose first; without pausing to shake out his cramped limbs he gave a roar and bounded out to the guards. One scream of terror came before the sounds of thrashing and ripping. Then the boar followed in swift silence. The wolf looked at her once, his yellow eyes seeming a source of light rather than reflectors. She saw his exultation, his wild gladness; then he turned and was gone.

From the camp of the Chigai came shouts of fear and alarm. She went out the back of the tent through the flap she had cut and tried to fade into the shadows, to escape to the west, but soon she was seen and run down by a guard who took her knife from her and carried her easily under his arm. He brought her to the nearest torch and looked at her eyes. "Blue like the sky!" he shouted. "I've got her!"

He carried her straight to Morl's tent. The guards in front stopped him and argued as to who should bring her in to Morl, for the one who did would be rewarded. It almost came to a fight, Jen being whirled around until she was dizzy as each of them grabbed for her, but finally another guard came out of the tent leading a half-wolf on a leash and stopped it, the half-wolf's snapping and gnashing of his teeth making them sober. The one who had caught her finally brought her in and stood her before Morl, who sat in a high-backed chair.

Morl was highly pleased. "Better!" he said. "Better and better!" His thick arms gleamed as he flexed them in satisfaction over his head. "Bring that lamp so I can see her eyes!"

The guard who had caught her held her up to Morl, whose broad, cruel face came close to hers as he looked into her eyes. "Yes, this is the other strange one. You have done well; you are now the sub-leader of your patrol."

Another guard entered then, visibly nervous and shaking. "Sir," he said. "Sir . . ."

"Are you a woman? Speak up!" Morl frowned down at him.

"The wolf, the bear and the boar . . ."

"Continue, before I have a wolf rip your throat out!"

"They've escaped, Sir."

Morl's face suddenly looked like a fist; he looked sickly, his forehead almost a shade of green. "Have the guards responsible disemboweled at once."

"They're already dead, Sir. Torn to pieces."

"Feed their bodies to the wolves. How did it happen? Tell me!"

"Their bonds were cut by a knife. A small flap was cut in the back of the tent . . ."

Morl's head jerked toward Jen. "A *small* flap? Where was she found? Near the place?"

"Yes, Sir," said the guard who had caught Jen. "And she carried this knife." He handed Jen's knife to Morl, handle first. Morl took it in his hand without looking at it, his eyes still on Jen. "I would kill her now," he said to no one. "Why did she come under the mountain? But she must die by the bronze knife on the altar, when her time comes." He pointed the small blade at her heart and sighted down it. "I don't like to have my plans disrupted, and my likes and dislikes mean life and death. *I am Morl!*" He shouted the last, and all the guards present blanched and straightened until they were as stiff as wood.

"Bind her wrists and put her with the other two!"

She was taken by hard hands, her wrists bound, then pushed through a hanging bearskin into another part of the tent, where she tripped and fell on the trodden grass that was the tent floor.

"Oh, Jen," Arel said sadly. She and Arn stood side by side, a burly guard standing behind them with a hand on each neck. Nearby three old women moaned softly as they sewed two sets of ornate clothes, the beading glittery in the lamplight. First Arn was forced to try on his tunic. Then Arel had to try hers on. When the ceremonial clothes seemed to fit, Arn and Arel were tied again and the old women left. Arn tried to speak, but the guard slapped him hard.

Only their eyes could speak in the dim light. They said fear, but they also said we are friends and at least we are together.

In the night, kept awake by the pain in her wrists and hands, Jen thought how the handsome doe had spoken to her mind and helped her escape the village of the Chigai, and how she should have gone to find Tsuga and Aguma. Once again she had acted without thinking, just on impulse, and here she was, captured again, having helped no one. Now she and Arn would die with Arel, and their mother and father would never know what had happened to their lost children.

The Evening
of the
Seventh Day

Toward evening of the next day, when the sun approached the western mountains, Arel and Arn were dressed by the old women in their fine new clothes of beaded borders and white trim of the winter weasel. The tents of the Chigai were struck, for after the sacrifice they would begin the journey back to their somber village. It was in the confusion of packing the carriers, changing the orders of the guards, posting the half-wolves to the patrols, that Bren appeared and was able to speak to them. Guards surrounded them, but the parts of the tent were piled on the grass, and the guards who might have heard them couldn't see them where they crouched among the piled skins, for a moment not under close watch.

Bren was dressed in the shaggy cattle skin of the Chigai. "Quick," he said to Arn. "Take those clothes off." He was taking off his cattle-skin parka as he spoke. "Quick! Do it!"

Arn began, but then stopped. "But, Bren! You don't have to . . ."

"Take them off," Bren said in a voice so unchildlike, so full of command that Arn did as he was told.

They made the switch of clothes quickly. Bren said,

"This is not your home, it is mine, and Arel's. You have done enough for us. When you killed the half-wolf you saved Runa's life, and Arel's, and even Amu's if he's still alive. One child dressed in cattle skin will be allowed to leave here, and it will be you. Find Tsuga or Aguma as soon as darkness falls. Maybe they can think of a way to save Jen."

"Yes, Arn," Arel said. "This is not your trouble. You've done enough."

"Go quickly," Bren said. "Keep your face to the east until the sun sets, then go west, to the Tree and the Cave of Forgetfulness."

Arn took his hand, but couldn't speak.

"Hurry, Arn," Jen whispered.

Keeping his face from the low sun, Arn walked as casually as he could past the ring of guards. They saluted him and let him pass. "Andaru's son," they said with respect.

Arn walked slowly through the camp to the southeast until he reached the border of the meadow, then turned west until he came to the shore of the warm lake. The wind had changed so that the mist rolled from the lake over the meadow and kept him hidden from the eyes of any patrols. This wind would bring his scent to the half-wolves with the patrols, but because he had been with the Chigai for many days and wore the cattle skin, they would have no reason to find his scent unusual or dangerous.

The warm mist swirled around him as it had when he and Jen first crossed the meadow looking for Oka. It seemed so long ago, their troubles so small then. He walked faster, stumbling sometimes when the mist thickened in the falling darkness. Perhaps Aguma and her people were already at the Tree, beginning the council fire.

As he came up the shore of the warm lake the mist receded, as it had before. He climbed the long slope toward the Tree. The dark foundations of the ancient village loomed up before him, the village in Ganonoot's tale of the man driven mad by power, and of the people who once lived here before the pestilence came and killed the impounded animals. He left the silent foundations behind and soon could see the top of the Great Tree rising higher as he climbed, a dark tower against the dim sky. He yearned to see a warm fire at the base of the Tree, to find the gentle people who called themselves nothing except the people—hunters, fishers, gardeners and gatherers. He ran for a while, but lost his breath on the steep slope and had to walk again. Always the Tree rose higher.

Finally he came over the rise so that the Tree and its ledges were wholly in his sight. There was no fire, only blackness so empty he caught his breath. The silent, ominous sentry stones stood before him in their circle, receding on each side into dimness, each carved of dead stone, yet stone shaped like headless men, with the stiff postures and ghostly dangers of men. He was lonely and afraid.

He went on past the ring of sentry stones toward the Tree. He had nowhere else to go, though nothing but cold darkness waited for him there. Maybe the Chigai patrols had waylaid the people and their councillors before they could assemble here, and killed them or taken them prisoner. Then Morl and his cruel power would be the only justice in this world.

But just as his courage was gone, just before he was about to give in to hopeless fear, a small spark appeared near the base of the ledges, followed by a bright flame that wavered and grew, and then grew taller and warmer and multiplied into yellow light that revealed all the people sitting there on the meadow grass, then the ledges and the councillors on the stone platform below the thick rising roots and trunk of the Tree, whose broad high branches turned green in the new light.

He ran the rest of the way, so relieved and grateful for their presence he began to sob, then forcefully made himself stop it. He had things he must tell Aguma and Tsuga, and little time. His heart was beating in his throat as he came through the sitting people and climbed the ledge to the platform where Aguma and the councillors sat. Aguma stood, her thick body leaning toward him in apprehension and concern, and made him sit down beside her. "The Chigai," he said, but found he hadn't the breath to go on. "The Chigai . . ."

"Wait, Arn," Aguma said. "Wait until we have given the bread to the Stag, and then you'll have your breath again."

"But Jen and Arel, and Bren . . ."

"Hush now." Her heavy arm came around his shoulders and squeezed him.

The fire rose up in its first surge, then fell into itself to burn more evenly. Only then did Arn realize that it was Tsuga who sat on his other side. He looked up into the lined old face that shone red in the firelight, the skin so transparent with age he thought he could see the bones of the skull shining through. Tsuga's bone-white hair hung to his shoulders, and his deep black eyes glanced down at Arn, just for a moment, before he rose to begin the council.

"Let the council begin," he said in his sad old voice. "I am Tsuga Wanders-too-far, and what I know I will tell you." Then he sat down again.

The man in the deer mask with the broad antlers appeared at the edge of the fire. Aguma rose, holding the loaf of bread. "Dona and Fannu have been chosen," she said, and broke the loaf in two.

Dona and Fannu got up from their places and climbed up to receive the bread from Aguma. They gave small, worried looks at Arn before they went back down to give the bread to the Stag, then resumed their places before the fire.

Tsuga rose to his feet again, leaning on his long, unstrung bow. "I am old enough to call you my children," he said in his dry, penetrating voice, a voice that seemed as old as the north wind. "And I say to you, what will happen tonight at the council fire, by the Great Tree and the Cave of Forgetfulness, will decide the future of the people. I cannot help you, for I am of another time, as you can see. I can give you advice you will not take, feel sorrow you will not share until it is too late. But I will ask you to listen to this boy who has just come from the camp of the Chigai. Do not be too impatient for that."

Aguma rose to her feet. "We must all listen to Arn, who came to us from under the northern mountains, who has seen Ahneeah in the form of an old woman."

From the people came sighs of wonder and also jeers: "We don't believe it! When did he last see her, in his sleep?"

Arn was afraid he couldn't speak to so many people, his voice would die to a breath; but the jeering question made him angry and he said in a high, strong voice, "I saw her last six days ago, in the pine forest west of the winter camp, just after Lado shot Amu in the back."

Silence from the people.

"And after Runa had shot Lado through the neck and a Chigai named Tromo through the body."

Tsuga spoke: "Perhaps you are more interested in the boy's story now."

There were jeers, but the people hushed them; they had heard Arn's strange accent, and seen the anger in him that was also strange in a boy his age who stood before so many. So they were silent as he told them about the sad village of the Chigai, its stench of carrion and the lowings of fear that were a pall over the village; how the Chigai patrol had left the wounded Gort to suffer; how Morl ruled by fear and would sacrifice children to the spirits of the animals he imprisoned and had killed and butchered by other hands.

But then Arn looked out to the meadow and was silent, because in the distance came the flickering of hundreds of torches. A chanting, like the wind in a hollow tree, rolled faintly from the east, where the people of the Chigai approached across the winter meadow.

As the chanting came nearer, all the people stood and looked down the meadow at the approaching torches; the torches themselves outnumbered the people around the council fire.

"There are so many Chigai," Tsuga murmured. "So many."

First came Morl's guards, the big men seeming even bigger in their tunics of shaggy cattle skin, their broad-axes hanging at their belts. They came walking abreast and surrounded the stone altar, moving the people away from it by pushing them with the ends of their bows, firmly and slowly, as if they knew their great strength could not be resisted. When the ground around the altar was cleared, the guards backed away to make a wide circle around it, admitting to the circle the masked men —the men in animal skins and the masks of bear, cattle, boar, antlered deer, wolf, lynx, crow, porcupine and the white mountain goat.

Then a thick, tall man, his black hair tied back away from his face, his chest naked and shining with oil, walked to the altar. It was Morl, and he held a bronze knife in his right hand. As he raised his knife to the sky the people of the Chigai, spread across the field, chanted their toneless chant of sorrow. "Hey-yeh, hey-yeh, hey-yeh, hey-yeh," the voices sang, neither rising nor falling, sad as the wind.

When Morl brought his knife down to his side the chanting stopped. All that could be heard was the creaking of the council fire as it burned, and the faint soughing of the wind high above in the Great Tree.

Aguma spoke, her husky voice carrying out over the meadow and the people. "Morl of the Chigai," she said. "We have come here to discuss your ways and to decide whether or not we will adopt them. Each of us will vote, each person equal in his decision. Tsuga has said that we are all one people in the world, and we must agree upon what is right and what is wrong . . ."

"Vote?" Morl said, interrupting her. He laughed. "Shall

I show you some votes?" He nodded to his guards; each man stepped aside to let a half-wolf leap forward and stop, all teeth and slaver, upon the end of a thong. "And here is another," he said. A huge half-wolf in a studded collar leapt into the circle and sat at Morl's feet. He was the largest of all the half-wolves. He seemed to grin as he looked around him, yet one brawny shoulder was slightly turned down in deference to his master. "Vote?" Morl said loudly. "Vote? Morl is the only one who votes, and his vote is law!"

Aguma said, "You are not greater than Ahneeah's justice."

"There are more powerful gods than your old woman who is never seen, and they have made me strong," Morl said. "I please them with blood, as I please my people with meat."

"Ah, Morl," Tsuga said, coming forward to stand with Aguma. "The gods of murder are simple, and voracious, and fickle; that is why you are afraid."

Morl laughed again as he looked around at his half-wolves, his guards, his thousand people covering a wide circle of the meadow. He raised the bronze knife again, and his people resumed their sorrowful chant.

Two men in cattle skins and masks then brought two children into the circle, the children dressed in clothes decorated with black and white beaded designs, trimmed in the white fur of the winter weasel. The children's hands were tied, their faces blank and cold, as if they knew their fate and must in their helplessness accept it. They were placed side by side on their backs upon the stone.

Then came the man holding the young evergreen tree, to place himself between the children and the bronze knife. The chanting grew in intensity, within its sadness a high call of hope, but when the bronze knife descended upon the tree and the green branches fell, one by one, the hope died back into the windy moan of despair.

"Bren!" came a deep voice from among the guards. Two of the guards in the circle were pushed aside, and Andaru, dressed in the cattle skin and armed with bow and broadax, came striding to the stone. "Bren!" He looked from the child on the stone to Morl, his black brows low over his glittering eyes. "You have my son upon the stone!"

Morl looked then at the children for the first time. He stared: again his plans had warped and changed before his eyes, and it was the children who caused it, always the children. He turned to Andaru and stabbed him in the side, then signaled to his half-wolf to kill him. "Your son will have to do," he said to the fallen Andaru.

Morl's half-wolf leaped at Andaru's throat, but Andaru rolled away. The half-wolf skidded on the grass as he turned to try again, snarling and snapping his white teeth. Then he froze still, for a long cry as thin and fine as a steel blade came from above, by the tree. This was neither the snarl nor the fawning howl of a half-wolf, but the clear, free challenge of a wild creature, cold as a winter moon reflected in ice.

At the sound, all the other half-wolves cringed and looked smaller upon their thongs. Morl's half-wolf didn't cringe, but turned toward his challenger, grimacing, the hair along his back stiffly erect, shivering as if in a rage to find a throat with his teeth.

Down across the ledges came the wild wolf, slowly and carefully. He was long and gaunt from lack of food; his yellow eyes were directed only upon Morl's half-wolf. He never turned his head, as if unaware of all the people.

Morl signaled his guards to let the wild wolf through, then took a bow from a guard and nocked an arrow to the string. "We will watch this," he said.

Morl's half-wolf, fed on beef, was the heavier one. His jaws, as he yawned in nervous anticipation, seemed wide enough to crush the wild wolf's skull. But the wild leader came steadily forward, his steps precise and firm, even delicate. Only his eyes shone with his fierce purpose.

When they were six feet apart they both leaped forward in attack. The half-wolf screamed in his rage, but the wild leader made no sound but breath and the clack of fangs. They met at an angle, in a blur of gray and black, and when they parted, a puffy cloud of cut gray hair settled to the ground. For a moment they were as still as two stones, then they met again, blood a new color in the blur of their bodies. Morl followed them with a half-drawn arrow, waiting. Many more times they met in a rush of slashing, until the ground beneath them was gray with shaved hair and spotted with blood. The half-wolf lost an eye and his studded collar, the wild leader two of his teeth broken off at the base. But after the last meeting there was stillness and silence, for the half-wolf lay on his back, his throat and scarred belly exposed in surrender and supplication, the wild leader's fangs around his throat. He had surrendered forever, as is the way of wolves. Though the half-wolf would have killed his enemy if he had won, the wild leader did not choose to close his jaws and kill.

Morl drew his arrow to kill the wild leader, but before he could let it loose, another cry came from above, along with the hiss and twang of a bowstring. "For Amu!" a woman's voice cried. "For Amu!"

Morl's bow fell from his hand, his thick left forearm transfixed by Runa's arrow. Without looking at his arm, he stared up at the ledges. "But she is dead!" he said.

Along the stone platform and above the Cave of Forgetfulness on the ledges a company of archers was assembling. "For Ahneeah and the Tree!" shouted a young man with a weathered face. "Hunters here!"

Others shouted that cry, but Morl's deep shout was the loudest. "Kill them! Guards of the Chigai! Kill them all! Loose the wolves!"

But now the half-wolves were no longer half-wolves, they were wolves whose leader had surrendered, whose human masters were busy elsewhere. When released, each turned tail and made for the darkness, leaving this human turmoil far behind, as is the way of wolves.

Morl's guards formed around him, big men with long bows and deadly axes, more of them than there were able men of the hunters. But the light of the fire and the torches was dimming now, and people ran here and there in confusion, screams of fear and panic everywhere. The dim air was full of the hiss of arrows and the clashing of steel. A tall guard leaned his whole length forward and hit the ground like a felled tree.

Arn had been watching the two children upon the stone, and when Morl had taken Runa's arrow in his arm he saw Bren push Arel off the stone, then roll over to fall on top of her on the grass below. When the guards formed in front of Morl and began to advance upon the ledges, Arn ran down the stones, ducking and jumping. The councillors had joined the fighting, but he had to get to his two friends. A dead guard, two arrows in his chest, lay in front of him. Arn took the large knife from the guard's belt as he passed. An arrow slit the shoulder of his parka, giving him a sharp sting. Others hummed and hissed overhead, meeting earth or flesh with the same *thuck, thuck.* He ran by the thighs of frantic men as if he ran past trees in a forest, until he found the stone altar and hid behind it with Bren and Arel. With the guard's knife he cut the thongs at their wrists.

"My father!" Bren said desperately. Arn held him, saying, "Wait, Bren!"

Morl stood on the grass with his broadax in his right hand, his wounded left arm at his side. With the ax he broke the arrow off on both sides of his arm. "Kill those archers!" he screamed to his guards. A guard stood at his side, and to him he said, "Kill the four children! Find them and kill them!" Then he looked back at the thousand people of the Chigai on the meadow. "Forward!" he shouted to them. "Come forward and fight for Morl and the Chigai!"

"Come," Arn said. The guard approached the altar, ax in hand. The three children ran through the screaming and the arrows, over bodies slippery with blood. To the guard they must have looked like a scampering of rabbits as they disappeared into the darkness. But he knew where the other child was tied to a sentry stone, so he went to kill her first.

Jen was tied to the boar stone, thongs around her chest and legs pressing her to the cold stone. The stench of carrion from the decomposing boar's head fell upon her like a thick pouring of the odor of death. It was upon this stone that the fresh head should have been placed according to the ritual of the Chigai, but there had been no fresh boar's head, so the old one remained. The people who had stood near her had all moved away now, and she was alone in the dim light, hearing the cries and the clash of battle at the ledges. She tried to get free, but the thongs had been wet, and as they dried they tightened. If she couldn't get loose somehow, the tightening thongs would compress her chest and kill her. She felt the gradual, inevitable clutch of them until it seemed she would be pressed into the stone itself, and become stone.

The silhouette of the guard grew as he approached her, walking fast and deliberately toward her. He grew taller and taller as he came on, his ax swinging in his hand.

"Help me!" she cried, though she had no hope.

The guard stopped and looked down at her. "I'll take her head back to Morl," he said out loud. "That ought to please him." He raised his ax to make a slanting cut, so as not to dull his edge on the stone, but a low sound came from behind him, a sound of distant thunder, unlike the battle sounds. At first he shrugged it off, but it grew deeper and more rhythmical and closer. It approached him, that deep pounding of the earth. He turned, but it was too late. A great black hump-shouldered thing hit him at the thighs and lifted him up, his ax flying. When he came down, one leg was useless, torn to the bone. He tried for his knife, but the thunder had turned, and the last he saw in the faint light was a gleaming yellow tusk like a saber that entered his side and split him into darkness.

The boar nosed the corpse of the guard, then turned to Jen. Battle thoughts roiled his mind, but then it began to settle, and the signals became fainter. He was a boar; he was wild and did not belong here. His instincts all cried out to him to run. But fading, fading, barely caught by Jen, was an acknowledgement of some service done, the faintest echo of gratitude and payment. Then he turned and ran toward the wilderness, his thunder fading across the meadow.

But the thongs tightened remorselessly, and soon Jen fainted, her head falling forward to her chest.

As soon as the three children knew they had escaped the guard, Bren said, "Jen! She's tied to the sentry stone with the boar's head!" They were at the edge of the fighting now. Bren and Arel both had knives they had taken from the dead, the knives almost the size of swords to them. "Come!" Bren said, and they ran back across the meadow, past groups of the people of the Chigai who didn't seem to know what to do. Some milled about like cattle, others merely sat and moaned. None did anything to stop the children as they ran on.

First they came to the wrong sentry stone, almost missing it in the darkness. Was the boar stone to the right or the left? "No good to stand here," Bren said. They ran to the right, on a guess, the only thing they could do, and found the boar stone at last. Arn tripped over the dead guard and was lucky not to cut himself on his knife. He went to cut Jen free, but Bren stopped him.

"Wait!" Bren commanded. "You'll cut her! I'll do it!" He felt carefully around Jen's ankles until he found where the thong was away from her flesh, then cut it once. Then it was a matter of unwinding the rest. "I saw them do it with one thong," Bren said as they unwound it. "It was wet."

Jen fell into their arms, but they warmed her with

decorated parka, and held her until she breathed breaths again and came awake.

The four friends were together once more, but they had little hope that the battle had gone to the hunters. There were too many of the Chigai, and of the big guards with their broadaxes. Over at the ledges the sounds of fighting had died down, although from across the meadow were still the shouts and clashes of battle. Someone had heaped more wood on the council fire, which flamed up again in light that illuminated the Great Tree. They decided to approach the fire, crouching and hiding as best they could, to see what had happened to Bren's father.

Creeping, and running crouched down in the odd shadows, they approached the place where all the bodies lay. In the fire's bright light a strange dance of violence was happening. They came close enough, hiding now behind the body of a bulky Chigai guard, to see two big men fighting with axes. Around the men in a circle were five Chigai guards, watching the fight. Andaru held his left hand to his wounded side, while Morl did the same with his wounded left arm. The axes rang and sparked when they met, the two men advancing to swing, turning and staggering back to avoid the deadly edges. They were both tired, both painted with blood that seeped down through the shaggy cattle skins they wore around their waists. Morl smiled and spoke as he motioned his guards back. "You are the only one of your thin people who could give me a fight, and if I want I'll split you down the center!"

Andaru, his eyes jet-black and intent beneath his black brows, raised his ax in answer. His face was pale from the hurt of his wound, but his big arm rippled along its length as it easily held the heavy ax, waiting for Morl's next charge.

"Wait," Morl said. "You are the last, now. All your people are dead or gone. You may still live and be the leader of my guards."

Andaru held his ax still in the air. "No," he said. "I must die for what I have done. Come at me!"

Morl smiled again and advanced. In the clash Andaru dropped his ax and went to his knees, looking at his right arm where it was slashed through the muscle to the bone.

"Now," Morl said, "here is another for my voracious gods!" and raised his ax high over his head.

But Bren was not through. He had found a thick Chigai bow and a spent arrow. He stood, the bow taller than he, trying to pull it. It was much too heavy a pull for him; his arms shook and trembled with the effort. But with one harsh sob he managed to pull it half of a full yard and sent the arrow on a high arc. The children watched its flight as it rose, black against the fire, orange against the blackness, to its full height and its unwavering descent upon the sweat-shining body of Morl, where it sank half its length between his neck and shoulder.

He gave a long cry as he dropped his ax and turned to see where the arrow had come from, then saw Bren, who stood with the long bow, and Arel, Arn and Jen, whose pale young faces shone in the firelight. "The *children!*" he cried in despair. "Gods of the Chigai, are you defeated by children?" and fell dead.

Three of the guards bent to Morl, while the other two came after the children. They got halfway before a whisk of angry arrows swept them down. On the ledges figures in brown buckskin appeared, bows drawn.

"Surrender!" they called to the three guards around Morl's body. The confused guards, who thought their side triumphant, tried to stand and draw their bows, but all three went down with several arrows in their bodies.

"Jen and Arel, Arn and Bren!" came a woman's voice, and the children ran to the ledges to find Runa and the young man with the weathered face, several of the councillors and others. Bren had gone to his father's side, where the big man lay beside the fire.

Arel's arms were around her mother. "But we thought they had killed you!" Arel cried.

"There will be a reckoning at daybreak," Runa said. "But no; we led them into the darkness, where our hunters' eyes knew better how to see."

19

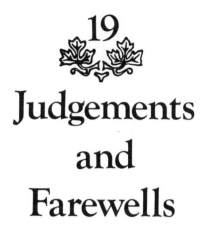

Judgements
and
Farewells

The council fire was kept fueled with wood throughout the night as the badly wounded, Chigai as well as those in brown buckskin, were brought in and placed near its warmth. Aguma, Runa and others tended them. Most of the people rolled up in their sleeping-skins and slept, exhausted by the fighting. Bren sat unsleeping near his father, who woke toward morning and called out for Tsuga.

In the cold light of pre-dawn the thin old man made his way down the ledges and stood, leaning on his long bow, over Andaru.

"Forgive me if you can, Tsuga. If not, I can't blame you," Andaru said.

"Your son has forgiven you," Tsuga said.

Andaru could hardly look at Bren. "I am proud and ashamed," he said. "I was bitter toward life and chose the powers of death; I do not deserve such a son."

"You did not serve death that obediently," Tsuga said. "You saved old Ganonoot from a soldier's ax—an act of mercy, no matter how little you thought it at the time."

"Tell Runa," Andaru said, his voice fading. "Tell Runa that I didn't know Morl would have them kill Amu, or sacrifice her daughter. I was told other things."

"Amu and Arel are alive," Tsuga said.

"Thank Ahneeah, then," Andaru said, and died.

Though Bren's face was wet, he made no sound. He looked once at the dead face of his father, the face so much like his own with its dark, overshadowing brows, then sat until full dawn staring into the moving embers of the fire.

At dawn the people gathered at the council fire. The dead were moved to a place on the meadow within sight of the Tree and the Cave of Forgetfulness, where they would be buried.

Most of the people of the Chigai had left during the night, in their confusion and panic, but a hundred or more had stayed. From this group a delegation had come to Aguma and Tsuga. Their leader, an old white-haired man, was the last of the former councillors, the rest having been imprisoned and killed by Morl and his guards.

"It will be hard for our people to go back to freedom," he said. "But we have been sad and lethargic under Morl's rule, frightened by the death-fear of the animals. We have yearned for Ahneeah's justice."

"We are all one people," Tsuga said. "May we remember that we do not own the world or its creatures." He looked over at the four children, Bren and Arel still wearing their sacrificial clothing. "This night may well have had a sadder ending—though it is sad enough for many.

"Now we will bury our dead, and may their spirits enter the Cave of Forgetfulness."

Later in the day, after the burial of the dead and a meal for the living, the people gathered again at the council fire. It was time to tell of the battle, and of the deeds of those who were no longer there.

Twenty men and women of the people had fallen. There would be empty hogans in the winter camp, orphans, old people with no families, but the people would take care of this.

The stories were told. The old councillor whose face had long ago been clawed into deep red furrows and his right arm taken by a bear swore that.three times in the battle, when Chigai came at his armless side and would have killed him, a great black bear had suddenly appeared out of the darkness and with a swipe of a paw killed his attacker and saved his life. "I swear it!" he said. "Their axes were no match for him!"

Jen found Tsuga's eyes upon her when the old councillor said that. Tsuga nodded, with almost a trace of a smile —or at least a brighter gleam in his somber old eyes.

Bren said, "It was Jen who set the wild leaders free— the wolf, the boar and the bear."

Runa told of the fight in the pine forest, and how Arn had shot the half-wolf before he could leap upon her, and how Amu had not died; he rested now in his hogan at the winter camp.

The councillor in goat skins and the councillor of the reasonable gestures sat quietly and said nothing. The people knew they had both run away during the fighting. Some of those who had been most in favor of the Chigai, however, had changed at the sight of the living children on the altar, and the news of Amu's being shot in the back, and Morl's arrogance. And aside from the guards, few of the people of the Chigai had fought for Morl.

All knew how Bren had taken a man's heavy bow and shot the arrow that ended Morl's life. No longer would they laugh at him for wanting to grow up too soon and be a great hunter.

Aguma said, "Now we will carry our wounded back to the winter camp, where there is food, shelter and medicine for them. We will remember this night as the Battle at the Tree, and when all of the story is known, it will be told at the evening fires."

As the people prepared to go to the winter camp, Tsuga came to Jen and Arn. "I know how much you want to return to your home, but first go to the winter camp. Arn's wound, though it may seem slight, must be treated with medicines, and there you may rest and prepare for your journey."

"Are you coming with us?" Jen asked.

"I must go to the village of the Chigai," Tsuga said. "Jen and Arn, I have not helped you, and I cannot help you. All I can give you is knowledge, but of that you have already gained much. I can tell you to begin your journey when you have rested, that you must go alone, as you came, and that you may come upon companions who may help you." He placed his old hands on their heads. "Now go with your grateful friends, and rest for your journey."

Carrying their wounded on stretchers of saplings and skins, the people began the long walk back to the winter camp. They rested that night in the forest and arrived the next afternoon. The four children went immediately to Amu, who lay propped up on a bough bed in his hogan. Runa hadn't stopped to rest in the night, so she was already there.

Amu put his hand on Bren's shoulder. "I have heard nearly everything," he said. "I am sorry for my brother Andaru, and proud of his son." Arel put her head in his lap. "And my daughter, who went with Arn into danger when I thought she was going to safety in the west!" He looked at Jen. "And Jen, who hears strange thoughts, and acts upon them."

He and Arn compared their wounds. The cut on Arn's shoulder, though shallow, was two inches long—a scar he would bear for the rest of his life. Amu's wounds, healing now, were raised dark welts on his back and chest, each a slashed circle.

For three days Jen and Arn rested, repaired their clothing and spent their time with their friends. Arn's wound was treated twice a day with medicine. On the second day he and Arel walked upriver to the crossing and retrieved their packs, sleeping-skins, Arn's bow and quiver, and their knives, finding the slightly rusty knives just where the patrol leader had made them throw them down. Arn had been afraid that Gort's body might be there by the ashes of the fire, and was relieved to find no sign of him. He still felt badly about how he hurt Gort with his knife, even though he'd had to do it.

He was grateful to Arel for having saved his life that morning. He said, "It wasn't told at the council fire, Arel, but I know how you saved my life, and I'll never forget it."

On the way back Arel took his hand as they walked along the riverbank. "Warm Arn," she said. "I'll never forget you."

He looked down at her pale face, her narrow shoulders that seemed so weak, yet were strong.

The morning of the fourth day was clear and cold; it was time to leave. More and more, thoughts of their mother and father, who would think them dead, came to both Jen and Arn. They saw the sorrowing faces, the cabin cold without wood or food.

The people were sad when they said they had to go. There were offers of gifts, much too many for them to carry. They told Runa and Aguma what Tsuga had said to them, that they must go alone but might meet help along the way. The thought of the bat cave and the dank black passages through the mountain made them cold, but the thoughts of home were stronger.

Bren and Arel, Fannu and Dona wanted to go with them as far as the northern mountains, but Aguma told them that Tsuga's words must be followed. Without a doubt, she said, Jen and Arn had been sent to them by Ahneeah, and only Tsuga would know her purposes.

All of the people of the winter camp came to the place in front of Aguma's hogan to say goodby. The councillors spoke, even Goatskins and Reasonable Gestures, though the people would never take them seriously again. The old councillor with the furrowed face and no right arm gave Jen a necklace made of the fangs and claws of bears, his own magic against night-fear. The bowyer had made an arrow to replace the one with which Arn had shot the half-wolf in the pine forest, its steel blade the silhouette of a wolf's head. Others gave them the seeds of squash, corn and beans, all known to grow large and fast. For food for the journey they were given shelled beechnuts, butternuts and hickory nuts, smoked shandeh, venison jerky, bannock and dried fruits and berries—all light and full of nourishment.

Finally Bren and Arel came up to them, carrying the parkas decorated with beadwork in black and white, made of the softest skins and trimmed with the fur of the white winter weasel. "This one was made for you, anyway," Bren said, smiling—a rare expression for him.

Jen said immediately, "We'll trade, Arel," took off her parka with the red fox fur border and exchanged with Arel.

Arn said, taking the decorated parka, "Then you must have my knife, Bren. I remember you said it was *yodehna*. I want you to have it."

Bren took a step backwards, his face stiff with surprise. "No," he said. "You don't want to give it away. It's too beautiful."

Arn took the sheathed knife from his belt. "You took my place in the sacrifice, Bren. Look, we'll trade knives; yours has cleaned a deer."

Slowly, still perplexed by the gift, Bren took off his plain sheathed knife and handed it to Arn, taking Arn's knife at the same time. "I'll always carry it," he said. "I'll always call it 'Arn's knife.'"

Then it was time to put on their new parkas, their packs, and turn to go. Fannu and Dona wanted to know when they would return. Runa embraced them both. They stood looking into the eyes of Arel and Bren, wondering if they would ever again see these friends with whom they had been through so much, whose bravery and loyalty had never wavered.

There were tears at the parting, stinging eyes as Jen and Arn turned to cross the field. At the top of the field they turned once to wave, the hogans and the people small now, the river blue beside the racks of drying shandeh. Many arms waved back at them; then they entered the woods trail to the north and left the winter camp, its fields, its river and its people far behind.

At noon, when the sun was in the south, they stopped by a small brook to drink and have something to eat. Jen said, "Do you think we can find our way back through the mountain?"

"I don't know," Arn said. "Tsuga said we might have help, but then he said he couldn't help us. I don't know."

"We've just got to go on anyway," Jen said. "But do you remember Ganonoot's story? He said there were many passages and only Ahneeah knows the way."

"Oh, Ganonoot," Arn said in disgust.

Just then came a spidery, scrabbling sound behind him in the brush, and a high cackle. "He he he! And did someone call my name?" Ganonoot scurried lightly out onto the trail, bent over like a crab or a table, and sat down before them. "Why, now," he said, his long fang pressing into his chin with each word. "It's Jen and Arn! We've met before, I can't remember when! But kind Jen and Arn, generous Arn and Jen, poor old Ganonoot is hungry, hungry! And I see you've been having a nice lunch of bannock and jerky!"

"Oh, Ganonoot," Jen said, "you're always hungry." She gave him bannock and jerky from her pack and he began to worry the food with his fang and lips.

Arn got up. "We've got to go, Ganonoot. We've a long way to go."

Ganonoot jumped spryly to his feet, his tilted head still on Arn's level. He held his bannock and jerky in one hand and his warped old bow in the other. "The thing about a . . . story," he said, his tongue cleaning his fang between the words, "is that it always changes when it happens again." Then he couldn't resist the bannock and shoved it into his mouth, still mumbling words as it soaked in there.

Arn and Jen put on their packs and began to walk on. They didn't want to be rude, but Ganonoot never quite seemed to hear anything they said anyway. Evidently he felt that he hadn't finished what he wanted to say, because he followed them, scuffing and tripping and running along behind in his scuttling way.

Near dusk they came upon a small field with a bog at one end of it where a kind of heavy grass grew and was green even in the winter. Then they saw the wolves lying on the field, their bellies distended with food. Nearby was the carcase of a cow, its red and ivory ribs arching over its hollow body. Its coat lay torn and bloody, partly inside out. The wolves saw Arn and Jen and Ganonoot, but merely raised their heads, ears upright, to look at them with lazy curiosity.

At the edge of the bog, several black shaggy-haired cattle grazed on the winter grass, not bothered by the sated wolves.

In the midst of the grazing cattle was a slightly smaller animal with a smoother, browner coat, with a large white spot on the side of its neck.

Jen grabbed Arn's arm and pointed. "It's Oka!" she said. "It is! Oka! Oka!"

The cattle raised their heads to look for the new sound. Their wide black muzzles all turned, slowly, their hairy ears alert, black eyes glittering beneath curls of shaggy hair. One large bull stamped his forefoot into the ground as a warning, and all the cattle came closer together, ready to run or to make their circle of defense. Oka stood still in the hock-high grass, making the children remember how often they had seen her standing this way in the small summer pasture at home, grass sticking out from each side of her wet, slowly chewing jaws.

Jen started toward Oka but Arn held her back. "Wait a

minute," he said. "We don't know what the others will do."

"I must go to Oka! Let me go, Arn!" Jen struggled with him, trying to pull her arm away.

"Jen! Wait a minute!" He turned her around toward him to try to talk to her, but her face was wild and disorganized, her blue eyes not willing to see him. All she did was struggle to get away. Her unreasonableness made him so angry he let her go, knowing that he shouldn't have. He felt in his mean places the words *serves her right!*

He watched her run through the high grass, a small child growing smaller as she approached the bulky black cattle. As she stumbled forward through the grass the big bull lowered his head, his thick curled horns directed toward Jen. He snorted and pawed up chunks of grassy turf that tumbled into the air along his sides. Suddenly Arn was running too, shouting as loudly as he could. He was scared and concerned for Jen and still angry. She had made a terrible mistake this time because she was not listening, not to him or to the animals the way she could when she opened her mind to them.

She fell in the tall grass and disappeared for a moment, then got to her feet again. He was beginning to catch up to her, but he had no plan at all. He just ran after her as fast as he could. He did what he thought he had to do, knowing that the bull would charge and if it did neither of them would get away. They would both be gored and trampled in the open field.

But as they came up to the cattle the bull saw them more closely and smelled them. It raised its head and stared; all the cattle stared—curious, a little nervous, but not really afraid. Jen, no longer running, went up to Oka, who gazed at her calmly and continued chewing the long stalks of grass. The other cattle went back to their grazing.

Arn came up beside Jen; she felt him at her shoulder, but all she could do was look into Oka's soft dark eyes. Oka blinked and went on chewing, slowly, evenly, her lower jaw sliding in the rich creamy green of grass and saliva. The thick odors of cow and sweet grass surrounded her. The evening light shimmered on her glossy hide.

She was a cow in a field, ingesting the richness of the world, making sustenance, content among all the natural dangers. The wolves lolled over there in the same dying light, and would again turn hungry.

"Oka?" Jen said. When she tried to put her hand on Oka's warm neck, the cow shook herself and moved away.

"Oka?" Jen asked, hurt and puzzled by her old friend's skittishness. "I've come to take you home."

Oka masticated the creamy grass; a green-white, foamy run of drool slipped from her lips and fell into the lush grass below. Jen could not hear her friend's thoughts, just the one contented hum of life from deep within her chambered body.

Why should Oka want to go home to the dark barn, to that hungry winter of ice? Perhaps here she might have a dark calf, bony and strong, with shaggy black hair. At home, back through the mountain, in that other world, she would be protected from the wolves and the winter-kill, but she would be a prisoner there, no matter how much she might be respected and loved. All this Jen heard in Oka's deep, basal hum.

She turned to Arn with hurtful tears in her eyes. "She won't come back with us."

"It's all right, Jen."

"We'll never see her again."

"We had that choice too—to stay or try to find our way home," Arn said.

Oka lowered her head and took another mouthful, smoothly wrenching the grass from the earth. The other cattle, sensing some change in the weather or the wolves, or the distant presence of some other stalking carnivore, moved off toward the woods, and Oka followed. The largest bull took up the rear in order to guard the cows as they slowly moved away.

Ganonoot waited for them on the trail, holding Arn's bow that he had dropped when he ran after Jen. "I presume the cow was an acquaintance of yours," he said. His old eyes watched them brightly, but he said nothing more.

They camped that night in a spruce grove, near a spring of dark water that emerged from beneath a granite boulder, flowed silently for a few feet and then sank back into the earth. Ganonoot was still with them, still greedily appreciating their food. After he had eaten he pulled his ragged, stained old buckskin tunic around him and began to snore, whistling and grunting and making drowning noises, each of which sounded like his last breath in this world.

When they had wrapped up in their sleeping-skins on the soft spruce needles, Jen whispered," Do you think Tsuga meant Ganonoot when he said we'd have someone to help us?"

"Someone to help us eat our food, anyway," Arn said.

One of Ganonoot's snores might possibly have been a chuckle just then, but they weren't sure. They were certainly tired, though, and soon were asleep.

When Arn woke up, at the first light, something was wrong. His sleeping-skin was so tight around him he couldn't move. What he first thought he saw was two of the spruce trees that grew near him, but he followed these two trunks up and they were the heavy legs of a big man who stood with a foot on each side of him, the feet holding his sleeping-skin tight to the ground. High above was a red face, and near the face was the glinting blade of a broadax. It was Gort, smiling a cruel and triumphant smile.

"Now I've got you, you little viper, so breathe your last!" Gort said, gritting his teeth.

"Run, Jen!" Arn shouted. He struggled, but couldn't move. Jen was waking up and didn't understand.

"She can run up a tree like a squirrel, for all I care,"

Gort said. "You're the little snake that gave me a limp for life and stuck me full of holes, that skewered my poor carcase till my life's blood filled my boots!"

All Arn could do was stare up at the big man's face, seeing in it revenge, a strange hard joy. He knew he was going to be killed. Jen couldn't help him. There was no help now.

Except that the broadax didn't come down; it stayed on Gort's shoulder while he went on talking. "Days and nights I've been waiting to get hold of you—nights of pain and days of hurt, and when it wasn't hurt, it was the itch you can't scratch, or the pain in the gizzard you don't even know where it's coming from. And now I may walk with a gimp and a lean, but I've got you where I want you, you nasty little stabber, so say goodby!"

Arn just stared at him. What could he do? Jen was struggling out of sleep, now, but it was too late even if she could have done something.

"Say something!" Gort said. "Say something!"

When Arn said nothing, Gort cursed and said, "I'm going to slice you thin as a jerked deer—make one piece out of you sixteen yards long and half an inch thick!"

Arn could only stare up at the big man who stood over him, now raising the broadax from his shoulder.

"Gort," a voice said. It came from the direction of Ganonoot, but it was low and clear, the one word moving surely into their attention with an authority that altered everything—the slight wind of the forest, the presence of the dark trees, the violent stance of Gort and the helplessness of the children.

"Gort," the voice said again. Jen had cried out once, when she had first seen Gort, but now she looked over at Ganonoot, and so did Arn and Gort. From under Ganonoot's ragged tunic where it was spread over his knees a long arrow protruded, nocked to his strung bow and half drawn. But it was the old eyes that drew theirs; no longer were they the shifty, somewhat vague eyes of Ganonoot, though the face was the same, with the long yellow tusk sticking down.

Then an old hand came up, took hold of the long tusk and carefully removed it. The bent old neck straightened, and next the bent body rose to its feet, to straighten and grow tall.

"Well, Gort," Tsuga said. "Is revenge worth an arrow through your middle?"

Gort stared at the tall old man who had been Ganonoot. Not moving, his ax still poised above his shoulder, he stared with an expression of wonder that seemed far beyond the threat of Tsuga's long arrow. He seemed paralyzed in place, unable to attack or to surrender. Finally he shook his head as if to clear his vision, then tossed his broadax aside.

"Ganonoot!" he said. "Ganonoot!"

"Yes," Tsuga said, glancing at Jen and Arn. "Tsuga is old Ganonoot, whose stories no one really believes until they come true." Then to Gort, "You can step off Arn's sleeping-skin now and move over there." He made a quick gesture with his arrow.

Gort looked down at Arn and said in a surprisingly calm voice, "You don't happen to want to reach for your knife, now, do you? I mean I don't feel like getting sliced open again."

"I never wanted to hurt anybody," Arn said.

Gort, still keeping a wary eye on him, stepped aside and let him up.

Then Tsuga did a strange thing. He laughed, unnocked his arrow and unstrung his bow. "Gort," he said, "I knew you years ago as a good man, and I saw just now you could not bring yourself to kill a child."

Perplexed, Gort scratched his head with both hands but said nothing.

"The boy was just trying to protect himself," Tsuga said.

Gort thought for a long time, looking at each of them in turn. Finally he said, "I guess he's brave enough, at that." Then he sat down cross-legged and rubbed his head, staring at the ground. After a while he said, "I never should've joined up with Morl's guards anyway. I used to be a hunter and a woodsman, not like those types that left me bleeding there at the river crossing. It was the pain that wouldn't let me think."

"All right," Tsuga said. "The time of hatred and murder is over—for a while. So let's have breakfast and do some thinking for a change."

Both Tsuga and Gort brought food out of their packs and pockets and they ate well. Tsuga told Gort, who had been alone in the woods during the battle at the Tree, most of what had happened, how Morl had died and the guard been disbanded.

"Well, that's good news to me," Gort said. "I wanted to quit that outfit, and now they won't come after me as a deserter and remove my tender skin."

"Go back to the Chigai, Gort. You can help them."

"All right, but first I'll help these children find their bat cave. I was there years ago. There's a trail along the rim that skirts the beaver dams and the blueberry bogs."

When they had finished eating and packed their gear, Tsuga said to Jen and Arn, "I'll leave you now. When you reach the bat cave, Ahneeah will provide you with a guide. She called you here, Jen and Arn, and you were worthy of what she asked of you. You lost a cow, but what you'll bring back to your mother and father may make up for that. Remember that Ahneeah is not all-powerful, but she is grateful, as all the animals are grateful."

He reached into a pocket of his ragged tunic and brought out two small leather bags, which he put in Arn's pack. "These are for your father, Tim Hemlock. No one can cure his sadness or his seeking, but in one bag is the powder of the needles, medicine for the sickness of his body, and in the other are seed cones of his name tree, which is the Great Tree on the meadow by the Cave of Forgetfulness. Plant them in your world, and when he sees them grow he will feel more at home. And tell him . . ." Here Tsuga laughed and shook his head ruefully, "Tell him that his great-great-grandfather sends him greetings."

"You, Tsuga?" Jen asked.

"Yes, you are all my children—the children of old Ganonoot, the buffoon. Tell your father to think on that."

Then Tsuga took Ganonoot's warped old bow, waved, and strode back along the trail. He turned once and waved again, a tall old man with white hair to his shoulders, dressed in stained and ragged clothes. Then he was gone.

Gort took them in a day, a night and a day to the entrance of the bat cave. "Jen and Arn," he said, "I'm sorry I scared you out of a year's growth back there in the spruce, but I was still out of my mind with pain and anger. Now I'll leave you. Ahneeah's guide won't show himself or herself or whatever it is to me, because I'm just an ordinary man. But here you are, and there are your funny-looking iron shoes the like of which I never saw before, so this must be the place."

They thanked Gort and said goodby. He waved and left them, walking, Arn was glad to see, with less of a limp than he'd had before.

When Gort was out of sight in the trees below, Jen and Arn looked back across the mountain-rimmed valley. Far to the south they could see the meadow and the warm lake. From here they couldn't make out the Great Tree, the hemlock that was the name tree of their family whose ancestors had left this world so many generations before. Only Tsuga Wanders-too-far had ever been allowed to return, went Ganonoot's story, and the others would forever be haunted by their loss.

Somewhere in the blue haze of the distance, beyond the forests and rivers, beyond the warm lake, was the river of the shandeh, and the winter camp, where their friends, the only ones they'd ever had, would now be going about their lives.

Behind them a pebble ticked against another, and they turned. Standing there was a large and handsome doe of the white-tailed deer, its coat a glossy reddish brown blending into pure white at its chest and belly. The large ears, as well as the deep brown eyes, were directed toward them with a great attention that held no fear, just calmness and sadness.

Jen looked deep into the doe's wide eyes. "It's Ahneeah's guide," she said. "I know her from before."

20

Home

One morning in March, Eugenia awoke to find the air in the cabin different. She could breathe more easily. Tim Hemlock, at her side, seemed to breathe more easily too. There was a moist warmth in the air she hadn't felt for the weeks and weeks of the iron ice. Maybe the cold had broken. Maybe spring would come again.

But then, as she had to at every waking, she remembered the loss. Her children were dead. They could not have survived the cruel cold, or the falling water. They were gone forever. The day turned bleak again, her life empty. Some mornings she would get up, weak from hunger and sorrow, and pick up the children's clothes, holding the small garments out before her to remember how the warm and solid little limbs had filled this shirt, these summer pants, that deerskin skirt of Jen's. Or how Arn's sturdy hands had flexed the leather of those gloves.

She would go on living as long as she could help Tim Hemlock, but the seeds for planting were nearly all gone now, even if they could survive until planting time and growing time. If the ice did break she could dig for wild roots, but she might not have the strength for that. She would have to kill the goats, and after that, Brin.

This very day she would have to kill the male goat, for she and Tim Hemlock were slowly starving. She would do it now, though the thought filled her with horror: the goats would know.

She got out of bed and dressed, then raked the ashes and put piece of a chair on the fire. The rope and sledge and sticking knife were there on the table. Quietly, so as not to wake her husband to his own weakness and hunger and loss, she took the instruments of slaughter and left the cabin.

The cold had broken. A bright sun had risen in a hazy sky, causing a broad glare on the melting ice. She was halfway to the barn when she happened to look up, half blinded by the glare, to the northwest, past the barnyard toward the woods. She looked back down again, but even in the glare spots in her eyes, or between those streaks of light, had she seen something—two small dark things—moving out of the woods? She looked again, rubbing her eyes with the back of her hand. At first she thought of animals—what kind could they be? But then the small figures came faster, running now, and calling. There was the clink of crampons on the ice, two small figures in ornately decorated parkas trimmed in white, running toward her with cries that seemed glad. Strange cries in another language she couldn't understand. "Matoneh! Matoneh!" she heard. But then they were upon her and the faces were those of her children, full of joy and tears. She wept as she held them against her.

"Tim!" she cried. She couldn't see through the glare and her tears, but Jen and Arn led her back to the cabin, where Tim Hemlock woke to find his children again and sorrow gone.

Jen and Arn unpacked the food they had brought with them. They made their father a rich broth from the powders Tsuga had given them—the same powders the old woman had brought so long ago as a gift. They made

Eugenia sit down and watch as they prepared a nourishing meal. And they answered questions—a thousand questions once the first joy had changed into a real belief that they were home. Occasionally Jen or Arn would lapse into the language of the people for a few words or phrases, but that happened less and less as they told their story.

But the Hemlocks would have a struggle to survive until late spring brought new growth from the earth. Now that the ice was going they might survive on wild roots and tubers, saving what seeds they had for planting. They scattered the seeds from the hemlock cones at the edges of the cabin clearing. There was the moist, receptive earth; the seeds of their name tree would grow in their world, too.

By day they gathered food and wood, and at dusk, after eating what little food they had, they settled by the fire while Jen and Arn told the story of their journey. Their father asked many questions. "You must remember everything," he said again and again. And they saw their father learning, his old sadness leaving him, his questions being answered in ways they sometimes didn't understand. But in the intense warmth of his interest they never grew tired of telling the story, its terrors as well as those parts they remembered with nostalgia. They never grew tired of telling the tale of the sacrifice, of Morl and Lado, and Aguma and Runa and Amu. And especially of Bren and Arel, though it made them sad with longing for their friends.

One night after the children had gone to bed on the loft, Tim Hemlock said to Eugenia, "The old woman was Ahneeah herself, and she came for Jen and Arn. For Jen and Arn, our children."

"The story tells me how lonely Jen and Arn are for their own kind," Eugenia said.

"Lonely! But all my life I looked for my own kind," Tim Hemlock said.

"And you were among them all the time," Eugenia said.

He turned from the fire and looked at her in a way she had never seen him look at her before. He had always been gentle with her and the children, but in some ways he had been a stranger. "You knew that all the time," he said.

"Yes," she said. "I always knew that."

In the days that followed they waited for the sun and its changes to warm the spring soil for planting. They were hungry, so hungry and weak they found it hard to do those things they must to find the wild food. Soon they would have to kill the goats, their source of milk and cheese. But then one morning while they were searching for edible roots near the alder swamp below the western field, a graceful white-tailed deer, a doe, stepped from the woods in front of them all, its deep eyes dark and sad, to wait while Tim Hemlock picked up his rifle. The one shot cracked in the morning air and the doe fell heavily to the ground.

They ran up to the deer, Jen and Arn getting there first. Jen looked at the deer and cried, "But it's Ahneeah's guide! She's dying!"

It was then they looked into the deer's wide eye and saw beyond. They saw a waterfall, a dark mountain rising, and black stormclouds moving. Then they saw a narrow trail along a ledge, the falling water on one side, and a black hole in the rock that now slowly, silently shut until it was solid stone, stone worn by centuries, with no seam or crack in the cold basalt.

The vision faded and the deer was dead. They would eat the deer's flesh and survive until the sun's gathering strength gave them other food. Though the doe's quick death seemed cruel, Ahneeah's last gift to them had been the gift of life.

Epilogue

Other Smoke
in the Valley

It was in the month of May, when the spring freshets had subsided and the river was no longer a froth of white water, when Jen happened to look down toward the landing.

"Mother! Dad! Arn!" she cried, running to find them, for coming up the near side of the river was a long canoe.

They met the Traveler at the landing, the man with the large arms and shoulders from paddling and poling his canoe.

"Thank God you made it through the winter," he said. "I couldn't come in the fall, so I came to see how you were and bring supplies!"

The Traveler tied the canoe's painter to a bush beside the landing, and looked downriver, where another canoe was coming into sight around the first bend, long poles moving up and slowly back. "And that's not all I've brought you," he said. "There'll be some other smoke in the valley, if you don't mind, Tim Hemlock!"

They all watched as the second canoe came up the slack water at the edge of the river. A man stood poling in the stern and a sturdy boy in the bow, their poles moving in a steady rhythm as the canoe surged forward at each double stroke. In the center of the broad canoe, between boxes and bales of cargo, a woman and a young girl paddled, one on each side.

"They're good folks and they won't crowd you. Fellow says he means to settle on the other side of the river somewhere. He was by here years ago, he says."

"We remember," Tim Hemlock said. "He seemed a good man."

Arn remembered the man in brown, with the brown beard, but of course Jen couldn't remember because she was just a baby then.

When the canoe came up to the landing the boy held out his pole to Arn, who took the end of it and pulled them in to an easy stop alongside the Traveler's canoe. The boy jumped out with the painter and tied a quick bowline to a rock.

"That's a good knot," Arn said. The boy looked up and smiled as they judged each other. His eyes were dark brown, slightly fierce, though willing to be friendly.

The little girl put her paddle down and smiled at Jen, then drooped her shoulders with a humorous shrug, to show how tired she was.

Their parents and the Traveler were laughing and talking as they walked up the hill toward the cabin, but the children looked at each other with a sudden and mutual gravity. Will we be friends? they all asked in silence.

It seemed they might.

ABOUT THE AUTHOR

THOMAS WILLIAMS was born in Duluth, Minnesota, went
to New Hampshire when he entered high school and,
except for army service in Japan and graduate work at the
Universities of Chicago, Iowa and Paris, has been living
there ever since. One of his short stories was awarded an
O. Henry Prize; others have been included in *Best Ameri-
can Short Stories*. Of his novels, *Town Burning* was nomi-
nated for the National Book Award in 1960, *Whipple's
Castle* was called "a masterpiece," and *The Hair of Har-
old Roux* won the National Book Award in 1975.

Mr. Williams has been a Guggenheim fellow, and was
awarded a Rockefeller grant for fiction in 1968 - 69. He
now lives in Durham with his wife and two children.